THE BIG BANG

MIKE HAMMER NOVELS
BY MICKEY SPILLANE

I, the Jury

My Gun Is Quick

Vengeance Is Mine!

One Lonely Night

The Big Kill

Kiss Me, Deadly

The Girl Hunters

The Snake

The Twisted Thing

The Body Lovers

Survival . . . Zero!

The Killing Man

Black Alley

The Goliath Bone
(with Max Allan Collins)

---- **THE** ----

BIG BANG

Mickey Spillane

&

Max Allan Collins

Quercus

First published in Great Britain in 2010 by

Quercus
21 Bloomsbury Square
London
WC1A 2NS

A CIP catalogue record for this book is available
from the British Library

ISBN (HB) 978 1 84916 041 4
ISBN (TPB) 978 1 84916 042 1

10 9 8 7 6 5 4 3 2 1

Printed and bound in Great Britain by Clays Ltd, St Ives plc

For Jim Traylor,
who saw the pages

CO-AUTHOR'S NOTE

This story takes place in the mid-1960s, when Mickey Spillane began it. With a deadline looming, he put *The Big Bang* aside, and substituted another Mike Hammer novel, *The Twisted Thing*, which he'd completed, and shelved, decades before.

In 1982, on a visit to Mickey's South Carolina home, I was handed by my host two substantial Mike Hammer manuscripts. I was flabbergasted – there hadn't been a Hammer published since 1970! I read late into the night, which was always my practice with Spillane novels, and the next morning at breakfast offered up enthusiastic reviews.

'Maybe we can do something with 'em someday,' he said casually. On a later visit, in 1989, he sent the partial manuscripts home with me 'for safekeeping'.

Mickey's words proved prophetic: a few weeks later, Hurricane Hugo destroyed his home, and *The Big Bang* would likely have been lost.

We had spoken about the novel in detail, including the ending, which Mickey said was one of his favorites. My hope is that readers will greet this tale as enthusiastically as I did back in 1982, when Mickey Spillane handed me a stack of manuscript pages for bedtime reading.

THE BIG BANG

Chapter One

T HEY CUT THE KID off at the corner, driving his motorbike into the curb and spilling him across the sidewalk into
the brick wall of an apartment building. Two of them came
out of the back seat of the old sedan that had skidded to a
stop, their shoulder-length hair flying, bell-bottoms flopping—one
in a leather vest and no shirt had a short, tape-wrapped billy and
the other in a tie-dye T-shirt sported a double length of bicycle
chain ready to whip into the head of the groggy short-haired kid in
striped top and jeans on the sidewalk.

What they didn't figure on was me being in the doorway and
when I stepped out and smashed the tie-dye slob with the chain,
his face seemed to explode into a bloody mess, and he backflipped
to the pavement and slid under the car he'd just left.

The other one stopped the swing of the billy halfway down and
tried to turn on me instead, and all I could think of was who the
hell these chintzy little shits thought they were with their scruffy
beards and spindly needle-pocked limbs, taking on an old tiger. I
broke billy boy's arm between the wrist and elbow, took half his

teeth out, snapped his jaw loose from its hinges, and sent the bastard's balls on a trip way up inside him with one beautiful place kick, landing him halfway out in the gutter.

That was when the blond-Afro-haired kid driving the heap suddenly unfroze and jammed his foot down on the gas. The car screeched forward over the one under the wheels, making a wild cracking that went squishy at the high point of its bump, and the vehicle lurched on, leaving the crumpled figure in tie-dye to die like a fish on a deck, flopping twice before becoming another statistic.

Leave it to New York, I thought.

One lousy day back in the city and the fun was starting all over again. One day away from the sun and pure white sand and back to scarlet-splashed concrete and an early fall already turning cold and a fat woman standing in a puddle of spilled groceries screaming her lungs out at the mess she'd walked onto.

A half block away, the would-be getaway car didn't make the squeeze between a double-parked truck and an oncoming bus and accordioned into a tangle of shrieking man and metal. For only two deep breaths a stunned, hushed silence held sway while the whole city seemed to pause in shock. Then the sounds of terror ended, and all returned to noise and normal.

This was *the* city, after all.

This was New York.

The lanky, narrow-faced, sharp-eyed character sitting across from me in Captain Pat Chambers' desk chair wore a lightweight blue suit and darker blue tie and might have been a young exec on Wall Street. He was instead an assistant district attorney named Vance Traynor, who had a cocky, smart-assy manner that meant we'd tangle sooner or later.

I'd gone down to Florida to recover from a knife blade that had opened my side like somebody wanted to slip in there and hide.

I felt okay but not in the mood to tangle, not even with this petty bureaucrat.

The windows were black with night. I'd been cooling my heels at Central Headquarters for hours. Pat had humored me by sharing the files on the three assailants—the dead driver was one Timothy Haver, 25, the tie-dye-kid-turned-speed-bump was Herman Felton, 26, and the billy-club boy was Norman Brix, 24.

"Thought you might like to know who you killed," Pat had said, which wasn't fair—two had gotten themselves killed, and as far as I knew, the other one was still breathing.

Anyway, I'd given two statements already, and now I was getting my official moment with one of the big boys. Swell.

Pat was standing just behind the seated D.A.'s man, leaning against some file cabinets wearing a hooded expression that said he would rather be anywhere else. A mousy bespectacled stenog was taking everything down.

"I suppose sooner or later," Traynor said, in a radio announcer's voice that would serve him well in the political arena, "I had to meet up with the great Mike Hammer."

That didn't deserve a response so I didn't give him one. I'd already laid the facts out for him. Now he was just fucking with me.

"I am supposed to believe that this was a mere coincidence," Traynor said, eyes slitted to cuts, "that a man with your background, your . . . abilities . . . *happened* to be there. To save the day."

"Mighty Mouse was out of town," I said.

"So were you, till this morning. You get in slightly before noon, and without even stopping by your office, you go directly to pick something up from a client. That's your story."

"No."

"It isn't?"

"It's not a story. I was doing business by phone while I was away. I was just following up back in Manhattan."

3

The eyes fluttered wide, then slitted narrow again. "One of the two corpses had needle tracks, Mr. Hammer. So does the hospitalized assailant."

"Junkies robbing somebody—who'da thunk it?"

He was shaking his head. "Any way you spin it, Mr. Hammer, that puts drugs on the table. And weren't you in Florida because you got knifed when Junior Evello's boys took you on outside Dewey Wong's on East Fifty-eighth?"

"That's a rumor. That's nothing that got on any police blotter."

Pat was staring at his file cabinets, like he was wishing he could crawl in one of the drawers.

"No," Traynor admitted. "But for a rumor, it has a certain weight, considering that two of Evello's top boys have not been seen since that night."

"Maybe they went on vacation, too."

"The permanent kind, right, Mr. Hammer? Let's leave it a rumor. Let's call it hypothetical—why would two of Evello's boys jump you outside a Chinese restaurant?"

I thought about trying a fortune-cookie gag, but instead said simply, "Junior thinks I was responsible for his late uncle's death, a lot of years ago."

"Were you?"

"Does it matter?"

He was too young to deserve a weight-of-the-world sigh like the one he expelled. "The Evello Family still controls narcotics in this town. And you have a long history with them—didn't you once upon a time cost them a major load of heroin?"

I shifted in the hard chair. "If you want to talk old times, buddy, send the stenog home and we'll have a beer somewhere. But if you want something on the record, I have no knowledge that this afternoon's incident has anything at all to do with the Evello mob or narcotics or anything except a couple of junkies needing fix money, taking down a guy who might have some cash on him."

4

He sucked in air. Then he let it out, saying, "You just happened to be on the scene."

"It's what we call in the business a coincidence."

"Do you believe in coincidences, Mr. Hammer?"

"Sometimes."

His smile was thin but nasty. "Young Billy Blue was just lucky you were there."

That was the kid on the motorbike I'd helped out.

"He was lucky," I said. "The punks weren't."

Traynor tasted his tongue. He didn't seem to like the flavor. "You *happen* to be there, and two guys get pulverized, and another is so badly beaten, he's in critical condition at Bellevue. At least you didn't *shoot* anybody."

"It's early yet."

Traynor grunted in obvious disgust. "Judging by your attitude, I would say the things I've heard about you from my associates are true."

"Probably."

"Your luck can't last forever, Mr. Hammer."

"No. But I've outlasted five D.A.'s since I set up shop. And I don't bother even keeping track of the assistants."

He rose, shoving Pat's chair back till its wheels collided with the wall. "I'm taking you at your word, Mr. Hammer, only because Captain Chambers vouches for you. But I'm going on record—if you get involved with this thing, your operating license and your gun permit will only be the *first* things to go. Clear?"

"It begins and ends here," I said.

"Good. Good."

Pat waited until the young assistant district attorney had taken his leave, then reclaimed his chair and nodded to dismiss the stenographer. She went out, and he flipped the tops off a pair of plastic coffee cups and handed me one.

He said, "You make new friends every day, don't you, Mike?"

5

"Pretty much."

He shook his head. "After all these years, and you're still a pisser."

Captains of Homicide Division can lay off-key intonations onto the most abrupt sentences. I couldn't quite figure his mood, so took a taste of the coffee and shrugged. "Don't sweat it, Pat. There were witnesses to everything."

He turned around and gave me a long, direct stare. "Buddy . . . I've asked you before. Two armed guys and a getaway driver, and you're the one standing? Where do you buy your luck?"

"Maybe theirs just ran out."

His expression was glazed. "You were the primary cause of two kids getting killed. Doesn't that even get to you—a *little?*"

I felt my face go hard and flat. "Kids, hell. They were punks—middle-twenties punks with a sweet list of arrests and convictions."

"You could have stopped it and held them there," he said, eyebrow arching. "You had a gun, didn't you?"

"Yeah, my .45, which means I could have shot them, too. I wasn't trying to kill anybody. I was just trying to stop a kid from getting hurt. Not pulling my rod, shit, I thought I was doing them a favor." I took another pull of the coffee. "Maybe I did at that."

"*Nothing* bothers you, does it?"

I shrugged a shoulder. "Not much anymore. Take a look around this town—it's that great big handbasket you heard so much about, headed to hell."

He grunted a laugh. "After all the bad guys you shot, you'd think it would be paradise."

I scowled at my supposed best pal. "Jesus, I just don't know what *you're* so bugged about. Those pricks could have killed that kid, if I hadn't stepped in."

Pat made a wry face. "I'm not talking about what happened today. I'm talking about *you,* Mike. There was a time when things

6

used to bother you. Now . . ." He shook his head glumly. ". . . there's no reaction at all. It's like nothing happened. What are you, dead inside?"

I frowned. Shrugged. "Okay, so it bothers me. Satisfied?"

His analytical mind bit right through my words. "Oh, you're bothered, all right. Just not about the two young men squashed to tomato sauce, *or* the other you put in the hospital needing an exploratory operation so the docs can find his nuts again."

I folded my arms. Stuck my chin out. "That's right, chum. I *am* bothered, but I'm bothered about the kid on the motorbike. He was a working stiff, holding down an after-school job, right?" Pat had filled me in before the assistant D.A. took over. "No arrest record, all character references good, yet there he was, about to be ripped off by lowlifes who want the rest of the world to subsidize their drug habit."

He held his hands up in surrender. "It's a crazy damn world, Mike. No argument. We live in one, they live in another."

"Or am I wrong? Was that kid Billy Blue just another user or dealer or . . . Come on, Pat, spell it out. *You* talked to the kid, I didn't."

Pat shrugged again. "Like you said, he was on a job. A messenger boy."

"What kind?"

Now the Homicide detective had to think for a moment. Was I just curious? Or was I curious because I was going to wade into this mess? Like I wasn't already hip deep.

Finally Pat said, "Special delivery of a certain antibiotic to a midtown doctor." He caught the way I was looking at him and gave me a negative sign. "No narcotics. We checked it out. Nothing in the package but capsules to be taken orally."

"Does Billy know why they attacked him?"

"No. But he has a guess."

"Reasonable one?"

Pat sipped his coffee and put his cup down. "The young man had just been paid two weeks' salary—a hundred and sixty bucks in cash."

"And that's enough for any freak to take a crack at. We have an autopsy report on the punks, or is it too early?"

Again he waited a few seconds, then gave me a tired grimace and said, "The one you left alive, and the driver of the car, were shooting H. The other had two dozen pills in his pocket."

"Not Bufferin, I'd guess."

"No. Speed."

I frowned, sat forward. "How'd the creeps know the kid had that kind of dough on him?"

"All three assailants reside, or resided, within three blocks of Dorchester Medical College. Everybody at Dorchester gets paid the same day twice a month, usually right after lunch. Apparently it's common knowledge. The Blue kid must've looked like an easy target."

"What about the one in the hospital? What does he have to say for himself?"

Pat's twisted smile had no humor in it at all. "He won't be saying anything for a long while, Mike. You made damn sure of that. They had to wire his jaws shut, he's in shock and going through withdrawal. The prognosis is that he'll probably live, but the doc I spoke to wouldn't bet on it. He's skinny, malnourished, and has hepatitis."

"We'll ask Jerry Lewis to do a telethon."

Pat didn't laugh at that. No sense of humor tonight. He said, "The damage you did won't kill him, but he's liable to check out during withdrawal. See, kiddo . . . your luck is still holding."

I felt my upper lip curl all on its own. "Screw his withdrawal. I couldn't care less what happens to that kind of human garbage. Those fucking drugheads are all the same, scumbags, all of 'em, and the gutter's too good for them. Hell, if I'd known what I do now, when this went down, I'd have knocked *his* ass under the car, too."

Pat's expression had turned grim. "Mike . . ."

"What?"

"It's a sour world. Don't make it worse."

I put both shoulders into a shrug. "Sure."

"These kids aren't born drug addicts. They're not 'scumbags' when they take their first breath. They have families, mothers and fathers who love them. . . ."

"Not enough."

"Christ, you're self-righteous today. Listen to you!"

"I'm not saying anybody started out bad. And the predators who get these kids hooked, they're the ones whose throats I'd really like to get my hands around. But you've seen the horror pictures, right, Pat? Once a vampire sticks his fangs in an innocent, that innocent turns into the next vampire, looking for a victim."

"You really think it's that simple, don't you?"

"I didn't say it was simple. I didn't say it wasn't tragic. But I see a vampire, buddy, I'm putting a forty-five-caliber stake through his goddamn heart."

His eyes were like quarters. "And I'm supposed to believe you're not getting involved in this?"

"I am involved! But . . . I made my contribution to society for today. I took two, maybe three junkie thieves off the streets, and that's enough. For today, anyway."

He was looking at me like I was the one out of a horror show. "Then lay off, Van Helsing. You got no counts against you right now. In fact, you come up smelling of roses for performing a public service. Even that old sedan was hot. The parents of those 'scumbags' aren't preferring any charges. Hell, they're glad to get their darlings out of their hair."

"What happened to the mothers and fathers who loved them you were crowing about?"

9

Suddenly Pat looked very tired. "Mike—as a friend. I'm asking you—lay off."

I gave him the innocent face. "Lay off from what?"

"From what you're thinking of, damnit! You have your back up about something and I can smell it all the way across the room."

"I wish you'd tell me what it is, then."

His eyes narrowed, his expression grew grave. "Think about it a little bit. Maybe it will come to you."

"Sure. I'll do that." I reached for my hat and eased out of the chair, stretched, yawned. Little man had a busy day. "Think our budding assistant D.A. got everything he wants?"

"He'll be overjoyed, we'll *all* be overjoyed, if you just get your ass out of here."

"My pleasure, buddy," I told him. "Feel like hitting the Blue Ribbon for supper?"

He gave me a "you gotta be kidding" expression, but it melted, and the cop became a friend again. "What's the special tonight?"

"Beats me, but I could dig some of that crazy knockwurst."

Pat leaned back in his chair. He even found a chuckle for me. "You buying?"

"Sure."

"Then you're on."

And we went out for a late dinner, leaving our conversation behind.

Anybody who walked into my office would have a hard time figuring out who it belonged to. Back in the old Hackard Building, it had been a cluttered, lovely mess. But they were giving the old landmark a major overhaul, and I'd had to move to new digs, maybe temporarily, maybe not. Anyway, now the address was classy, the view scenic if you liked towering Manhattan tombstones, with a doorman who after six months still looked at me like I didn't belong.

Velda had added decorating to her secretarial duties, keeping the place rugged enough to maintain my occupational image without scaring off the more timid clients. The outer office was inviting, furnishings modern but not metal, nice lush dark wood and a couch with dark leather padding. Wood panels bore framed newspaper stories about her boss and various sharpshooting plaques I'd racked up, and even a couple of civic awards from groups not afraid to endorse my brand of rough justice.

She was still the teaser, though. In her own area outside my private office she had installed an antique but functional desk, at which she could be seen when my inner office door was open, so I could take in both of those lovely, disconcerting legs crossing and uncrossing down in the desk's well.

And if that wasn't enough of an invitation, she'd smile over her Smith Corona and inhale deeply so the tight jersey tops she always wore would swell out with an open challenge to give her more breathing room.

Velda.

Wide shoulders, deep, dark tresses falling in a pageboy that fashion had long since left behind, yet still the most beautiful hairstyle of all. A tall woman, with dark almond-shaped eyes, rich with mystery, and a lush red-lipsticked mouth that made a guy consider doing the kinds of things that get you arrested in some states. . . .

Morning sun was slanting through the blinds and throwing horizontal patterns on the hardwood floor as I stepped into my new, modern suite of offices, and closed the door behind me. "Hello, kitten."

Her teeth flashed in a smile so white, the sunlight seemed to bounce off and get brighter. She stood behind her desk and reached out to take my hands in hers.

"Mike, you bastard," she said, and held her mouth up for a fiery little office kiss. Then she tugged me back to my favorite sitting spot on the edge of her desk.

"'Mike, you bastard'. . . what kind of welcome is that?"

Her pout was a phony. "You could have stopped by when you got back. You didn't even call me last night. You *were* home, weren't you?"

"Not till fairly late. I got caught up in something."

She frowned. "Yeah, I know. Pat called me. *He* can call me, but you couldn't take the time?"

"Listen, last night when I got back, I hit the rack and was asleep before I could turn out the light. I'm not a kid anymore, you know. You're up on what happened?"

She nodded crisply. "I read about it in the evening papers, and this morning the coverage was more detailed, but still with plenty of lines to read between. . . ." She tucked her lower lip between her teeth, waited a moment, and said, "Pretty nasty scene?"

"Nasty enough." I shrugged. "Could have been worse."

"Oh?"

"This Billy Blue—he's apparently a nice kid, and those punks were out to tear him up."

Her head cocked in that RCA-Victor-dog fashion, only she was no dog. "What were you doing there, Mike?"

"Hey, just delivering that report to Klein. I'd just come out of his damn building. I was on my way up here."

She sighed, shook her head, and all that auburn hair shimmered. "Oh, Mike, how do you always manage to get involved in these crazy scrapes?"

"Like the man said—just lucky I guess."

Velda gave that a little laugh, which was more than it deserved, then looked into my eyes. "Good vacation?"

"Plenty of sun, caught some fish, got my paperwork done, and managed to locate Klein's missing shipment by telephone."

"The private eye's best weapon." Now her eyes got narrow. "Get laid?"

"What a question."

"So answer me."

I shifted on my desk perch. "Number one, it's none of your damn business."

"And number two?"

"Number two, let's just say I didn't have any decent offers, and number three, maybe I didn't feel like it."

"I'll ignore number two, and politely pretend number three can be taken seriously."

"Hell," I said, "I was saving it all up for you."

"That I won't ignore." She kissed me again, lightly, then ran her hand gently down my side. "How's the wound?"

"Healed, but still sore. Hurts like a son of a bitch when I sneeze."

"So don't sneeze. But I bet you feel better than the two guys who jumped you outside Dewey Wong's."

"I don't know, doll. When you're dead and buried, like those clowns, nothing much hurts. Even in a landfill."

She was stroking my hand now. "That little brannigan yesterday, that didn't do you any good either, did it?"

"I'll survive."

"That's what some people are afraid of, I think." She gave me an odd look of resignation. "Was that dustup the end of something, or the beginning?"

"You and Pat can throw a lot of curve balls, sugar. What's with you two?"

She shook her head. "We've known you too long, maybe. Way ahead of you—like a dog who brings in the newspaper before his master even realizes he wants to read it."

I said it before, but this time out loud: "Baby, you're no dog."

She smiled impishly, reached over, picked up a folder from the desk, and handed it to me.

"What's this?"

"A rundown on those kids."

I gaped at her. "You been working on this already?"

"Think of it as the newspaper you didn't realize you wanted to read yet."

"Oh yeah, where's my pipe and slippers?"

She slapped me gently on the leg.

"Kitten, I appreciate the effort, but I went over the police reports and Pat filled me in a little. Do we really need to dig into this thing?"

"How about where Billy Blue is concerned?"

"According to Pat, he's clean."

Velda nodded, looking at me thoughtfully. "He seems to be, but I found a store owner in his neighborhood who had seen him talking to two of his future assailants—Felton and Brix. It looked like an argument, but he couldn't be sure."

"What are you, a witch? How'd you find this stuff out so fast?"

Her smile said she liked the implied compliment, witch remark or not. "I been working the phone. Private eye's best weapon, remember?"

"Naw. A good secretary, *that's* a private eye's best weapon. Who's the beat cop in the area?"

"Officer named Sherman—you can thank Pat for that tidbit. Sherman knew the players in your little melodrama yesterday, including Haver, the driver? But Officer Sherman never saw all four together. He gave the Blue kid a clean bill, but said the others were all just biding time before jail or an O.D. Real hardcases for their age. Haver had just beaten up his mother the day before. She doesn't even want to go to his funeral."

"There's a picture Norman Rockwell could paint."

She frowned thoughtfully. "But, Mike, it was a shop teacher in the high school Billy Blue goes to who put me onto something. Mr. Lang thinks both Brix and Felton were hustling narcotics to some of the kids. With Billy working in the hospital, they might have seen a potential source in the boy—tried to make a supplier out of him."

I nodded. Smart cookie, my Velda. "You check at Dorchester Medical College?"

"I haven't had time." She nodded toward the phone and the fat directory on her blotter. "I could only let my fingers do so much walking. . . . Anyway, I thought you might like to poke around your-self."

I flipped the folder open and gave a slow scan to the four pages inside—four life histories with pertinent remarks contained on one page apiece. Idly, I wondered how many pages it would take to summarize my own life. Of course, just the fatalities I'd racked up would rate more than four.

I said, "Now I know what Pat meant."

"Oh?"

"Why he told me to lay off, I mean. These boys have interesting records. Interesting ties."

She was studying me warily. "Are you going to? Lay off, I mean?"

I gave her a big ugly grin. "If you thought I would, baby, then you wouldn't have bothered with the legwork."

"Fingerwork," she said, holding up pretty red-nailed digits. "All *that* means is, I know what you're going to want before you do."

"You're a good little doggie after all, honey."

"Then why don't you pet me?"

She leaned toward me, half rising, and I leaned toward her, and I was half rising myself, though I was still perched there. My fingers started in the softness of her hair, touched their way down over the firm slope of her breasts and slipped lower till nestled snugly against her flat belly. In this position, that was as far as I could reach. I stopped, cupped her face in my hands, and kissed her again.

When I pushed her back, she said, "That was mean."

"You asked me to," I reminded her.

"I meant stopping," she said.

I got off her desk and stood there and straightened my tie and said, "Just trying to maintain a little office decorum."

She was laughing and pointing at me. "What's that, our new hat rack?"

I said, "I told you I was saving it all up for you," then I covered myself with my porkpie hat and went back out into the hall. I could still hear her laughing behind the glass of the door as I headed off to find out just what it was I'd gotten myself into, playing Mighty Mouse for a kid called Billy Blue.

Chapter Two

DORCHESTER MEDICAL COLLEGE was an old, reputable, well-funded institution that specialized in rare-disease research. It was housed in two baronial-style mansions joined by a modern white-brick structure on the upper edge of Manhattan, quietly exclusive and staffed with the finest minds available courtesy of generous endowments from several giant corporations.

The nurse at the personnel desk had received her own generous endowments, but no corporations had been involved. Her hair was red-blonde and her freckled nose was almost as cute as her long-lashed blue eyes, which she batted at me when I made my inquiries.

Seemed she didn't usually give out information about employees, and unlike some people, she didn't mistake the ID card and badge for a city cop's. But the name on the ID made her eyes widen.

"I saw in the papers what happened to Billy," she said, and the blue eyes spiked with indignation. "It's all anybody around here is talking about today."

"I bet."

"It's lucky you were there. On the scene. You're a real *hero,* Mr. Hammer."

"Maybe, maybe not, but I'm doing follow-up and wanted to get some background on Billy."

She almost frowned. "As I said, we don't usually give out information about employees, Mr. Hammer. . . ."

"That's a shame."

She fluttered some more. "But you *are* sort of *almost* a policeman, aren't you?"

I leaned a hand on her desk. "I never heard it put better."

Then she fetched the file on William R. Blue, age 17, and the rear view while she fished in a filing cabinet was worth the trip. She allowed me to copy down the kid's local address with references from school, clergy, and neighborhood shopkeepers.

Billy Blue was engaged in part-time work on weekdays, with a full day on Saturday, and he always accepted overtime if it was asked of him. There were no complaints from his supervisors and in seven months he had only taken off one day, for a dental visit. He had started with light janitorial work, moved into the dietary kitchen, then got assigned to Dr. David Harrin, chief of staff at nearby Saxony Hospital, who regularly taught at Dorchester.

I asked the nurse, "What does he do for Dr. Harrin?"

"Everything from sterilizing equipment to delivering supplies. The doctor has taken a rather personal interest in Billy, after seeing how enthusiastic the young man is about his job. Billy works very hard at his studies, too."

"But he's not a student here at Dorchester—he's still in high school . . . ?"

"That's right, but Dr. Harrin took the boy under his wing. He's a nice kid, Billy, and I think Dr. Harrin sees a lot of potential in him."

I gave her a lopsided grin. "It's nice to know there are still *some* people like that around."

A touch of concern creased her brow. She lowered her voice as if sharing a secret: "Well, you know, the doctor lost his own son two years ago. The boy died of a heart attack a short while after a track meet."

"Damn," I said. "That's rough."

She nodded. *"Especially* so, what with Dr. Harrin being widowed a year earlier. His wife was killed in an automobile accident on Long Island. I imagine he feels a kinship with Billy, since the boy's an orphan himself. Did you know Billy practically supports his grandparents?"

I handed the file back to her. "Doesn't sound like Billy's exactly a problem child. But I just like to check everything out."

The blue eyes widened. "You could talk to Billy."

"I plan to."

"Or his friends at the high school . . ."

"Naw, that's not worth the bother. You know how it is. They're usually reluctant to say anything about other kids."

"How well I know. I have a sister that age."

"There's more at home like you?"

She didn't have a reply for that, just a smile. Then she glanced at her watch and said, "Billy and Dr. Harrin are quite close—you might want to speak to the doctor. You'll probably find him in the staff cafeteria about now." She pointed to one side. "Up those stairs and first door on the left."

"Appreciate it," I said.

"Any other information I can provide?"

"Nope."

But she gave me more info just the same, by way of her phone number.

I took the slip of paper and thanked her for it, but I'd pitch it.

Not that a redhead like her couldn't soothe my pains, but if Velda ran across that scrap of paper, I'd need a doctor not a nurse.

Up in the cafeteria, a gnome-ish waitress in a hairnet who didn't exactly spark my appetite pointed out Dr. David Harrin. Though he sat hunched over a coffee by a window, he was clearly a tall man. He had a distinguished air and a bony, Lincolnesque physique. At the moment, he was studiously going over some handwritten notes in a spiral pad.

When I approached, the white-haired, bespectacled physician looked up and I knew at once that he, too, wasn't the kind you could fake out with a state license and a metal badge. His eyes were a washed-out blue, set in a firm, friendly face that had looked upon life and death a thousand times, searching for answers to ten thousand baffling questions.

"Dr. Harrin?"

"Yes?"

"I'm Mike Hammer."

He stood up and held out his hand, and I took it—there was a secure, tensile strength in his grip.

His smile was quick and genuine. "Ah, yes. The celebrated Mr. Hammer. Hero of the hour, and star of a dozen tabloid tales."

That was delivered in good humor, so I just said, "Guilty as charged."

"Sit down, Mr. Hammer, please. Coffee?"

Before I could answer, he signaled to a perky little waitress who was filling coffee cups and water glasses, and she nodded and went off to do his bidding.

Then he pulled his chair around so he could face me.

"I'm very happy you dropped by," he said. "It's a pleasure and a privilege to have you where I can thank you in person for helping Billy out of that jam."

"No trouble."

"I would think a *world* of trouble. Society has a way of punishing good Samaritans."

I'd been called a lot of things in my time, but good Samaritan wasn't one of them.

The doc was saying, "I hope you won't be having any difficulty yourself, with the, uh, messy aftermath."

"No," I assured him, "I'm clear. There were too many witnesses and, anyway, those punks had plenty of strikes against them already. How's Billy?"

His smile was one of relief. "Strictly bruises, lacerations, and a badly sprained ankle from that fall he took when the car swiped him. I'm making him stay at Saxony another couple of days—he doesn't relish the idea, but doctor's orders are, as they say, doctor's orders."

"Rank's got its privileges, all right."

The coffee came and we both thanked the perky little gal. This one was cute enough that the hairnet didn't defeat her.

As I stirred some cream and sugar in, I said offhandedly, "Billy mention why those clowns went after him?"

He looked up with a thoughtful squint. He reminded me of somebody—the actor John Carradine, maybe?

"Mr. Hammer, I'd say they were after his money. He'd just been paid, you know. Must it be anything more sinister than that?"

"No. That's sinister enough."

His eyebrows, which were as black as his hair was white, rose high. "The same thing happened twice last month to an orderly and a nurse. Open, daylight muggings by apparent narcotics addicts."

"What does Billy have to say on the subject?"

"He doesn't. He couldn't give any reason for the attack at all." Harrin made a wry gesture that was matched by his facial expression and said, "It doesn't matter much *now*, does it? That is, thanks to your quick action, Mr. Hammer. Two are dead and the other one is under arrest, and in critical condition."

"There are plenty more shitheels where they came from."

His look turned grave. "And we get them at Saxony, poor wretches."

"You feel sorry for them?"

"Not for them. For the human beings they once were."

"You know kids—they think they're going to live forever."

He said nothing, and I realized what I'd said.

"Sorry, Doctor. I know you lost your son. That's a hurt that doesn't go away. Sometimes I'm a tactless bastard."

He hardly seemed to be listening. But then he said, "Mr. Hammer, it's these times, these changing times. There are things about them that are positive—freedom of expression, that's a good thing. Certain shackles of society *need* to fall away."

"I kind of dig this sexual revolution myself."

"I would imagine. From what I understand, Mr. Hammer, you may have fired the first shot."

We both smiled at that, but then the doc said, "It's these narcotics that are the most troubling. A kid smokes a little marijuana, and really what's the harm? Jazz musicians have been doing it for years."

Couldn't argue with that.

"But it's a minor high, Mr. Hammer. Don't believe this nonsense about 'gateway' drugs. It's not the drug that intrinsically leads to harder stuff. It's the urge, perhaps a natural one in a young person, to experiment, to seek a, well, *higher* high. And now we're finding teenagers, *teenagers,* Mr. Hammer, addicted to heroin."

"Thanks to the bastards who sell them the stuff."

His shrug was eloquent in its sorrowful resignation. "I'm afraid it's a vicious circle almost impossible to break. Nothing seems to deter this idiotic need for thrills that inexorably leads the immature to a slow and sure death. It becomes so important, the users will even kill to obtain it . . . or perhaps I should say, kill while *it's* using *them*. More coffee?"

"Sure. That's my drug of choice—caffeine."

"And I would imagine beer is another one."

"Guilty again."

His smile was world-weary. "But you are an adult, Mr. Hammer. You can make these choices. Our children can't."

I cut my sigh off with a grunt. "Too bad somebody doesn't wipe out all the dealers and the traffickers, way on up the ladder. But even I only have so many bullets."

He laughed at my kidding-on-the-square, and said, "You know, Mr. Hammer . . ."

"Mike."

"Of course . . . Mike, you did a bigger service than you knew when you stopped that attack. Greater than just removing a couple of minor drug dealers."

"How's that?"

"The antibiotic Billy was delivering was something we had just developed. The police car that got it to the clinic arrived with about ten minutes' grace to save a woman's life."

"How did the cops know to deliver the stuff?"

"Billy remembered it when he gained consciousness in the emergency room."

I shook my head. "He's in a world of hurt, and his first thought is that? This is a kid I'd like to meet. I could use a boost in my opinion of the human race about now."

His smile was wide but thin. "Good. I know Billy would like to thank you personally." His eyes went up to the wall clock. "You know, I'm about to go over there myself, if you'd care to join me. It's only a two-block walk to the hospital."

"Fine."

He rose. "Then let's go up to my office so I can change."

We took the service elevator to the fourth floor of the east wing,

23

where Dr. Harrin showed me into his modest office. He smiled when he saw me surveying the simple layout—a desk, two chairs, filing cabinet, and washstand. The only wall hangings were framed parchment scrolls, each with a one- or two-line quotation, from Admiral Dewey's *"Keep Cool and Obey Orders"* to Marie Antoinette's *"Let Them Eat Cake."* A couple were in Latin, which I flunked, but another said, *"The king can do no wrong,"* coined by somebody who never heard of Lyndon Johnson.

"Not a very pretentious place," the doctor told me. "Here, space is too valuable to waste on large, lavish offices. This is where I hang my hat, and do a little paperwork. If we had time, I'd give you the grand tour."

"Of a medical college? No thanks. I wouldn't want to walk in on a cadaver getting cut up or anything."

"Who knows, Mike? Maybe you provided it."

I grinned, shrugged, and pointed to the framed items. "What's with the wall hangings?"

He traded his white smock for a suit coat and joined me at the wall, snugging his tie.

"A hobby of mine," he said. "Famous quotations and slogans, all pertinent to some phase of my life or some belief or even phobia of mine." He indicated the one at the far left. "My father gave me the first of these when I was ten."

I moved down and had a look at the faded yellow sheepskin with its flowery script: *"The man who says it can't be done is interrupted by the man who did it."*

"Anonymous," I said. "My favorite poet."

"And a sentiment apropos to practically any situation," he said, tapping the glass with a forefinger. "Remembering that simple phrase helped me earn my way through college and medical school. Whenever I think something is impossible, I just repeat that line to myself, and keep on."

"There are worse philosophies of life," I said. "So where does Marie Antoinette fit in?"

He moved to that framed phrase and stared at it wistfully before saying, "During the Second World War, three of us were sprawled in a trench. I was a medic and my patient had just died. I was griping about having to eat K rations. The other survivor looked at the mangled body beside me and said, 'Oh yeah? Like that French broad said, "Let 'em eat cake."' Rather put things into perspective. From then on, I often brought to mind those words, and that time. Somebody is always worse off than you are."

"True," I said, "though sometimes I wonder. But to me, Doc, that phrase has another meaning."

"Really? And what is that?"

He was expecting a wisecrack, but this is what he got: "Something can happen that wakes a sleeping giant. Sometimes it's an event, the Alamo, Pearl Harbor. Sometimes it's one individual, Churchill talking about blood, sweat, and tears, or your French broad saying, 'Let 'em eat cake.' But right after, the shit hits the fan."

He studied me with a thoughtful smile, then walked back to the desk and picked up a corrugated wrapper and slid out another framed slogan, holding it up for me to see.

"Here's my latest acquisition, Mike—'Caveat emptor.'"

"Let the buyer beware." Even my Latin covered that. "What consumer advocate magazine are you subscribing to?"

"Actually, this is a gift from my colleague and friend Dr. Sprague. He considers me something of an impulse shopper—he's trying to cure me of my bad habits through my own psychological devices."

"Will he succeed?"

"That," he said cheerfully, "is about as likely as me convincing Dr. Sprague to mind his own business. . . . Come on, Mr. Hammer . . . Mike. Let's go see Billy."

• • •

His right eye was black, the side of his boyish face skinned up, one arm wrapped in bandages from wrist to shoulder, and his swollen ankle taped and propped on a pillow.

Dr. Harrin gave him a warm smile, and said, "You look lousy, Billy," and when the dark-haired kid chuckled through his sore mouth, the doc checked the damaged areas and nodded approvingly.

"This is no worse," he told the kid, "than something you might get playing football."

"Yeah," Billy said, "on *pavement* maybe."

That made Harrin smile again. "Who's ever seen grass in the city, except perhaps apartment-house patios?" He gestured to me and I stepped forward, my hat in hand. "Billy, this is Mr. Hammer. He's the one who stopped those characters from jumping you."

I said, "Hiya, Billy."

"Hello, Mr. Hammer." He tried to straighten or sit up a little and the bed squeaked. "I'm just sorry it got so . . . so out of hand."

He was giving me a strange look, his bright blue eyes trying to classify me for his uneasy mind, which couldn't find the right category.

Sharp, these kids. They live in this city, too, and can pick up on things—I knew what he was thinking because I had seen that same expression on other faces dozens of times before.

Who is *this guy? Cop? Hood? Citizen?*

The marks of each category had left their scars on me, but Billy couldn't locate the fence that divided them into their own specific compartments and it scared him because at his age, after what he'd just been through, he couldn't afford to make mistakes anymore.

Dr. Harrin said, "Mr. Hammer is a private investigator, Billy. He was a little concerned about you."

A small light of relief showed in the kid's eyes. "Hammer. *Mike* Hammer?"

"That's right."

"I heard of you. You're famous."

"Infamous, maybe."

Then his eyes clouded again. I got the message before he realized he'd sent it, and assured him, "I wasn't part of this, son. I wasn't tailing those druggies or anything. I just happened to be coming out of a building where I had a client, when it went down."

"I see." He was still holding back.

I shook my head. "A rough go, son. Who *were* those creeps?"

His eyes tightened, his forehead, too. "Mr. Hammer . . ."

Like the good-looking redheaded nurse had known, these kids don't talk about each other—it's worse than prison, the inmates not wanting to rat the other cons out.

And I didn't want to have to trip him up in a lie in front of the doctor, either, so I went right on: "Felton punk have it in for you, after that argument?"

Harrin's eyes tilted toward me curiously, then shot back to the boy in the bed. "Billy, I didn't realize you *knew* them. . . ."

"Well . . ." The kid licked his lips and swallowed. "Herm Felton and Norm Brix . . . they used to go to my school. They dropped out a long time ago. I hardly knew them at all."

I said, "They knew *you* though, didn't they?"

After a few seconds of strained hesitation, Billy nodded. "Yeah, I . . . I guess so."

I pressed: "What did they want from you, Billy?"

He squirmed, not caring to look at either of us, his savior or his mentor.

Harrin said, calmly, coolly, "You can tell us, son. There's nothing to be afraid of. We're both on your side."

A sudden denial leaped into his eyes, then he saw my face and knew no bullshit would get by that puss, and it subsided quickly. Speaking to the doctor was easier than dealing with me, so he rolled his head over and looked at Harrin. "You won't get pissed, Doc?"

"Do I have reason to, Billy?"

"Maybe. That I . . . didn't tell you before, I mean."

"No, I won't get angry with you, Billy."

The kid locked his lips and nodded, his face resigned. "Felton . . . he knew I worked for you. Somebody told him I could go any place I wanted to, at the college." He stopped and waited, as if that explanation were more than enough.

It wasn't for the doc, who urged, "Go on, Billy."

"They wanted me to get them . . . stuff. Cocaine and other drugs. From the medical supply cabinets? They said they'd pay me more snitching stuff for them in a day than I made working for you, Doc, in a month."

When neither Harrin nor I said anything, Billy added, "I told them to go . . . sorry, Doctor, but I told them to go fuck themselves."

I smiled a little.

"But Felton . . . he said he'd make me change my mind, and have a good time doing it."

I heard Harrin say under his breath, "Unregenerate bastards . . ."

I asked the boy, "Could you have done that for them, Billy? Were the drugs that accessible?"

The kid shook his head. "Not really. They didn't know what they were talking about. That didn't stop them from putting the squeeze on me, though."

Harrin turned his cadaverous gaze my way and said, "Mike, there are two keys to the lock on the medical supply room. Authorized personnel can check one out, the supervisor on duty has the other and accompanies everyone in. Inventory control is tight and security is first-rate. There was *no* way Billy could have gotten in there without getting caught pilfering. Dorchester, as a medical college, is not run like the usual public hospital."

28

I said, "Except those punks didn't know that."

"Apparently not," Harrin said.

Then he patted Billy's hand, straightened, and smiled. "Well, son, don't fret about any of this. I appreciate your attitude and I'm glad you took the stand you did. In the future, you come to me, if anything like this ever comes up . . . understood?"

Billy's face brightened. "Understood, Dr. Harrin. And . . . look, I'm really sorry."

"I'm sorry, too—that you got bashed up. Now you stay put until Dr. Sprague releases you. I'll only be gone for a week, and you can get back to work when I return."

"Then you *are* going?"

Harrin nodded, smiling. "Finally decided somebody might know more on a subject or two than I do, and that I'd better catch up." He glanced at me and explained, "Medical convention in Paris. Haven't been there since the war."

Billy, his voice lighter now, said, "See if you can snag me Bardot's autograph, would you, Doc?"

Harrin chuckled and patted the kid's arm. His affection for the boy was nice to see.

Outside the building the doctor put a hand on my shoulder. "Anything I can pick up for you in Paris, my friend?"

"When you're getting Bardot's autograph," I said, "tell Bebe her Mike misses her, okay?"

We exchanged grins, and I flagged down a cab to get me back to midtown. I gave the driver the address of the Blue Ribbon on West Forty-fourth Street and fired up the last butt from my pack of Luckies.

The city unwound past the window, the sidewalks sparse with people, the work force on trains heading home by now, the city enjoying its temporary lull before darkness settled in and the night people took over. Everything seemed peaceful enough.

But so does dynamite until somebody touches a flame to the fuse.

Pat finished his knockwurst, washed it down with a beer, and belched. "Damn, that was good."

"Sounds like it."

He smirked at me. "And I suppose you never belch, Mike?"

"Naw. I got too much class to belch in public."

"Yeah?"

"I fart instead."

Pat's face twisted sourly. "Man, you are one nasty piece of work."

"Which is why the dolls dig me. They go for Neanderthal types."

"That's the best explanation of your appeal I ever heard."

Two after-dinner coffees arrived, and Pat said, "Tell me you've been behaving yourself since last we met."

"What do you think?"

He took on that same old troubled look and he shook his head. "I thought I told you to lay off. . . ."

"Hell, I was curious, Pat. I poked around a little bit. Can you blame me?"

"That's how it all starts with you, buddy. You get curious, then somebody gets suddenly dead. I don't know how it goes down, but it *does* go down, and then everything turns to shit. You make things work out so that you only get dirty around the edges, not enough to need a bath or anything, and me? I wind up having to go around holding hands and pacifying the damn politicos who are screaming for your head."

I just shrugged and said, "So what are friends for?"

"Balls," he scowled.

I changed the subject to improve his digestion, but somehow we got back again to those charmers who took Billy down. The one in the hospital still couldn't be interrogated, the docs said, and his condition hadn't changed any.

I asked, "Anybody going to look into the drug scene in that neck of the woods?"

"Mike, the narco squad is busy *all* over town. We haven't got enough manpower to bust every little pissin' pusher. Hell, you know how these courts are today—the kids say they're sorry and get their wrists slapped and are dropped right back onto the streets. The only way we'll ever control this beast is if we can figure a way to stop the flow of stuff into the country."

I shrugged. "If our government ever puts a financial squeeze on the countries growing the junk, we might just manage that."

"How, in God's name?" Pat tried his coffee and put it down when it was too hot. "Look at opium. They grow it legally, supposedly for medical purposes. They sell only so much straight, because they have to, and hold back the rest for the black market, where they *triple* their take. Hell, man, the growers are only poor farmers who don't know any better since they only handle the raw product. It's the ones processing the stuff into heroin and shipping it out who need to be nailed. But right now, old buddy? They have the large loot to make payoffs, and the political power to keep the lid on the racket."

I said, "It has to end sometime."

"Yeah. When the world does." He shifted in his seat. "Right now there's an alert out for a massive heroin shipment being held for delivery someplace on the European coast. The syndicate operation here, your old pals the Evello Family, seem to have a cute little operation for getting the stuff in that nobody's been able to figure. For the past six months, the stuff's been delivered in small lots until they're sure their new procedure is foolproof. Now they're ready to go for the big bang."

"Oh? *How* big?"

"About fifty million dollars big, when it's cut and hits the street."

I let out a low whistle. "Pretty big at that, chum. Adds up to a whole lot of needle marks."

"Shit," Pat spat out. "Whole lot of robberies, muggings, and murders, you mean. Whole lot of kids dead, not to mention your occasional decadent celebrity. You got a damn good look at it the other day."

"Nothing I haven't seen before."

"And don't give me your crap about stopping the traffic in drugs. There's too much money to be made. It *can't* be stopped." He searched my face and scowled again. "What's so funny about that?"

"Just something I read today. A slogan."

"Yeah?"

I repeated, "'The man who says it can't be done is interrupted by the man who just did it.'"

Pat looked up at the ceiling in total disgust. "Oh great, just great. Hit 'em with a slogan. That'll do it. That'll show the big boys."

"Maybe it will," I said.

His eyes came down slowly, watched me, got mad for a second, then he grunted through a sarcastic smile. "You're just talking, right?"

"You been doing most of the talking."

"You're not getting into this . . ." He was frowning so hard he was inventing new lines in his face. "You're not tilting at *this* windmill, are you, Mike?"

"What windmill?"

"Drugs. Narcotics. Junk. Shit."

"No," I said.

"No?"

32

"No. I talked to Billy Blue, he's resting up, healing up, the bad guys are dead or maybe dying. My work here is done."

Pat was studying me now, the way you do a junkyard dog that's just sitting there wagging its tail at you. "I wish I could believe you, Mike."

I wasn't kidding, but I knew there was no convincing him, so I let it go.

I had sat too long in one position and the wound on my side was feeling like leather drying in the sun, pulling everything in with it.

Pat offered to drive me back to my apartment, but I opted to walk, told him so long, and took off east on Forty-fourth Street at an easy lope.

At Sixth Avenue a pair of hookers in miniskirts and blouses that were all chest almost gave me a pitch, but turned it off after a second glance. Sometimes vice cops can even look like vice cops, and I grinned at them for giving me the benefit of the doubt.

"Business must be off," I said, waiting for the light, "if a couple dolls like you don't have any takers."

This was generous but not a total lie.

The brunette with the pretty, green-stockinged legs flashed me a smile. Either I was a native straight who knew the dodge, or a cop skipping the entrapment angle—making the first overture louses up the case for a cop when there's a witness around.

"Sometimes," she said, "I think I shoulda hung on to my fuckin' pimp."

I shook my head. "But that cuts the pie in half, cutie."

"Half a pie beats hell out of a whole cookie."

Wisdom is where you find it.

She took a risk. "You looking for some company?"

"Thanks. Not tonight."

She nodded, then indicated her friend. "The two of us, honey, we could turn this dull conversation into a real lively party. . . ."

"I imagine you could."

The light changed to green and I winked and started across the street. On the opposite corner, another pair who'd gathered that I'd turned down the other gals didn't bother chasing this foul ball, and let me go by with barely a glance.

On Sixth Avenue I walked north, remembering the way the street used to look and trying to picture it after the city planners and developers would finally get through. The decay had taken hold twenty years ago, but instead of treating the rot and restoring the originality, they had decided to extract each structure, replacing the street's aging smile with architectural dentures that seemed to be trying to take a jagged bite out of the sky. In between, where the holes were, the decay still showed, the infection deadly—right down to the gums of the sidewalk.

When I reached Forty-ninth Street, I cut east again, threading my way through another parade of faded fun girls looking for the tourist dollar, and almost made the middle of the block without having to deal with any wilted flower's offer.

An ancient rose of thirty in a too-tight dress split up the middle to where her wares showed was about to fall in step with me; her unlit cigarette in its long, slender holder was the opening gambit for the "got a light" come-on.

But her eyes, which had seen too much already, suddenly reached behind me and widened just enough to touch off all those old reflexes and I twisted out of the way of the knife that was supposed to have gone into me, hit the guy on the shoulder to spin him my way, and smashed a fast right to his face that splintered his nose into fragments of bone and flesh, then got him twice more before he lifted off his feet and plopped into the gutter between parked cars.

I kicked the six-inch open switchblade knife over beside him and looked down at the mashed face bubbling with blood. My mugger was damn well-dressed—that was no off-the-rack suit he was wearing. But he was too slippery and red for me to walk away with a decent description, so I knelt and patted him down until I found his wallet, took out his driver's license and social security card, shoved the wallet back, and stood up to grin at the ancient rose.

She was wondering whether to puke and I was in no mood to help her decide, so I left her standing there, unable to take her eyes off the smeary human fingerpainting in the gutter.

No crowd had collected, nothing seemed to have upset the ecology or the decorum of the street. A few eyes looked and a few mouths spoke, but there was no change in the tempo. It was simply a moment of waiting to see what would happen next.

When I crossed the street, I didn't even bother to pick up the pace. I was in no hurry.

But I knew that what I'd told Pat was wrong—this *wasn't* over, not when a "mugger" in a tailored suit had tried to knife me. Billy might not need my help anymore, but somebody did.

A guy named Hammer, who person or persons unknown had decided needed killing.

Chapter Three

UNDER THE PAGE FIVE photograph, the mini-headline read MIDTOWN MURDER, and beneath that the caption: *Uniden-tified Man Knifed in Mugging Attack.*

I was behind my desk and Velda was draping the *Daily News* across my blotter with narrow-eyed accusation. I had called her last night and filled her in on the day's events, including the attempted mugging.

I shrugged, flipped the paper closed, and handed it back to her. "Doll, he wasn't like that when I left him. Scout's honor."

She gave me a long, slow look and I saw the tension creeping across her shoulders. That same old worry was back in her voice, tight, low, and a little breathless, as she said, "Then this *is* the guy who came at you?"

"Yeah." I gestured with open hands and gave her as innocent a look as I could muster. "The bastard tried to knife me and I splashed him—what do you want from me?"

"Mike . . ."

"Hey, he was flat on his back when I left the scene—out cold, plenty the worse for wear, but breathing, baby. Breathing."

She opened the paper again, held it out in front of her. I couldn't see the page she was perusing—the front page faced me, full of Casey Stengel, recently retired as Mets manager—but I knew she was studying the face-down corpse in the crime-scene photo.

"If this *isn't* your handiwork . . ."

"It isn't."

The dark eyes flared. "Then whose *is* it?"

I shrugged again. "Plenty of easy answers, kid. Either there was a backup man, to pay the guy off the hard way, if he bungled the job—which he did, remember—or maybe one of those faded flowers started frisking him for his loot and the guy started coming around and the gal had to kill the son of a bitch, to keep him quiet. I mean, that knife was right there beside him, kitten, when I took off. It was only later the thing got stuck in his back."

She pulled up the client's chair and sat, her expression empty of accusation, full of thought.

"You had just left Pat," she stated, "and were on your way home. The guy really could have been just trying to mug you, you know."

I shook my head. "No dice, honey. Open street muggings are usually strong-arm attempts and involve two people, one to latch on to the mark and the other to beat and bash him. This was a solo kill, carefully set up to be enough like a mugging to be written off as one."

"You just said yourself there may have been a second person. . . ."

"Yeah, but not in the mugging-team sense. Hit men often have a backup, you know, running interference, waiting with wheels." I batted the air. "And even from that newspaper photo, couldn't you catch how wrong that bozo's threads were?"

"Not exactly typical mugger attire."

"Naw. That was one sharp suit. Tailored, British kind of cut."

38

She was shaking her head, the dark tresses dancing. "But, Mike—you weren't working on anything."

My eyebrows went up. "I'm beginning to wonder. Anyway, that isn't the point, whether I was working on something."

"What is?"

"Whether somebody might have *thought* I was."

I pulled the license and social security card out of my coat pocket. The name was the same on both: Russell Frazer—address, the Avondale Hotel on upper Broadway.

I reached for the phone and dialed Pat's number. They located him in a police cruiser, gave him my message, and told me to stay put until he got there.

Fifteen minutes later, Pat brushed by Velda at her desk with a polite nod and locked himself in with me in my private office, obviously trying to decide whether to haul my ass downtown to the cooler or listen to me try to worm my way out of the bind. He tossed his hat on my desk, deposited himself in the client's chair, and his eyes dared me to win him over. It took me all of three minutes to give him the details, and he was good enough not to interrupt. Then I let him check Russell Frazer's ID cards.

When he was finished looking those over, he gave me the long-suffering face and said, "I'm supposed to ignore you walking away from an attempted mugging? A mugging where you beat the hell out of the guy? The day after you send two other guys to the morgue and another to the critical ward?"

I lifted a shoulder and put it down again. "Would you rather I called it in, and the two of us had another scintillating session with that assistant D.A., Traynor?"

He just scowled at me.

"What did the medical examiner come up with?"

Pat tucked the cards away, gnawed at his lip a moment, then said, "It could have been a fight that ended in a knifing. Or it could have been a mugging. Poetic justice—mugger gets mugged. Guy's

39

pants pockets were turned inside out, some loose change was in the gutter nearby, and his wallet was missing."

I held up an honest-injun palm. "I didn't take the wallet—just his license and social security."

"Any dough in the thing?"

"There were bills in it when I stuck it back in his pocket, yeah. You got any witnesses?"

He smirked without humor. "You kidding? Right now, you'd think that corner last night had been as deserted as Sunday morning. Nobody saw a damn thing, and the girls who work that block must be working some other block today." Then he shrugged. "But just as soon as we let a little heat loose, we'll get it put together."

"You're giving this that kind of priority?"

"I am now that I know *you* were on the scene." He crossed his arms and glared at me, tiny lines showing at the corners of his eyes. "So—what's your angle, Mike?"

"Quit playing the heavy," I told him. "All I did was protect myself."

"That's all you ever do," he said sarcastically. "Why did you lift his IDs?"

I got up, walked over to the mini-refrigerator, took out a can of Pabst beer, and popped it open. Hadn't had time for breakfast. Pat waved it off when I offered him one.

"You didn't answer me," he said.

"Because," I said, settling back behind my desk, "if there was another reason for the attack, besides a mugging, I wanted the bum to know I could finger him."

"Don't give me that mugging crap, Mike. You're not exactly the kind of target those guys pick on. They go after little old ladies or rabbity tourists who won't fight back. Most of these muggers have a habit, and they don't want to do any cold-turkey time in a jail cell."

I leaned back in my swivel chair. "Okay, so there's only one angle left—somebody had to be tailing me."

"And the great Mike Hammer didn't notice?"

I batted that away. "Hell, Pat, I didn't have any reason to sweat it—I wasn't on anything active. Only you and Velda knew I was going to be at the Blue Ribbon last night, so they had to pick me up someplace before I got to the restaurant."

He was frowning. "Why would they bother tailing you? And if this wasn't a mugging, who wants you dead? Scratch that—*plenty* of people want you dead. . . ."

"It's bugging me, too," I said, ignoring his last statement. "I'm going to have to think about it."

Pat and I had been friends too long for him not to know when a conversation of ours had come to the end of the line. The gray eyes narrowed and he was very likely still considering putting a hold order on me for my own good; but we were both pros, and he would hold the reins loose until I started to bolt. My sources of information weren't as broad as his, but sometimes they were a lot more specific when some long green was handy to grease the way.

So he nodded curtly, a silent acknowledgment that I could try to satisfy my curiosity just a little bit. A very little bit. He plucked his hat off my desk, put it on, and headed out.

At the door, though, he stopped, turning around and saying, "By the way, Mike, where *were* you before we met up at the Blue Ribbon?"

I made a face and shrugged. "Pat, believe it or not, I was visiting a sick friend."

"Horseshit," he said.

But it was fairly good-natured, and he even threw me a kind of wave.

I heard him tell Velda so long and, when he was gone, she came into my inner sanctum and up to my desk and handed me a memo.

"You didn't exactly put a big smile on his face," she said, though she was smiling.

"He should buy me a six-pack for what I gave him. Right now he's one up on every other cop in town."

"Not on us." She flicked the memo. "I took the liberty of calling Bud Tiller to do a little work for us."

"Yeah? He does owe me a favor."

"Not anymore. Bud pried a little information out of the desk clerk at the Avondale Hotel, which is not a flophouse exactly, if only a couple rungs up."

"My mugger in the mod suit was living in less than luxury?"

"So it would seem. Russell Frazer moved out of that place six months ago after a two-year stay. Apparently he never bothered changing his address on his driver's license. Anyway, he moved someplace up near his job and gave his work as his forwarding address, in case he got any mail." She gave me a look that said another shoe was about to drop. Then she dropped it: "Russell Frazer was employed six blocks from Dorchester Medical College."

I let out a low whistle. "Isn't that interesting? Where exactly did my well-dressed attacker work?"

"It's a ceramics shop. Apparently he drove the delivery truck, but we'll need to do some more digging. And you'll *want* to do some digging, because I've got a connection between Frazer and one of the freaks who jumped Billy Blue."

If I had straightened any more, I'd be standing. "Spill it, sugar."

"Before Frazer moved to the Avondale? He lived on the same street as the Brix kid—just a few blocks away."

My eyes tightened; so did my hands. "What a cute little play this is. . . ."

She cocked her head. "Mike—if they were friends, hitting you could have a revenge motive."

"Naw, it's thin."

42

She arched an eyebrow. "People *have* been known to kill other people, over *revenge,* you know."

I gave her a look. "Sarcasm doesn't become you, baby."

She was smiling. If I weren't preoccupied, I would have smashed her in that mouth. With my mouth.

"So," I asked her, *"were* they friends?"

"Bud didn't get that far. But it's possible. Frazer was three years older, and that's roughly the same age bracket."

"It could make sense," I said, and sighed. "But where could he have picked me up? Nobody knew I was going to the hospital. Not even you. Not even me."

Her smile had settled on one side of her face, and she shook the dark tresses again. "You're not exactly hard to find, Mike. The papers didn't carry your address, but we're in the book. It wouldn't have been tough. He could have tailed you all day, waiting for the right opportunity, and you wouldn't have known it."

"He'd have to be good for that."

"Not necessarily. You weren't expecting anything."

I'd made the same point to Pat. "You'd like it that way, wouldn't you? Just somebody settling a score?"

"Well, if it *were* a simple revenge factor, it'd all be over now."

"Unless there are some more out there who'd like to try their hand at the same game."

"What happened to Frazer," Velda said with an eyebrow high again, "wouldn't exactly encourage them to try again."

"Maybe . . . but I think I'd better emphasize the point a little."

She smiled at me and went back to the outer office and her desk, leaving the door open. I sat there and stared at her legs and she parted them to give me a better view and then stuck out her tongue at me, in that taunting, tantalizing way of hers.

She was damn lucky I was preoccupied.

I flipped a paper clip at her, but it only made half the trip. Then

I got my .45 out of the top desk drawer and checked the clip, and shoved the rod in the holster and got up.

Outside it had started to rain.

The state of mind called Greenwich Village had gone through another of its periodic shifts, though you would find the same zigzag streets and street-corner poets and shaggy-haired oddballs selling canvases that would make Picasso say, "What the hell?" But the beatniks were gone and the hippies were here, the folk music electric now, and the shops had tourists in mind, not the local populace.

Both large windows facing the street read VILLAGE CERAMICS SHOPPE in Old English lettering, the rain hitting their surfaces and blurring the multicolored pieces on display behind them. It was a three-story renovated building tucked between two newer, higher ones, faced with stucco and stained timbers like an old London townhouse. A pair of young housewife types, heads tucked under those silly mushroom umbrellas, ducked around me, went inside, and I followed them in.

The interior was bare brick walls and a hardwood floor with aisles of pine shelving displaying glazed pottery, mostly in shades of green and brown but with the occasional more colorful item. The feeling was of spare simplicity and, for a few minutes, I just went up and down the aisles, looking at the finished pieces with price tags that landed somewhere between reasonable and outrageous. A few aisles were devoted to the practical—vases and bowls, plates and cups and other dinnerware—but the majority were decorative pieces, cats and leopards and female nudes as well as abstractions.

Eventually the heavyset woman at the counter waiting on a customer noticed me, hit a hand bell, and the curtains to the rear section flipped open and a lovely blonde in a paint-stained smock stood there filling the archway. She was in her mid-twenties, maybe five five, with the kind of curves even a loose-fitting outfit like that couldn't hide, her eyes big and brown and generously lashed.

She used those remarkable orbs to look around until she found the unattended customer, then smiled and happy-hipped over, trying to wipe the stains from her hands on a paper towel. A little smear of green highlighted one cheek, but that only made her prettier, and then she asked, "May I help you, sir?"

It was in a voice that fit the rest of her perfectly—smooth, rounded, and velvety.

I shook the rain off my hat and said, "Maybe. But I'm not exactly a customer."

She gazed up at me, still smiling. Nice dimples. "I didn't think you were," she said, vaguely amused. "You don't, uh . . . look like the kind of person who makes or buys ceramics. Of course, you never know about people."

"No argument there." I shifted on my feet. "It's about Russell Frazer. Any place we can talk privately?"

The smile faded—not into irritation, but sadness. "A terrible thing. Terrible." She paused, then nodded toward the archway. "You're another investigator?"

"That's right."

She nodded, businesslike. "Then we can speak back in the studio."

I followed her through the curtains and across to a large table loaded with partially painted figurines, and surrounded by a half-dozen beat-up wooden chairs. The rest of the room was a maze of shelves and bins packed with chalky molds, raw bisque, and greenware. It wasn't anywhere near the season yet, but holiday items seemed to predominate, little Santas and reindeer and elves that didn't quite fit with the artier junk out front.

She noticed me eyeing that stuff and said, "Christmas underwrites the rest of our year."

"You and about every other shop in town."

45

When I had pulled out a chair for her and sat down myself, I said, "I take it you just found out about what happened to Mr. Frazer?"

She shuddered. "Not thirty minutes ago. There was a call from police headquarters, then a squad car stopped by, and right now, Mr. Elmain—he's the manager—is on his way to identify the body. But then you must know that."

"Pretty standard procedure," I said evasively.

She frowned just a little. She had smooth skin and, at her age, such frowns had only delivered glancing blows. "Mr., uh . . ."

"Hammer," I said. I hadn't bothered to introduce myself. I'd wanted to connect with her before we got around to the ugly reality of who I was in this.

But she was no fool. When I said "Hammer," she must have caught the lack of rank before my name. Because now she was cocking her head, looking at me peculiarly. "You *are* a policeman . . . ?"

"I'm a private investigator, Miss . . ." And this time *I* let it hang, because she hadn't introduced herself, either.

"Shirley Vought." She may have been suspicious, but her manner remained direct and essentially positive.

"Miss Vought," I said, and gave her a serious smile, "I was involved in helping the police identify Mr. Frazer. There's an odd set of circumstances at play here, which might make Mr. Frazer's death relate to a problem of mine."

"Oh?"

"You might be able to help me."

Again, she remained direct and positive: "Certainly, if I can."

"Do you know any of Mr. Frazer's friends?"

For a moment she looked puzzled. Then she answered, "Well, there was a young woman, just a girl really . . . Susie something . . . who met Russell a few times, after work. . . ."

"Know where she lives?"

46

"No, but she works in the market on the corner. I can point you there." She gave me directions, briefly.

"Thank you. Any men Mr. Frazer hung around with?"

She thought again before shaking her head. "Outside the shop, I can't say I know any of Russell's friends."

"What exactly did he do here?"

"Pickup and deliveries. In between, he poured slip in the molds, loaded the kilns, waited on customers."

"Well paid?"

She nodded, chin crinkled. "I'd have to say, yes. Mr. Elmain is an exceptionally generous employer. Russ made over a hundred a week for what you'd have to say was menial work."

I nodded, remembering that tailored mod suit, and the wallet in his pocket, thick with big-number bills. Whoever had rolled the late Mr. Frazer was walking around fat and happy. But even at a generous hundred bucks a week for unskilled labor, how had my buddy Russell rated In Crowd threads and a wad of dough like that?

Somehow she picked the thought out of my mind and said, "Russ lived by himself, Mr. Hammer. He *did* have rather expensive tastes in clothes, but he didn't have much else to spend it on."

"No family?"

"He originally came from Chicago, I believe." She thought harder, then said, "I can't say I ever heard him specifically mention anybody back home, either family or close friends."

"Where did he live?"

"Let's see—I think on Peck Street. That's one block from the new housing development this side of Saxony Hospital. But I'd better check it."

She got up and went to a counter; she had black slacks on under the dusty smock and, where it tied, a glimpse of nicely rounded rear peeked out and said hello.

She riffled through a card file a moment and came back to the table and sat. "Peck Street, all right," she said. "Number 1405. Before that he lived on the Boulevard."

"Miss Vought—have you ever heard the names Herman Felton, Norman Brix, Timothy Haver, or William Blue?"

Those lovely dark eyes angled into mine a second and twin narrow lines formed a brief furrow between her brows. "Yes."

That perked me up. "You did?"

She nodded. "I read about them in the papers. And, of course, I knew Billy Blue."

"You *knew* him?"

"Know him. We deliver a quantity of greenware pieces to the hospital for their therapeutic program . . . in the children's ward? Billy often came by here to pick up some incidental supplies— brushes, paints, that sort of thing."

I waited, thinking.

"And Mr. Hammer—I remember reading about *you* now, too." There was a wise glint in her eyes.

I gave up half a grin. "I've been around too long to bother trying to con anybody, Miss Vought. I never misrepresented myself."

"Yes, I know," she said. "I pay attention to such things." She gave me a small smile.

"I guess in the pottery game, you have to pay attention to detail. Same in the detective game."

"I'm sure," she said, the velvety voice making a purr out of it. "You know, I rather appreciate your indirect approach. No lies, but not terribly generous with the truth."

"No use showing your hand until you have to."

She was studying me now, the big eyes going narrow. "Then your interest in this matter is . . . personal?" Her voice remained calm. "Rather than professional?"

"It's always personal when somebody tries to kill me."

48

The eyes got big again. "Well, Mr. Hammer—you *are* Mike Hammer, aren't you?"

"Yeah."

"I seem to remember a rather sensational magazine that made mention of another violent incident involving you . . . a few years ago?" She smiled again. "The publisher tried to sue you, after you did something, uh . . . detrimental to his well-being?"

"He caught an acute case."

"An acute case of what, Mr. Hammer?"

"Broken ribs." I shrugged. "No big deal. He withdrew the charges upon advice of counsel, after receiving a ten-cent phone call."

"Anonymous call, you mean?"

"Oh no. I gave my name loud and clear."

The smile had something flirtatious in it now. I'd told Pat the dolls went for Neanderthals.

She said, "Who tried to kill you *this* time, Mr. Hammer?"

"Your friend Russell Frazer."

The smile vanished, and she tilted her head. "That doesn't make sense. . . ."

"Murder never does," I said. "At first, anyway."

"Russell rarely raised his voice around here. He was nice, rather funny, I'd even say charming. I can't imagine him trying to kill anyone, much less . . . much less someone as, uh, formidable? As you, Mr. Hammer."

"It's like you said, Miss Vought."

"What?"

"You never know about people." I pushed the chair back and stood up. "Thanks for the conversation. I hope I wasn't a bother and kept you too long from your work."

With her penchant for detail, Shirley Vought was watching me carefully and the eyes were wide again, curiosity twinkling at their corners.

Very abruptly she said, "I was wrong."

"Wrong?"

"You are *anything* but indirect, Mr. Hammer. I would say . . . you are remarkably *di*-rect."

"Thanks."

Her expression grew slyly catlike, and openly sensual. "Tell me, Mr. Hammer . . . do you make love with that same direct approach?"

I grinned at her, taking the invitation of that remark to allow my eyes a sweep over her body. The streak of green on her cheek glowed like some sort of psychedelic beauty mark under the fluorescent lighting.

"No," I told her. "I'm a little more devious in my lovemaking. I like it nice and lazy, after a good, long chase . . . so I can appreciate the explosion, when it comes."

She couldn't hold back the laugh, throaty but still velvet all the way.

"You know," she said, "I believe it."

I gave her another half grin. "Interested?"

This time her eyes smiled, too.

"This," she said softly, rising from the table, "is where I say 'Thank you . . . call again.'"

I was almost through the curtains when I glanced back and said, "Don't you mean 'come again'?"

She gave me a little shrug. *We'll see,* she seemed to be saying. *We'll see. . . .*

Her name was Susie Moore, she ran the checkout register at counter number two in Supermarket East, and she was glad to have a sandwich with me at the rear table at a lunchroom around the corner. She was twenty-three, shared an apartment with two other girls who worked in the neighborhood, and was saving her money to enroll in a secretarial school that winter.

Susie wasn't exactly pretty, just cute in a pug-nosed way with brown pixie-cut hair, a lithe figure, and a bubbly charm that was attraction enough—one of that new breed of kids you see leading peace marches and waving out of the window of a police van on the way to being booked at the local precinct house for having disturbed the tranquility of the Establishment.

We were next to a window in the unpretentious little deli restaurant. The rain had stopped but its tendrils were trickling down the glass nearby. I had pastrami, corned beef, and Swiss cheese on rye, and she had a tuna salad sandwich. She didn't eat meat, she said. That would be news to the tuna.

Analytical eyes picked me apart across the table, trying to separate me into beast or benefactor, or maybe just plain lecher looking to add a few female flower children to his well-thumbed black book.

She had accepted the invitation of a free lunch with a knowing smile—as long as *she* picked the place—willing to cross swords with me just so it saved her another couple bucks for her secretarial kitty. She was wearing her pale blue checkout uniform, which was miniskirt short, showing off her long, bare Go-Go Girl stems.

Before she had finished her sandwich, she had rattled off most of her life history without bothering with any of mine, and when she suddenly realized that, she paused between bites and said, "You play it pretty cool, don't you, Mr. Hammer?"

"Do I?"

"Uh-huh." She swallowed down her last bite of tuna fish sandwich, and sipped her Coke through a straw. "Here I've been waiting for the big pitch, figuring there might be a new angle, and it's like it's *never* gonna happen." Her tongue flicked a crumb from her lower lip and she put the glass down. "You play it nice and cool—let me do all the work."

"Maybe I'm just interested."

"Maybe . . . but what's your ult?"

"My what?"

"Ulterior motive?"

"It's not like that."

She grew a knowing, smirky look that didn't become her. "Isn't it?"

"No. Honey, I'm not after your body."

That surprised her, and probably hurt her feelings a little, but that's what she got for getting too cute. She gestured down at herself and back to me. "I haven't had any complaints before."

I shrugged. "You have a nice figure. Like a model. Only, my tastes go back about ten years, when women had some meat on the bone—more hips, bigger boobies."

Now she was really puzzled. "Well, that's not today's scene."

"It'll come back," I said, not convinced it had ever left.

Susie didn't like to be sidetracked. "Let's get back to your ult. If it's not me, what is it?"

"Suppose we start with Russell Frazer."

This time she squinted and wrinkled her nose at me. "Why?"

"Isn't he a friend of yours?"

"Until he got to be a drag. I used to date him. Just broke it off, like, the other day. What about him?"

She obviously didn't know he was dead, but she had dated him, so things could turn ugly, even with a cutie like this. Still, there are ways of saying things without having to lie or actually say anything at all.

"Maybe," I said, "the best way to put it is that I'm looking for character references on him."

"Is Russ in some kind of trouble?"

Once again I could be truthful about it. I simply said, "Nope."

After all, Russell Frazer would never be in trouble again, not unless his coffin got caught on a tree root, getting lowered into the big hole.

She refused the cigarette I offered her, and I waited. This time the computer eyes had hesitated because the keyboard was sending out odd vibrations. She shook off the confusion, trying the Coke again. Her mouth working the straw was pretty cute, but I'd rather she talk.

Finally, she did: "Listen, I said he was a drag, but if you're checking up on him, really, Russ is okay. I met him right here, you know." She gestured to the little deli sandwich shop around us.

"You dated him? How serious did it get?"

She shrugged and tapped out a rhythm on the tabletop with her fingernails. "Not serious at all. Oh, I *balled* him plenty of times, sure. He thought he was God's gift, but he was all show and no go, you know? A wham-bam type who figured a girl could get her jollies just because he pulled down his zipper. He was hung like a horse."

She said this with full frankness and volume, even though we were hardly alone in the little restaurant. She might have been saying he had dark hair or his name was Jones.

Now she got confidential, leaning forward. "You know, a guy who is *too* big, he never gets *really* hard. Plus, he can only get part of it in."

I think maybe she was trying to shock me or possibly get me interested in her, despite my tastes in fleshier dolls. I ignored it, but didn't insult her. Just let her prattle on. . . .

"You have to fake it for a guy like that," she said, sitting back, almost wistful. "They should pay girls for faking it so convincingly. That kind of guy, you'll hurt his feelings, if he thinks you didn't come through the roof. I hate to hurt people's feelings."

"Did I hurt yours?"

Her smile was a little too big. "Come on, Mr. Hammer, feelings are all *any* of us have. You have *got* to care." Her expression was more teenager than twenty-three-year-old.

"I've been known to care," I said.

"Have you?" She shook her head doubtfully. "Or do you really understand at all? Over thirty and the compassion just goes. *Phhffttt.* I'm sure you were really nice, once. But now? No compassion, no understanding at all."

"You're wrong, Susie."

"Am I?"

"I was never nice."

That caught her by surprise and made her laugh. It was a childish giggle, but appealing.

"Understanding is one thing," I said. "Toleration is another, Susie. And some things just can't be tolerated."

She had her chin up. "If we ever made it, Mr. Hammer? And you didn't ring my bell? I swear, I'd go right ahead and hurt *your* feelings."

"I might hurt more than your feelings, kid. But let's get back to Russ."

"All right," she said with an agreeable shrug. "I've known him for over a year—ever since he began working at the Village Ceramics Shoppe. He liked to show a girl a good time, and didn't mind spending money. He had . . . well, ambition. Someday he was going to be somebody big, he always told me."

"You kidding? Working in a ceramics shop?"

"He had other interests, and real possibilities, big opportunities."

"Such as?"

"Oh, he didn't tell me about them, but I believed him, all right." My face said I didn't believe *her,* and she frowned indignantly. "Well, I *did* believe him!"

"Why, Susie? You said he was all show and no go."

"In the bedroom. But when somebody gets calls from Hawaii and Rome and has Cadillacs sent around to pick him up, it's because he has *some* kind of potential, right?"

"Right," I said pleasantly. "But it depends on who's making the calls and driving the Cadillac."

Her smirk was supposed to put me down. "This Cadillac had a chauffeur, Mr. Hammer—an Oriental chauffeur in a proper uniform."

"Careful, girl. You're cultivating Establishment tastes."

She let another giggle escape her lips and her shoulders moved in a childish gesture. "It *was* cute, though, getting the limo treatment. My roomie, Elsie, was real jealous. Before then, she thought Russ was just a big-mouth drag."

"All show and no go again."

She smirked and nodded. "Like, I been flapping my lips and what you wanted was a character reference for Russ. I guess I haven't done him any favors."

"Depends on how you look at it."

"How *are* you looking at it, Mr. Hammer?" She lifted the Coke again, slurped the last dregs down in the ice, and put it back on the table.

"Through a Coke glass, darkly," I said.

She let half a minute go by while she made designs on the damp table with a fingertip. "Lay it on me, Mr. Hammer. What's this really about?"

"Russell Frazer is dead," I told her flatly. "Last night he tried to stick a knife in my back."

There was no doubt about her believing what I said. It was there in the dull shadow of her eyes and the tight lines around her mouth. Her voice was a bare whisper when she said, "And you . . . *you* killed him?"

"No, I didn't kill him. I knocked him on his ass, into the gutter, and left him there. Later, somebody rolled him for his loot, and stuck Russ's own shiv through his heart in the process."

She blinked at me, as if in time with her brain processing the information. Then she blurted, "I saw something about that incident . . . in the papers? But it don't show the man's face, or—"

"Papers called the victim an unidentified man this morning. They know who he is now. Later you'll probably get some visitors from Homicide."

"Are *you* one of them?" Her expression had turned nauseated. *"You're* not a . . . *pig?"*

"I oink in a different tone of voice, Susie." I gave her a business card. "The others who come around will have a little more pork behind them."

She started to change somehow, like the slow cracking of an ice floe. Her tongue made a nervous pass over suddenly dry lips and she shook her head in bewilderment. "But Russ was never . . . I didn't *know* . . . didn't *see* anything that . . ."

"Everybody hides things," I said. "You're a hip chick, not some teenybopper, even if you like to act like one. You didn't notice anything hinky when you were at Russell's pad?"

"I . . . I just didn't think much about it."

"About what?"

"Like . . . well, his apartment. He made over the loft in that funky old building, and laid out a lot of bread on it. The big stereo with the record collection, and the tape recorders and the big color TVs—all of that was awfully expensive. You can buy toys like that on time and all, but he bragged about paying cash. I thought it was more of his big talk, until, you know . . ."

"The phone calls and Cadillacs?"

Susie nodded, her eyes worried. "One time I answered his phone and got an overseas operator."

"Remember the conversation?"

"No. Russell took the call in the bedroom. I was in the living room."

"When did you see him last?"

"Just two nights ago. He was going to take me to that new 'in'

56

place—the Pigeon? Then he called it off because something came up."

"What?"

"He had to meet somebody."

"Who?"

"Russ didn't say. He was all excited and sort of, well, secretive. Like, I offered to go with him but he didn't want me along."

"He say why?"

"No." She stopped and looked down at the table again and the watery designs she'd made. "I broke it off right after that. Funny. You know, before that? I was set to see him tonight. He was taking me to a ball game to celebrate."

"There aren't any ball games in town tonight, Susie."

Her eyes came up expressionlessly. "Not *that* kind of ball game. I mean, the swinging kind we played at his apartment—you've really got to stay with it, Mr. Hammer, the new culture, the new language."

"I'll try to catch up with you kids. Susie, you've obviously been to Russell's place lately—I was told he moved out."

She shook her head. "He had a hotel room somewhere, where he'd been staying, but I think that was for business, mostly."

"Were you ever at this hotel room?"

"No, and I don't know what hotel or even what part of town. I do know, with his loft pad? Russ had some troubles with the neighbors, and stopped having parties there, and kept a way lower profile. I gave him a bad time about having to sneak around going into his own place."

"You have a key?"

She nodded, fished in her little purse, and held out a key in her palm.

I didn't make any move to take it. "Susie, you can hold that for the cops or give it to me. Your choice."

Her hand stayed outstretched. "Why break the door down?

57

Besides, whatever you are, you're not exactly an Establishment type."

"That's a character reference I can appreciate, sugar."

That made her smile a little. I plucked the key from her palm and dropped it in my pocket.

When I paid the bill, and walked her to the door, she stopped me with her hand on my arm. "I feel awfully funny, Mr. Hammer, now that I think back."

"About what?"

"Having balled a dead man."

"He wasn't dead then."

She took her hand away and let it drop at her side. "Yes he was," she said.

Chapter Four

USSELL FRAZER'S APARTMENT was everything little Susie had said, and more.

She had apparently never opened the mahogany box with the heavy-duty diamond cufflinks and the Cartier jeweled watch. She had not found the two packets of fifty-dollar bills, or seen the empty wrappers for three others, because they were tucked in back of a bottom bureau drawer otherwise occupied by black silk socks, the kind worn by guys with dough or as the primary costume of some stud in a stag reel.

Frazer hadn't lied to Susie when he said he'd paid cash for everything. His receipts were all filed in one compartment of a black-lacquered wall unit with built-in storage cabinets and shelves for his hi-fi components and enough electronic gadgetry to make NASA turn green.

The living room motif was black and white, from the thick white pile wall-to-wall carpet to the black couch and stacked black cushions and white ones that apparently took the place of chairs for guests. The walls bore black-lacquer-framed black-and-white nude female photos that must have been art because the pubic deltas weren't airbrushed out, and the built-in bar in one corner was mirrored where it wasn't a black-and-white checkerboard design.

With the exception of the white carpet, though, the bedroom was in shades of brown and black, since the center-stage round bed's leopard spread seemed the focal point—a mirror above said Russell Frazer was no spring sybarite. That opinion was confirmed by the lavish bathroom's big sunken tub with its water-jet sprays, perfect for two. Or more.

Oh, it was an expensive, elaborate layout all right, taking one hell of a lot of bread, too heavy for a hundred-plus-a-week ceramics worker to handle; but if you had a good sideline going for you, it could be bought.

That character reference Susie had sketched for me was turning into a full-scale portrait as I shook down the rooms. This was all just one big playhouse and these were a little boy's toys. Russell Frazer probably never had the likes of them before, except in his fantasies or reading *Playboy* magazine.

But he sure had made up for lost time. There wasn't one sign of anything of solid investment value—just the ephemeral junk of a have-not who'd been given his head in some overpriced, trend-happy department store. The black satin sheets and the brass cigar humidor on the nightstand were the crowning touches.

Except the humidor didn't hold cigars—it was packed with dozens of condoms topped by a dozen fancy French ticklers, so he could do his entertaining in style. Either he had never heard of the Pill or he was understandably paranoid about VD.

One thing he did have: sense enough not to leave anything around that had a name or a number that wasn't his. And if he had a drug stash, I sure didn't find it. I was starting to wonder if I'd been the first guy to look this coop over.

Because I know how to shake a place down, and nothing pertinent turned up. I double-checked to make sure I hadn't missed anything, then finally headed out. The Homicide team could take it from here and put it through their own system of analysis, and maybe those sharp-eyed boys you never see because they live in labs could work out better answers than yours truly.

All I had going for me was a tight feeling across my shoulders and those funny fingers flexing in my mind and tapping out the message that something in this horny bachelor's pad was emitting a bigger smell than even my trained nose could sniff out.

Near the door, a four-shelved niche showcased a set of male-joined-to-female statuettes depicting just about every sex act imaginable. These weren't the kind of knickknacks you found for sale back at that pottery shop. They were arranged in an almost studied progression, lessons in a book to be learned and practiced, each one more acrobatically ambitious than the next.

Apparently Frazer was pretty serious about his Don Juan image. I could picture him hopping out of bed for a quick run to his knickknack rack to review a posture, then scurrying back to correct his technique. I grunted out a laugh.

His collection was pretty complete, plaster figures based on the most famous Hindu temple reliefs, hand-painted with loving care for detail . . . and nothing that was new to me at all.

I could have told my pal Russell Frazer that he was missing at least one good arrangement Velda had devised.

Hell, I had muscle cramps for two days after.

It took me three hours of talking to half a dozen merchants and citizens, but I made the connection between Norman Brix and Russell Frazer.

Alex Singer, a retired tailor whose stone front stoop was his bleacher seat on the world, remembered them both and didn't have a good word for either.

He was a small blue-eyed man with thin white hair, looking lost in a dark woolen suit the temperature didn't call for. No doubt he'd perfectly tailored that number for himself some years ago, but age was shrinking him.

"Mr. Hammer, that Frazer was a real nogoodnik. The kind of slimeball that can bring a neighborhood down. The kind of crudder that can give young kids the wrong idea about what is 'cool,' and send them off down the wrong path."

"You make him sound like Fagin."

"I don't mean to say he paid any attention to the younger kids, nothing more than a grin and a nod. But when they saw him usher sexy young women up his front steps, and watched him getting in and out of expensive cars with a driver no less, well . . . it gives those kids the wrong kind of ideas."

I didn't point out to the old gent that he seemed to be paying pretty close attention to the dolls parading in and out himself.

"Now *older* kids?" the geezer was saying. "That's another story. Like that Brix boy. Ever since Frazer moved into the neighborhood, occupying that apartment by himself? It turned into the worst kind of hangout for street punks and these trashy little girls they attract. Sometimes I'd see him go in with about five of these punks, Brix and these other greasy-haired bums, and just one girl . . . and she would come out looking tired and frazzled, but counting her money."

"Any specific girl?"

"No. A good half-dozen of them. Skinny with dead eyes, all of 'em."

"There's a little doll named Susie, with a short haircut and long legs, skinny like a model—you see her?"

He nodded. "She'd go in there with him, sometimes. She looked nicer than the others. She wasn't one of those, uh . . ."

"Gang-bang gals?"

He shivered as if the early fall evening had turned bitterly cold. "Not her. Those parties of his, though . . . you could smell the stuff coming out of his windows at night."

"What stuff?"

"Marijuana!"

How much of the old tailor's tale was envy for the younger generation—he probably went 23 skidoo with Charleston fillies and drank hooch in speaks in his day—and how much was righteous indignation, I neither knew nor cared. But the picture of Russell Frazer having dough to throw around, and maybe access to narcotics, kept getting clearer and clearer.

Singer suggested I talk to Angelo Sito. I knew the name—Sito had been a heavyweight back in the '40s, had been a contender for a couple of years, then in the '50s became a semi-name who could throw a fight and build a younger slugger's rep. The fight racket had made Sito enough dough to retire, not to luxury, but to an apartment on this almost respectable street.

I bought the old boxer a beer at the corner tavern. He had been a mauler and had come away with the requisite cauliflower ears and bulbous nose broken so many times, it qualified more for decoration than breathing apparatus. With his full head of salt-and-pepper hair, he had a rough-hewn dignity about him, wearing a white short-sleeve shirt and tan slacks that were clean and fairly new.

"I heard of you, Hammer," he said, his grin big and white and store-bought. "You had a few fights yourself in your day."

"Not in the ring."

"Safer in the ring. They don't shoot at you."

Not unless you don't throw the fights you're supposed to, I thought.

But I said, "Alex Singer told me you could fill me in on Russell Frazer. Your neighbor who got stabbed to death yesterday?"

Sito sneered. "He should have only bought it sooner. He was a miserable lowlife bastard."

"That's okay, Angelo," I said, and sipped my Blue Ribbon. "They probably don't need you to deliver the eulogy."

The fighter's lopsided grin said he liked that crack.

Then he went into it: "I got a kid in his twenties. He's married, has a little boy, and he's got a decent job in the Garment District. Then he starts hanging around that fuck pad across the street. Pot, booze, broads."

"Some people would say that's just a good time."

"Not when you risk your job and marriage and your kid's welfare." His eyes managed to narrow, despite their puffy surroundings. "I think there was more'n pot up there, Mike. Hate to say this, but . . . my boy, I think, was maybe doing harder stuff. Not horse or anything, but the nose candy, might be."

"You said he was in his twenties. He's a big boy."

He shook his head. "I can't give you anything but a feeling, Mike. A hunch. But I think that this louse Frazer was trying to get my kid into some kind of . . . illegal crapola. I don't know what. Could be dope. Could be a goddamn bank robbery, I don't know."

"No offense, Angelo, but it's no secret you got your hands dirty back in the old days."

He just shrugged. "Doesn't mean a guy can't want better for his kid. Anyway, what harm did I ever do anybody? Fight game's just entertainment."

"So is dope, some would say."

"You don't O.D. watching boxing."

I sipped the Pabst. "So you told your boy to stay away from Frazer?"

"I did. And his mother did, and his wife did, and he's straight as an arrow now, Mike, I swear to you."

"And that's all it took?"

"No. I also went across the street and told that lowlife bastard Frazer to get lost or get broken up."

Even in his fifties, Angelo Sito could put the hurt on a guy.

He added, "Bum moved out."

"Wise decision. You know where to?"

64

"Some hotel downtown, I think. I ain't seen him around since."

"You know a kid named Norm Brix, Angelo?"

"Yeah. He's in the hospital, I hear."

"I put him there."

His scar-tissue-heavy brows beetled. "He tried to jump some other kid, right? Yeah, it was in the papers! Were *you* mixed up in that . . . ?"

"What about Brix?"

"His parents used to live on this street. Mom was decent, Pop was a drinker. The father burned himself up in bed, smoking and drinking. The mother moved upstate with her sister, but the kid stayed around here."

"What *about* the kid?"

"Nasty. A bully. A dropout. He was pals with this Frazer slob, you know. That's one thing I can give my son credit for—he never liked the Brix kid."

"Well, thanks, Angelo."

"Thank you, Mike." He got up and slid out of the booth. "I'll buy next time."

"Deal."

I stayed put and finished the beer I'd only nursed along, talking to the old pug. Just sat there, thinking it through. . . .

The connection was there, all right, and maybe Velda had it figured—these punks have strange loyalties, and Frazer trying to knife me really could add up to revenge.

I let it go through my mind once more, then threw the notion on the discard pile. So I'd caused Brix some grief, so what? Brix was still just a punk. Frazer had something going for him, something bringing in real dough. Punk loyalties stop when one of them jumps from the minors over into the big league.

I couldn't help but picture those hippie kids in Frazer's fancy pad, a guy in mod threads and Beatle boots lording it over kids in T-shirts and jeans, playing the big-shot host. He would not view the likes of Brix, Felton, and Haver as equals, or even associates, much less the kind of friends whose misfortune might inspire him to take it upon himself to go wipe out the guy responsible.

Frazer was a god to these punks, but in the greater scheme, he was just another minion—*a minion someone above had dispatched to take me out.*

I picked up the afternoon paper and read it over another cold beer. On page three I found the story that Frazer had been identified, but was still classed as a victim of a mugging-kill. When I finished the funnies and the coffee, I threw a buck on the counter and went outside.

Saxony Hospital was two blocks away.

Billy Blue had been released from his bed and was back working, taking inventory of boxed medical supplies in a storeroom. The short-haired kid, in blue-and-red-striped shirt and jeans and tennies, was moving awkwardly, holding himself stiff. It hurt his face when he got a smile through, but he was clearly glad to see me.

He perched on a carton, and I did the same. I asked if it was okay to smoke and he said it was, but turned down my offer of a Lucky.

He told me, "Dr. Sprague figured I might as well be hurting down here as in a bed."

"How'd you manage it?"

"Ah, I psyched him out. Told the doc I was getting stir-crazy, and said I would sue if I got bed sores." He shook his head. "I couldn't take it, man, those nurses are always fussing around with me. Gives me the jumps."

I grinned and shook my head. "You don't know when you've got it good."

He made a face. "I don't like older women."

"Why, how old are these hags?"

"Late twenties, early thirties, I guess—flirting and flitting around like a bunch of girls."

"Yeah," I said, letting smoke out around my grin, "that does sound like hell."

"I mean, they're nice enough, but what if you want to sleep or read or watch TV? They don't give a guy a minute's peace. Like with that cowboy actor, who got tossed off his horse at the Garden? Nonstop attention. You better not be some old guy with a hernia or some housewife with a broken ankle or something, when there's a man around here, under thirty, with a pulse."

"Sounds like sheer agony, kid."

"Or like when that Evello guy was in there. He wasn't even some good-looking actor. I mean, he's an *old* guy, fifty or something. But he's a celebrity, and of course that's how it goes in the celebrity suite."

I frowned at him. "Who are we talking about?"

"You mean, the actor?"

"No," I said. "I know who the actor is—Lance Vernon." I also knew those nurses wouldn't get very far with Lance. "You said 'Evello'—did you mean Junior Evello?"

"Yeah, yeah, Evello. Right name, Carlo Evello—old-style don, head of the sixth Family. Don't you know about him, Mr. Hammer, in your line of work?"

"Yeah, I do, but where do you come off?"

He laughed through his cracked lips. "Menial staff at a hospital doesn't exactly draw executive types, Mr. Hammer, and I work in the basement. Some of these neighborhood guys tell some pretty crazy stories. Sounds like Junior Evello's a real big shot in their backyards."

"Sure, when it comes to extortion, drugs, prostitution—you name it."

Billy's nod was age-old and unconcerned. "You name it," he agreed, "and wherever you are, you'll find it. They say Junior was behind a hundred hits but never got indicted once."

"They aren't wrong."

Billy cocked his head. "Why is it he's called Junior, Mr. Hammer? He's no kid."

"He was named after his uncle, a Syndicate guy who bought it back in the early '50s. He looks a lot like his uncle did, and got nicknamed Junior as a kid, and it held, even as he rose to a similar position of power. He's a bad apple, Billy. You don't want to get too friendly with the likes of Junior Evello."

"Funny thing," Billy said, shaking his head, "but you'd never know that. He was nice to everybody, Mr. Hammer! Hell, he gave gold watches to the nurses, money to the orderlies—I got a ten-dollar tip for mailing a letter for him."

"What was he in for?" I asked.

"Not what you'd think," Billy said. "You'd figure maybe one of his enemies would get him, or he'd get shot up by the cops over something. But instead he started to cross against the light on Lexington Avenue, and got clipped by a lady driver making a turn. He made them bring him up here, because he didn't want to be too far from where he lives. Dr. Harrin took care of him, personally. Junior left a beaut of a watch for him."

I wondered if Harrin had kept it.

"That actor was something else, too. The nurses went crazy trying to keep the girls out of there. But at the same time, they were swarming all over that poor guy themselves. Half of them bawled when he was released, would you believe it?" Billy stopped, and a half-embarrassed smile blossomed. "Was there . . . something you wanted to see me about, Mr. Hammer?"

"Yeah, there was," I said, letting more smoke out. "You familiar with the Village Ceramics Shoppe?"

"Sure," he said with a shrug. "Dr. Harrin's sent me over there for materials a few times. The kids in therapy use the stuff. Dr. Harrin started the project last year and it works swell. They seem to—"

I cut in: "A guy name of Russell Frazer worked there. You know him?"

After a moment's thought, he said, "Tall, slim fella, kind of slicked down, about twenty-five?"

I said that could fit him all right.

"Didn't know his name," Billy went on, "but he took the doc's order from me once. He delivers the ceramics here for the shop. Why?"

"Somebody killed him."

Billy frowned. "That's too bad. I mean, I didn't really *know* the guy, but . . . why are you telling me this, Mr. Hammer?"

"Frazer used to live close to the Brix kid. He could have known Felton and Haver, too."

The blood drained from his face, leaving the abrasions more prominent than ever. "How was he killed?"

I gave him the whole thing, from the attack on me through the discovery of Frazer's corpse.

"Christ," the kid said, breathlessly.

"Billy," I asked him, locking eyes, "the other day when we were talking—are you *sure* you gave it to me straight?"

His answer was quiet, but very direct: "Right down the line, Mr. Hammer."

"Nothing you might have left out?"

"Like what?"

"This ceramics shop is a new wrinkle. You knew Frazer from there, a little. Did you ever see those punks hanging out there— Brix, Felton, Haver?"

"No, but . . . well, I might have seen them *near* the place. On the street. I mean, it's the same general neighborhood, but never in the shop or loafing in the alley or anything."

"Okay," I said with a nod.

And when I nodded, he knew that I believed him and he smiled back, the color returning to his face.

I was getting up from the carton when he added, "But, Mr. Hammer—I didn't tell you everything I was *thinking*."

That stopped me. "Want to try it now?"

He took a deep breath and looked right at me. "You have any idea what hospital security is like in this city?"

"From what I read in the papers, pretty lax."

"Lax is right. Get an addict in for treatment, and he'll still get his junk. Try the big hospitals, and they're buying and selling all over the place. Somebody even stole the copper roofing off Bellevue to pay for the stuff."

"So I heard."

"Mr. Hammer, some of the guys who work here at Saxony worked other places, before, and when I hear how they schemed to lay their hands on narcotics, I get sick. They brag about how they used to switch stuff around, so the loss wasn't noticeable right away."

"You report this, Billy?"

"No. Could just be talk, and I got to swim in these waters, don't I? I go around finking, and something bad will happen."

I didn't remind him that his face was battered and he'd just crawled out of a hospital bed.

"Anyway," he was saying, "it can't happen at the college, and because Saxony is small, it's pretty tight here, too. But even in this place, when you match the inventory sheets with the checkout lists, you can see the shortages."

I sat back down on the carton. "Go on, Billy."

"I don't use, Mr. Hammer. But I know people who do. . . ."

"What *kind* of people?"

"Various kinds. Please don't press me on it."

"Okay."

"I'll just say, you'd be surprised how young some of them are right now. And I *hear* things."

"What have you heard?"

We couldn't have been more alone, but his voice dropped to a hush. "There's a shortage of stuff on the street. It isn't hitting the

70

guys with the big money, but it's got the nickel- and dime-bag buy-
ers in a real bind. Hospitals are getting forced withdrawal cases
all over the city. Either the dealers are holding back, to jump the
prices, or the stuff isn't coming through."

"Which is why Brix and Felton put the squeeze on you to supply
them."

"Exactly right, Mr. Hammer. They figured, with me on the inside, and them pushing? We could grab off all the small stuff, and
really clean up."

"*Could* you have gotten the stuff?"

He shook his head. "Not at the college."

"What about here?"

His half-smile was more a smirk. "I could have figured something out," he told me honestly. "If I had *wanted* to."

"And your old schoolmates knew that."

He nodded glumly. "They knew it."

I dropped my cigarette butt in the half-empty soda bottle somebody used for an ashtray, and stood up. "Thanks, Billy." I handed
him my business card. "Keep right on thinking. If anything comes
of it, let me know."

"Sure." He tucked the card in his back jeans pocket. "And, Mr.
Hammer—this Frazer guy? *You* didn't . . . didn't come back and
take him out, did you?"

"No, son," I said. "Somebody else beat my time."

Dr. Alan Sprague, friend and colleague of Dr. David Harrin, also
worked at both Saxony Hospital and Dorchester Medical College.
I caught up with him at the latter.

He was a round little guy with bristly gray hair and a tired but
ready smile. He was in a short-sleeve white shirt with a blue bow
tie, his white coat hanging on a hook, and was rocking in the chair
behind Dr. Harrin's desk, the office being about the only quiet
place on the floor.

71

Harrin had left that morning for Paris, to make the first three days of seminars before touring the hospitals where experimental work in cancer research was in progress. Sprague had taken over Harrin's caseload and his classes, and right now was catching a breather from his work.

I settled in the chair opposite him. I had a Lucky going and he his pipe.

I said, "Paris isn't bad this time of the year, Doc. You should have joined him."

Sprague waved off the idea with a grunt. "We have enough of that right here in the States," he said in his gruff baritone. "Finding time to keep up with all the new medical developments, and just getting the work done, is bad enough, let alone taking a trip on the social side of the scientific world. I'm surprised David even bothered with it."

"Why's that?"

"He's a damn workhorse." Sprague glanced at the pipe in his fingers and scrubbed the bowl with his thumb. "And I'll tell you one thing—if ever anybody needed a break in his routine, it's David. I've been trying to get him to take a vacation ever since his son died, and all I ever managed was two days on a golf course. He drives himself too hard, too *goddamn* hard."

"I've seen it happen before," I told him. "Not much left when you lose your family."

"Oh, it's understandable, all right. Just not conducive to good health. Even machines wear out if they're mistreated." He rocked back. "Now, Mr. Hammer . . . what can I do for you?"

He was familiar with what had happened and, when I mentioned what Billy had told me about lax security at the hospital, agreed Saxony had its flaws in that area and admitted he didn't see a solution.

"In most cases," he told me, "it's a plain case of oversize institutions with heavy traffic in and out of restricted areas. Keys can be lost, duplicated, and used before locks can be changed. Because of a supervisory shortage, one person will be in charge of a maintenance crew or cleanup team. Then again, you can even have the problem of some authorized person removing drugs without accounting for them."

"Medical personnel?"

He raised an eyebrow and nodded. "There *have* been such cases. We had two right here, where underpaid interns were so far in debt they took the chance. And they blew their careers right out the window."

I nodded, then asked, "Much pilferage lately?"

"Holding at the usual rate. Why?"

"They say things are getting tight on the street."

He tented his fingers before his face, and his eyes narrowed. "Wait until the Snowbird gets back. It'll loosen up, then."

"Who?"

His smile was a world-weary one. "His right name is Jay Wren, a little joke his mother played on him. Locally he's known as the Snowbird, a big-time pusher who moved in on this . . . I believe the word is . . . 'turf,' a few years ago."

I sighed smoke. "I don't know which surprises me more, Doc—that I never heard of this Snowbird, or that you know all about him."

He shrugged. "On the latter score, Mr. Hammer, we deal with more than our share of drug-related illness here, from infection caused by dirty needles to O.D.'s and full-scale addiction. So we have a better than layman's knowledge of what goes on in the world around our facility. As for your lack of knowledge of the Snowbird, he would have been until very lately too minor a player to have made it onto your singular scorecard."

"But he's moved up?"

"And beyond. He represents a new generation, and possibly a threat to the older one."

"You mean the Syndicate? The Evello crowd? Your former patient, Junior?"

"Yes. Our former patient." He puffed at his pipe while he weighed what to say. Then: "My understanding is that there's an uneasy alliance between the Snowbird and the old-guard mob. He has the means and the methods to get the product to a, let's call it, younger audience."

I sat forward. "Wren wasn't on my scorecard till just now. What about the cops? Is he on theirs?"

"The police have him pegged, all right, but they haven't caught up with him . . . yet." He made a disgusted face and a sound to match. "It's a shame to watch these people living it up on the blood of school kids."

"Where is the Snowbird now?"

Sprague shrugged again and sucked on his pipe. The fire had gone out and he picked up the crystal lighter from the desk, flicked it a half-dozen times without getting a flame, then put it down in annoyance.

"I give David a nice new present," he said, "and he doesn't even bother to put fluid in it—just like him."

"He doesn't have your slogan up yet, either," I said with a little smile, gesturing to the framed *"Caveat emptor"* parchment leaned against the wall.

"He *has* seemed preoccupied of late," Sprague said. "But then, most doctors are."

I handed him my Zippo across the desk and, when he was stoked up again, he handed it back and said, "Wren was here, or rather at Saxony . . . we discharged him a month ago. He still had the cast on his leg, and all I know is he told David he was going to take a vacation until it came off."

"What happened to him?"

"Automobile accident."

"Like with Junior Evello?"

74

Sprague gave me a twisted smile and laughed. "Billy tell you about the celebrity suite?"

"He mentioned it."

"No, Wren didn't get clipped by a lady driver. He was getting out of his limousine on the driver's side in heavy traffic and got swiped by a truck. Far as I'm concerned, it's too bad it didn't roll over him, although that wouldn't have done more than put a temporary dent in the drug scene around here." He shrugged. "Somebody else would have taken over anyway."

I asked, "How bad is it up here?"

He was inspecting the chewed end of his pipe. "We only get to see the ones who are crippled by it, of course, but it's a good indicator of the trend. In brief, it's growing fast. The sad part is that the growth rate is largely in the younger group. Our methadone program here never stops expanding. Right behind it is the VD problem. Until a few years ago you rarely saw an under-eighteen-year-old patient. Now they're coming in sucking lollipops."

"And that's not all they've been sucking," I said.

He gestured with an open palm. "Free love is expensive for these children. When the Pill replaces condoms, social disease has a field day. But what I truly despise is the way these children treat it all like a big joke—no concern for themselves or anybody else."

"Doc, you said it—they're children. They don't have the maturity."

"They're mature enough to mouth the phrases—society pushed them into it, society can take care of them—only society can't tell them what to do, because they're 'doing their own thing.' Over fifty percent of our drug-abuse patients are repeaters, Mr. Hammer, and fifty percent of those have arrest records . . . and who *knows* what percentage will die early, and bring others down with them."

"Any answers?"

Sprague made a face and spread his hands. "If you could pick out one specific group as being responsible and direct your attention toward them—maybe. But it's spread to the rich and poor, educated and uneducated, and all the strata between. Nobody gives a damn because it's *their* life, right? But if things go awry, society will take care of them."

"Drug chic, they call it."

"A disease, *I* call it." He shook his head in grave frustration. "David and I have spoken about this so very many times. And yet he seemed to get along with both Wren and Evello—treated them with the deference and courtesy you would *any* patient."

"Doesn't that have something to do with that oath you took?"

His eyes flared. "But we don't have to be *friendly* to them. Businesslike is enough! I've asked David why he . . . fraternizes with such scum, but he's never had a reason that makes sense."

"Why, does he have one that doesn't make sense?"

"Several times he's said to me, 'Alan, it takes dead cells to create a vaccine.'"

"What's that supposed to mean?"

"Who knows? He's said it so often, it ought to be on parchment in one of these stupid frames." He tapped the sludge out of his pipe and leaned forward on the desk, looking at me carefully. "Which brings me to you, Mr. Hammer. In view of your reputation, and your profession, your interest in the matter here is a little disconcerting."

I grinned. "Ever been knifed, Doctor? Stabbed?"

"I wield a blade myself, but in the manner you suggest—I can't say I have."

"It isn't very pleasant, having a knife shoved in your back. That was tried on me last night."

He leaned forward. "Tried . . . ?"

I told him what had happened.

"And you think it was related to the attack on Billy Blue?"

"'Think' isn't exactly the right word, Doc. It's an oddball feeling

I have that for some reason somebody is trying to toss my ass in the wringer. Like being in the jungle—you don't always go by what you see . . . you go by what you feel, or else something's going to drop on you from overhead, or kill you from the blind side."

"What do you propose doing?"

"Just making a nuisance of myself maybe. Antagonize something or somebody into coming out in the open where it can be clobbered."

"That isn't a very antiseptic method, is it, Mr. Hammer?"

I grinned at him and got ready to leave. "Look at how long Madame Curie worked at it before she isolated radium."

Dr. Sprague smiled gently, his eyes thoughtful. "You might keep something else in mind, Mr. Hammer. Madame Curie died of radiation poisoning."

Chapter Five

SOMEWHERE IN PAT CHAMBERS' private collection, not on public display, are four medals for wartime valor, nine commendations from the New York Police Department, and a couple of civilian citations for exceptional bravery. He had faced down armed gunmen, rescued little old ladies from burning buildings, and driven mad chases in pursuit of bandits.

All that without batting an eye.

Right now, however, he was scared shitless.

The knife in his trembling hand didn't want to go through a filet that should cut like butter, and when he tried to stir his coffee, the spoon rattled like a blind beggar shaking the pencils in his cup.

I grinned at the terrified captain of police, that bachelor brute of the Homicide Division, whose words were choking up in his throat when he was asked to make simple, polite conversation.

All because Velda had brought a friend to supper who had this crazy typing-paper-colored hair and big, full breasts that tried to burst through a semi-sheer, laced-up blouse, and seemed about to succeed any second. The air-conditioning in Finero's Steakhouse, just off Broadway, wasn't really necessary, but it did make the dame's nipples stand out like bullets, which was fitting because that was what Pat was sweating, electric breeze or not.

Helen DiVay had started out as a stripper and never forgot it, even though she'd long since come up in the world. One day maybe half a dozen years ago, she had taken five grand out of her savings from traveling skin shows, invested in a then-unknown stock issue called Xerox, and now, ten years later, she had a few million bucks from a company that had seen one stock split after another.

And yet she was still looking for a husband.

Velda said it was because Helen intimidated men, too rich, too shapely, too pretty—guys usually thought she was out of reach, a dream that couldn't come true. So the big beautiful broad could find herself on a blind date like the one Velda set up with Pat, only without the handsome, gray-eyed lug's knowledge—much less permission.

Helen was rather delicately eating the shrimp salad that was the only food she'd ordered.

She was saying in her husky, knowing, yet ever-so-feminine voice, "It must be terribly exciting being a detective. I mean, your friend Mike here is a detective, but to be captain of Homicide! The things you've seen, the pressures you've been under . . . and yet you look so *young*. . . ."

Pat said, "Uh . . . th-thanks."

She gestured with a speared shrimp. "I dated a fireman once, and he seemed so *calm* all the time, and I just couldn't understand why. He told me it was because when he was with me, he wasn't at the firehouse. Said he saved his nerves for on the job. But, you know, I think he was just naturally brave. He was just one of those men who are innately cut out for dangerous work. Are you one of those men, Captain Chambers?"

"Puh."

"Pardon me?"

"Puh-Pat. Call me puh-Pat."

He sounded like a tugboat.

I couldn't figure whether Pat was shook up because Helen was deliberately pouring herself all over him, or because he was one of those guys Velda talked about, afraid he couldn't handle what was on offer.

When the two girls left to go to the powder room, I just sat there and laughed at the big chump, who was still trying to get down the last of his steak, and said, "There's a slice of cheesecake available, buddy, if you're up for dessert."

"Mike . . . you have no shame, no class, no sympathy. . . ."

"No shit." I grinned, and looked off into nowhere. I molded the air with a hand. In the background a jazz piano seemed designed to accompany my words. "Try to imagine that work of art making you coffee in the morning, wrapped up in a little shortie terrycloth robe that keeps falling open. . . ."

"Show respect. She's a nice woman."

"Very."

"I find her most intelligent."

"I'm sure she was impressed with your dinner-table conversation, too, old buddy. All five words."

He pushed his plate aside. "Is that all you think about?"

"What?"

"Sex."

"Sure. I admit it. What're you saving it up for? Waiting for the sperm bank to raise its rates? Civil-service pay just doesn't cut it, huh?"

He gave me a disgusted look, then let a smile twist the corner of his mouth. "Boy, you sure can back a guy into a corner."

I nodded toward Helen's empty chair. "With those babies prodding you, is there a better place to be?"

"You ought to know, you lecherous bastard," he said.

"Not lecherous," I said, and raised a teacherly finger. "It's just that I have my own means of interrogating certain suspects of the female persuasion. Too bad the department regulations don't give you boys a little more leeway."

Pat shook his head at me. "You're lucky you went private. You'd never have made it, over the long haul, as a real cop."

"Maybe not," I said, and sipped coffee. "But I bet I could have tracked down a mugger who carves up his victims, by now."

It was his turn to grin. "Don't look so smug, you slob—we *did* find him."

"Yeah?"

"Yeah. Those hookers returned to their favorite street corner, finally, and we ran 'em in and turned the screws, and two of 'em made a positive identification."

"How about that?" I fired up a Lucky with my Zippo. Snapped it shut. "Tell me about your suspect, Uncle Patrick."

The captain of Homicide waggled his own lecturing finger at me. "He's *more* than just a suspect. He's a middle-aged drifter who's been in the city the past two years. Wanted in Oklahoma on a burglary charge, and Texas had a warrant out on him for man-slaughter. We picked him up dead drunk in a hotel room uptown, along with a whore who had just lifted his roll."

"How much did he have on him?"

"A little under three hundred bucks."

"From the Frazer punk?"

"So he admits."

I blew a smoke ring. "Does he also admit stabbing the guy?"

Pat drank water. Didn't look at me. "No."

"Did you find the knife?"

"Hell, no! That would've gone down a gutter. You know that."

"No, I don't, not if stabbing his marks after robbing 'em is this guy's M.O."

"Mike, he's the guy."

"He may be the guy who rolled Frazer. But is he the guy who stuck him?"

Pat seemed ready to take me on again.

So I held up a palm. "Okay. All right. Then let's go back to square one—what would Frazer want to mug me for? A guy like that, with sharp clothes and lots of bread coming in?"

"Maybe he didn't like your ugly face," Pat said, but he had an odd expression, so I knew there was more.

I just stared at him till he gave it to me.

He said, "The Chicago police sent through Frazer's rap sheet on request. He had six mugging arrests before he was twenty, one conviction for an eight-month stretch, then he dropped out of sight. Mugging seemed to be his game."

"Swell, but he wasn't trying to mug me."

"Mike . . ."

"It was a knife attack, Pat, plain and simple. Or maybe not so simple. Anyway, it was going to be a hit-and-run deal, and if he hadn't been a little sloppy about his approach, you'd be renting a tux to bury the corpse about now. One jab through the heart from the rear, and I wouldn't have been able to clear my rod. You stagger a couple of seconds, hit the pavement like a tired drunk, and the killer walks away."

"You're sticking to that, huh?"

"This thing smells of orchestration. Frazer is told to shiv me, during what seems to be a mugging, and whoever sent him knew that if his boy got exposed, you smart cops would soon learn that Russell Frazer had mugging in his rap sheet."

"That's far-fetched even for you," he said.

A waitress refilled my coffee. Pat was still working on his first cup.

"Since I'm on the sidelines on this thing," I said, stirring in cream and sugar, "I wonder if you could do me a favor."

"I'm listening."

"That kid, Billy Blue—what if Brix and those other punks targeted him for more than just turning them down when they wanted him to supply them with pilfered drugs?"

He frowned. "Such as what?"

"Not sure. These players are all bumping into each other at odd angles. I think we're missing something. Maybe the kid witnessed something at the hospital he shouldn't have."

"Suppose he did."

"Then he'd still be a target. How about assigning some men to keep an eye on him—stake out where he lives. He's staying with his grandparents, I understand."

"Yeah, I know. They have an apartment over a cigar store." He thought it over. "You may have a point. I'll put some men on him. You want the boy notified?"

I held up a hand in a stop motion. "No. Strictly sub rosa."

He frowned at me some more. "You don't suspect Billy Blue of anything, do you?"

"No." I let smoke out my nostrils, and grinned. "But we've been surprised before."

He smirked and nodded. "That we have. That we have."

"By the way, Pat," I said, as if casually shifting the subject, "the narcos keeping tabs on the Snowbird?"

He didn't say anything, but the lines deepened around his eyes.

"How about my old pal Junior?" I asked amiably. "You know . . . Junior Evello?"

Through a clenched mouth, Pat said, "Man, I should have seen it coming. I should have remembered you're nothing but a package of pure trouble, because you can't let things alone that are none of your damn business."

He had forgotten about the big blonde and the jumps in his hands were long gone. He was nothing but a calm, inscrutable cop

84

now, with eyes of solid gray ice. "You faked me out, Mike. You've really learned to act."

I shrugged. "We're off-Broadway, aren't we?"

"Sidelines my ass. You damn near had me believing you were out of this. That the old days were gone."

"They are," I said. "We're starting fresh. Now . . . how about those two solid citizens, Jay Wren and Junior Evello? What's new with them?"

"Go screw yourself. I don't work narco detail. And, anyway, how do you even *know* the Snowbird? That's way off your beat."

"Don't stall me, Pat. Why do I think if you goose the Snowbird, Evello will jump? And vice versa?" I shrugged, sipped coffee, then asked, "Besides, what's the harm? It's only a question. After-dinner conversation . . ."

He crumpled his napkin and tossed it on the table. "Jay Wren's in Miami nursing a broken leg. We've kept in touch with the PD down there, but there've been no beefs reported. The Snowbird sits in the sun by a swimming pool, with some dame for a companion, makes no contacts, and doesn't seem to be doing anything more than recuperating." He paused, and added, "Why the interest in somebody you don't even know?"

"Maybe I want to widen my circle of friends. Maybe some of my old buddies don't appreciate me."

"Maybe you should tell me what you're getting at. . . ."

I shrugged. "I gather there's a short supply of junk on the streets in the area the Snowbird services."

Pat's small grin was pleased and tight—I knew its meaning: he loved it when he knew more than I did.

"I told you before," he said. "Stuff's short on the street, buddy. Like the man said, things are tough all over."

I didn't want to push him, so I took a drag on the butt and watched the smoke drift toward the ceiling.

Somehow, my silence prodded him.

Softly he said, "You may have a low opinion of real law enforcement, Mike, but that's how the supply got choked—solid police work. The Treasury Department nailed four heavy shipments, the Border Patrol got two, and when they tried an airdrop into Arizona, the state police were there to intercept it. If that kind of heat stays on, there's going to be a lot of hurting junkies between here and L.A."

"Maybe," I reminded him, "but for every T-man in the field, the Syndicate has a hundred operators on the streets."

Pat looked at me sideways. "But what are they selling? Dribs and drabs from here and there. To serve their public, the Syndicate needs huge quantities—the stuff has got to come in in bulk."

"What's with that big load you told me about," I said, "that's stashed in Europe somewhere?"

His shrug was eloquent, but he elaborated anyway: "Wouldn't tell you if I knew, pal. It could be a big fat lie, designed to keep the cops over there too busy chasing a myth to spot other, smaller, real traffic . . . or it could be a fact."

I frowned at him. "You didn't sound so uncertain when you first mentioned this super shipment."

"Myth or fact," he said with a shrug, "a couple hundred pounds of pure H has to be taken seriously. Call it a de facto fact."

"Cute," I said, and took a last drag on the butt and snubbed it out in my saucer. "Then why hasn't anybody come up with anything? You were bragging about solid police work a minute ago."

"Let's put it this way," Pat said. "Some countries don't consider illegal narcotics traffic in the same light we do—especially those countries where the profit can filter up into political hands. And some have outlets for handling the stuff legally."

"And our agencies haven't got a lead, and are getting ready to cover their asses with the myth angle."

Pat batted the air with his palms. "Hey, I don't have access to what's on the mind of the federal boys."

I studied him. "Myth or fact, chum—what's your opinion?"

"Don't have one."

"Sure you do. I can see you thinking, and because you're an idiot, it's *not* about getting into Helen DiVay's panties."

Though I doubted she was wearing any.

"All I'm thinking," Pat said defensively, "is how the hell the Syndicate figures they can get that much stuff in at one time. Security might be less than ideal, but it's tight enough that they couldn't take the chance of that kind of loss . . . and the way the demand is, they can't afford to waste the market value, trying to dribble it in. They seem to have got something going for them, some kind of smuggling system . . . but even the federal experts can't figure it out."

My tone was innocent but my expression wasn't: "Maybe I ought to ask Junior Evello. He used to be top man in the dope racket before he retired into an advisory capacity. Make that, *supposedly* retired."

He gave me that flat look of his. "You'll live longer, Mike, if you keep your hands on your pecker and out of my business."

I spotted the girls coming back, giggling and talking, and grinned at Pat. "You've been a bachelor too long, kid—it's showing in your table patter. These days a guy doesn't have to hold his own—there's always somebody else to play with it for you."

"Play with what?" Helen DiVay smiled broadly.

Pat got red and started to stammer again.

Helen laughed and said to Velda, "Isn't that sweet, a great big man like Captain Chambers . . . blushing."

Maybe Pat wasn't going to have the fun evening that was his for the asking, but I was having a blast, watching the "great big man" squirm.

I was going over the log of incoming calls when Velda came out of her kitchen carrying a coffee tray and, after she caught the way I was gaping at her, she gave me a typical feminine smirk of satisfaction.

She had nothing on but a cobwebby-thin yellow robe that must have come out of a Times Square fetish shop, and with that beautiful dark hair she was a study in contrasts that could give a dying man the will to live.

All I could do was drop the book and ease back into the end of the sofa and gawk like a kid at a carnival hootch show.

"Will you either get naked or get dressed?" I asked her. "I can stand you either way, but not in between."

She put the tray down on the coffee table, still smirking. "Knowing your penchant for ripping the clothes off women, I deliberately bought something inexpensive."

"My ass. You got two weeks' salary tied up in that thing."

Velda leaned over and filled the cups and handed me one, her eyebrow raised in mock disdain, while her breasts under that filmy stuff swayed like tempting fruit. "What a romantic you are . . . and you make snide remarks about *Pat's* bachelorhood."

"Sure. To him a bed is something you sleep in."

When she sat down next to me, she leaned over and kissed me on the neck. "Oh, and what is it to you?"

"A workbench," I said.

She smiled prettily, then gave me a devious look. "Someday . . . if you ever decide to terminate our somewhat nebulous engagement in a legal ceremony, you'll need to undergo a rigorous brainwashing."

"Long engagements are recommended by the best shrinks to ensure lasting marriages, baby."

"Ten *years* long?" The pout was starting now. "Don't you ever get tired of playing permanent houseguest?"

"Nope. Kind of fun. No wife would be looking like you do right now."

The pout relaxed into a smile, but her dark eyes were still devious. "Oh, but you're wrong. I would. I guarantee you I would."

She kissed me again, and I felt that familiar surge of warmth. "Sometimes, Mike, I wish I'd never told you I'd wait for you. . . . That you could sow your wild oats and I'd still be here, waiting."

"Who says I'm sowing any wild oats?"

"Shut up," she said, and kissed me again.

Then she tensed her expression, a pretend-mad I knew so well. "What I ought to do is cut you off—no more fun and games until you get serious. . . ."

I put her hand somewhere. "That's serious, isn't it?"

We necked a while, then she took my chin in her hand and said, "But you bring something home to me, Mike, it better be flowers. I don't take drugs and I *include* penicillin."

"I hear you, honey. . . ."

I sipped and supped on those lush, ripe lips for a while.

Lazily, her dark eyes hooded, she said, "Sometimes I think I'll just go ahead and have a baby."

I drew away, grimace-grinned at her, put the half-empty cup back on the tray, and checked my watch. "Right. Yeah, well, I think I better blow this coop right now. I'm beat."

Velda seemed half amused, half hurt, then gave me a nudge with her elbow. "Easy, my love. I was only kidding. When you're ready, we'll do this thing. Do it right. Only for now, let's sort of keep the idea in mind, okay? A little Mike or a little Velda?"

"Deal. As long as it's an *idea*."

I didn't say it, but it wasn't a bad idea at that. Sowing wild oats was one thing—coming home to a feast like her every night was another.

And it must have shown on my face, because she got a little misty-eyed for a second before she turned her attention back to her coffee.

When we had seconds, Velda said, "I cleared out all the details at the office."

"Yeah?"

"The Jordan Agency is going to handle the Redding contract, and Bud Tiller said he'd cover the Murphy-Baine deal for you. No charge. You just owe *him* one, now."

What was this about?

"The rest of the business," she said, "I can handle myself. The bills are paid, and you have about eight thousand in the bank, if you have to do any check writing. So you're free to do this thing, and anyway, I know I can't stop you."

For one minute I was all set to climb her frame for being so damn presumptuous . . . then the years went by in microsecond flashes, and I remembered the bullet scar on her back and the other one across her palm, and the irritation ebbed away into cold relief and I said, "Thanks, kitten."

"You were going to do it anyway, Mike," she said with a shrug. Her breasts rose and fell under the sheer yellow and keeping my eyes off them was hardly worth the effort. She was saying, "It works better if you don't have to worry about other things."

"Honey, you're a pisser," I said.

"Like I said . . . ever the romantic . . ."

"An even bigger pisser than Pat." I shook my head. "All I do is nudge around the edges of something that may not even be there, just to relieve the monotony . . . and you two get ready for a war."

Velda twisted around on the sofa, drawing her knees up under her. "So go ahead and nudge. Just keep your head down, your tail covered, and send back a signal if you need help at the front."

She wasn't kidding. She was the other licensed P.I. in our agency, after all, and she packed almost as many rods as I did, and in much more interesting places.

I could feel my teeth showing, and a relaxed, easy feeling settled in and replaced the tension around my shoulders.

It was on now, and I wouldn't have to make any excuses for it.

I reached out and ran a hand under the sheer yellow cobwebs and touched the satiny roundness of her breasts, their erect points daring me to do something about them.

"I appreciate it, kitten." I took my hand away and covered her up again.

Velda asked softly, "Would you *really* like to show me how appreciative you can be?"

"Uh-huh . . . but maybe I'd better save my strength."

"You're finking out. Sometimes I think you're as bad as Pat."

"Not really." I buried my face in her neck and nuzzled.

Then I told her ear: "This tomcat doesn't want anything else on his mind when he tangles with a beautiful pussy like you. . . ."

Droplets of night rain speckled the streets and the wind had a little bite to it as it blew out the last remnants of summer. Occasionally empty taxis would cruise by, but I ignored them, sticking to the nearly deserted sidewalks.

A jumpy drunk on the corner hustled me for a buck, but the young hippie in the doorway farther down got a fast brushoff. When I reached my block, I picked up the early morning edition of the *News*, and cut down toward my apartment house.

You've come a long way in a few years, Mr. Hammer, I thought. *Used to be a West Side walkup, crappy but comfortable. Now here you are across town in a fancy pad with all the goodies, where you can stand on the ridiculous little patio and see both rivers at either end of the asphalt artery. From the street you can look up and see your quarters jutting out like a balustraded pouting lower lip, marked by the glow of the red overhead light.*

The rain almost caught me, but I made it under the canopy in time. Having a uniformed doorman usher me in had become one of life's little pleasures, but this time I had to shoulder the plate-glass barrier open myself, because the guy was sneaking a smoke beside the service elevator.

He dropped the butt, squashed it out, and came dutifully over, looking guilty, forefinger flipping a sloppy salute. "Good evening, sir."

"Hi," I said. "Thought Jerry was on tonight."

"Supposed to be, but he called in sick."

"Bad?"

"No . . . nothing serious. One of those virus deals."

"Oh. Well, lot of that going around. Good night."

"Good night, sir."

I walked around the bend and punched the UP button on the elevator panel.

Then I stepped back against the wall and got the .45 in my right hand and when the little uniformed bastard came around the corner with the silenced Luger in his fist, I smashed the cold steel of the Colt into his forehead and left one eyeball plastered to his cheek to dangle there and look at me with absolute horror.

Pain-racked reflexes twisted him into me and we both hit the floor next to the gun that had dropped from suddenly nerveless fingers just as the other one came out of the service entrance. He was a big guy with a raincoat and no hat and I could see the huge bulk of the Magnum in his hand, obscenely tipped with a muffler, and I knew it was time to die, because the slugs that rod spat could whip through three people in tandem before they slowed down and my own piece was caught in the folds of a doorman's uniform.

And it *would* have been time to die if he hadn't used hollow points designed to flatten so they could churn up guts like an egg-beater. That sadistic desire cost him, because each slug was like a fist pounding into the body I held in front of me, hitting without penetrating all the way, and he was trying for a head shot at me when my fingers found the corpse's hand with the Luger and I squeezed off one nine-millimeter *phutt* that took him in the throat and rocked him into a gurgling death twitch against the door.

For a second I lay there, waiting.

Across the foyer a leg gave an involuntary jerk as muscle tissue died in sequence. A foul intestinal smell hung under the cordite and something was making dripping sounds and it wasn't the rain.

But it *was* over.

I pushed the body away, making sure the Luger stayed in the lifeless fingers of the guy who didn't know that this was an expensive building with permanent, bonded doormen who only covered for each other, and each had a uniform that didn't have rolled-up pants cuffs or sleeves too long. And who were allowed to smoke on the job if they felt like it.

I found Jerry in the locked mailroom, alive but unconscious, a purple welt behind his ear. Tomorrow he'd have a hell of a story to tell and maybe a few tenants would put another lock on their doors and a couple would move out. Whoever walked in on the mess would have a ball talking into the TV cameras and be a celebrity for a day.

The job was too professional for me to be bothered frisking the bodies. Nothing would be there and I'd only waste time, and get in even deeper. I made sure no blood or gore showed on my clothes, and went back to the street through the rear entrance, ducking under the scope of the remote TV lens that monitored the doorway. I went up the four steps to the sidewalk and turned left.

All was still quiet on the eastern front.

For now.

Velda's place didn't have a doorman, but I had the key and nobody saw me go in. I told her that if any questions were asked, just say I had been there all night.

She didn't bother querying me. Not Velda. Not when something was *on*. She knew to let me play it out any way I wanted to.

But she did give me one of those sloe-eyed smiles and say, "It's going to cost you, Mike."

Her fingers did something and the transparent yellow cobweb hissed to her feet in a silken puddle and the Velda I loved so much was right there, starting to arch toward me in all that crazy nakedness.

"Get ready to have your strength sapped," she told me.

"I better catch a shower," I said.

"We can start there," she said, and started unbuttoning my shirt.

Chapter Six

I T W A S A N H O U R later before we decided to use the bed for
sleeping and at least two hours after that when the phone
rang.

Velda sat up, and clicked the nightstand light on. The covers were around her waist and she was nude as a grape and a half-
lidded glimpse of those full, lush, unbound breasts was enough to
snap me wide awake, if the phone hadn't already.

Even from my side of the bed, the imperative but trying-too-
hard-to-be-casual voice could easily be heard, apologizing for the
late call, and asking Velda if she knew where I could be reached
on an urgent matter.

She nudged me and said in a sleepy tone that didn't go with her
alert expression, "Why, yes—yes, he's right *here.* . . ."

Before she could hand me the phone, the voice chuckled, like
one old friend catching another in the act, and said with a laughing inflection, *"Don't tell me he's been there all night?"*

She could sure play the game, embarrassed confusion, the
stammer and inadvertent confession all in one run-on sentence of,

"Uh, yes—that's right, I mean . . . well, what business is it of *yours* if he spent the night with me?"

All the while her shrewd, dark eyes were locked on mine. With her nakedness to distract me, keeping my eyes on hers shows you how seriously we were taking this. And how severely she really had sapped my strength. . . .

She was saying, "Who *is* this?"

"I'm sorry to have bothered—"

"Here, let me put him on and—"

"No," the commanding voice said. *"No, never mind. Thank you, ma'am, and again I apologize for the lateness."*

And hung up.

She cradled the phone, propped a pillow, sunk an elbow in it, and rested her chin against a fist, looking at me with tousled accusation.

"Friend of yours?" I asked her lightly.

"Not hardly."

"Oh?"

"I get the occasional middle-of-the-night call from a strange man, but not a wide-awake, sober one, and with a teletype clicking and deep voices in the background."

"Wasn't our friend the captain of Homicide?"

"No. I'd like to have let *you* give that character your *own* performance." Her eyes narrowed. "Offhand, I'd say that was the esteemed Vance Traynor."

"Oh, laughing boy from the D.A.'s office. He must be riding Pat's back again." I let out my own chuckle. "I wonder if he had to run Pat down and shake him out of Helen DiVay's bed."

She arched an eyebrow at me. "You really think Pat was up to that challenge?"

"No."

She reached over and clicked off the bedside lamp and yanked the covers up and said, "Turn the other way."

96

I turned the other way and she snuggled herself against me.

I was enjoying that warmth and the darkness, and the near silence of Manhattan after midnight where even the occasional muffled siren had a dreamlike quality.

Then she whispered, "Mike—don't keep secrets from a girl. Who did you kill this time?"

I reached behind me to trace the smooth rise of her hip. "Nobody you know, sugar."

The warmth and the silence began lulling me again. Then I realized her lips were near my ear.

"Want to try killing *me*? With kindness maybe?"

"That might take two or three weeks."

"What's time anyway?" she said, and she was crawling on top of me.

Where was a can of spinach when you needed it?

The morning papers and early TV shows headlined the gruesome find in my apartment-house lobby with a publicity-conscious fat woman giving the vivid details of how she had stumbled over the corpses after returning home from a party at her son-in-law's.

Jerry the doorman was okay, telling the cops how the guy they found dressed in his uniform had approached him about a supposed tenant, asked him to verify an address on a letter, and then coldcocked him while his attention was diverted.

Velda and I hadn't been in the office long enough for me to make it into my inner sanctum, from sharing coffee and Danish at her desk in the outer one, when our visitors arrived.

One was the kind who could drop by unannounced anytime, no problem—Pat Chambers, his eyes puffy from a long rough night that I guessed was not courtesy of a certain wealthy ex-ecdysiast. His suit was the one I'd seen him in at the restaurant and it looked almost as rumpled as he did.

But he wasn't even the first through our door. That honor was reserved for the ambitious young assistant D.A. whose suit was almost as sharp as his eyes. Vance Traynor, with his lanky frame and insincere smile, still struck me as a guy who might go far in politics.

Not a compliment.

"I'm sorry to just drop by, Mr. Hammer," he said.

"Phones out over at City Hall?" I asked good-naturedly, wiping some Danish off my mouth with a paper napkin.

"No, I just took a chance."

"I've taken a few of those. Velda, get our guests some coffee, would you? Captain Chambers, always a pleasure."

Standing behind Traynor, Pat gave me a look that was half apologetic and half annoyed. Pissed off at me as he might be, he did not take kindly to carrying anybody's water, especially a slick young political rung-climber like Traynor.

Soon I was behind my desk, and Velda had served our guests coffee in plastic cups, and refilled mine. I asked her to join us and take notes on the conversation.

"That's not necessary," Traynor said, opposite me in a client's chair, Pat next to him in the other one.

"This is my office," I said. "Not yours. I'd like to have a record of what's said."

"That's a fairly extreme reaction, when you don't even know why I'm here."

I grinned at him. "There were two men killed in the lobby of my apartment house last night. I read the newspapers. I sometimes even listen to TV and radio."

Pat, looking embarrassed, said, "Mike, if it had been up to me—"

"Anyway, I'd say," I cut in, "having an assistant district attorney and the captain of Homicide drop in on you, first thing in the morning, also qualifies as 'fairly extreme.' Velda?"

She went out for her stenog pad and came back in and got settled. She was in a white blouse and black skirt and black pumps and yet still looked like a damn pinup girl. But she sat with her knees together, not crossing her distracting legs. Always thinking of the boss, my Velda.

"At this point," Traynor said, in a voice so smooth you could bead water off it, "I'm not looking for a formal statement. Captain Chambers suggested we just have a friendly talk, and determine whether any further steps are needed."

"And I assume Captain Chambers has told you," I said, "that he and I and Miss Sterling, my secretary, had dinner together at Finero's Steakhouse. The captain's date was a young lady named DiVay, and I'm sure he's given you information on how to contact her."

Pat shifted in his chair. "Actually, I didn't get her contact information. I thought you or Velda might be able to help with that."

I glanced at Velda. Her expression said what I was thinking: *Poor dumb schmuck.*

Velda told Traynor she'd get the phone number and address for him before he left, and I told my story of how my secretary and I had left Pat and Helen at the restaurant, and had walked home, and then never left her apartment.

Traynor listened quietly but his expression was rather glazed. Pat had no doubt told him exactly what to expect out of me.

Then the assistant D.A. folded his arms and smiled on one side of his face and said, "And here we are again, Mr. Hammer."

"Where would that be, Mr. Traynor?"

"At that improbable place where you expect me to accept a wild coincidence. It's been only a few days since you expected me to accept the last one."

"What coincidence are we talking about this morning?"

"That two men were murdered in the lobby of your apartment

house, and you were conveniently away at the time. One of the men was battered in a manner so brutal as to suggest an assailant of considerable strength, and with a reckless disregard for human life."

"Was I seen there?"

". . . No."

"Any witnesses place me there?"

". . . No."

I grinned again and leaned back in the swivel chair. "Not wishing to embarrass my secretary, Mr. Traynor, I invite you to steal a glance at her and determine whether it's far-fetched that I would rather spend time at her place than mine."

She was smiling just a little as the assistant D.A. couldn't help himself but to steal that glance.

Then I said, "And I don't have the statistics—you'd have to check with Captain Chambers about that—but my guess is there were a whole lot of murders in New York City last night, and the night before that, and before that. This is that concrete jungle you hear so much about. And I am not necessarily involved with any of those homicides."

"You aren't necessarily *not* involved, either."

"No. But unless you have evidence or witnesses or a motive— little details like that—I need to remind you that I am not on the city's payroll. I have a business to run. And if you don't have any other questions, I would respectfully ask you not to let the door hit you on the ass on the way out."

Pat hadn't said anything during my indignant denial of the innuendos, but I knew he'd be out checking taxicab trip sheets and my route home the minute he left, and if he reached that newspaper stand, my tail would be in a sling.

Give Traynor credit. He merely smiled, shrugged, and said, "Point taken."

He rose and turned to the Homicide captain.

Pat said, "I'll hang behind, sir. If you don't mind. I can find my way back."

Traynor gave Pat a nod, too, and went out. Velda followed to get that DiVay info for him, and Pat got up, went over, and shut the door behind them. He took the client chair where Traynor had been sitting.

"Where do you get your luck?" he asked.

"Same place as my nerve."

He shook his head. I offered him a cigarette and he took it. We both fired up and he sat there and laughed. I didn't know what was so funny.

Finally, he told me: "Somebody saw you last night, Mike."

I felt the back of my neck prickle.

"Somebody saw you when you went in Velda's place after walking her home."

So Lady Luck did *love me.*

He filled me in. Across the street from Velda's building, a plain-clothes cop on a stakeout on an unrelated matter was sitting in a parked car, and spotted us going in . . . and swore he never saw me leave. He had been surveilling the area the past eight hours.

Pat and I both knew that if the flatfoot had fallen asleep, he obviously wouldn't say so; and if he had missed me, because his attention was elsewhere, whether on a sandwich or a girlie mag, he couldn't even know he had. He could only present himself as the ever-vigilant watchman of the NYPD, and along the way provide me with one lucky alibi.

Move over, Sky Masterson and Nathan Detroit.

"Then what the hell," I said, "was Traynor dropping in about?"

"He wanted to see if you'd spill something before you knew you were covered by a cop, no less."

I laughed and, to his credit, so did Pat.

Also to his credit, Pat didn't bother to ask whether I had or hadn't taken that lobby pair out of the action. He could see it was my style, but what he didn't know couldn't hurt me.

"Give me one reason," he said, heaving a smoky sigh, "why I should share police information with you?"

I hadn't asked for any, but I said, "Because I saved your life a couple times?"

"I've saved yours three times."

"Who's counting?"

He grunted. "The two lobby stiffs have been positively identified as a pair of contract hit men from St. Louis."

They were importing help to deal with me. I felt complimented.

Pat was saying, "Even though the slugs, the prints, and the paraffin tests for gunpowder tell the story of an angry shootout between the pair, nobody in their right mind's going to believe it."

"Why not?"

"Two reasons—first, why would they come all the way from St. Louis together just to shoot each other? And second, how did this falling-out between a couple of St. Louie hard guys just happen to happen in Mike Hammer's lobby?"

I spread my hands. "The things some people will do to rub up against a celebrity."

He didn't even smile at that. He just got up and went to the door, where he stopped and glared at me.

"You may be a celebrity, Mike. But you're going to look like just another dead nobody wrapped up in a rubber body bag."

He went out quickly, not shutting the inner-office door.

Velda ambled in, in her catlike way, and asked, "What's his problem?"

"Ah, he's just pissed because we set him up with that broad Helen."

"Why would that make him mad?"

I pawed at the air. "The sap just can't handle the steep banks and the dark tunnels."

That got a nice purring laugh from her, and she dropped off the notes of the Traynor meeting, already typed up.

"You're fast," I said.

"Took *you* long enough." She perched on the edge of my desk, plucked the Lucky out of my mouth, and sucked on it. She let the smoke curl out and I gave her a *don't-start-with-me* look, and she said, "So why the charade?"

"Huh?"

"Don't play dumb. That lobby bit was self-defense that you rigged to stay out of it. Why did you bother? You could have walked away clean."

I waved that off. "So soon after nailing Billy Blue's attackers? That clown Traynor would have kept me downtown forever. Might have charged me on manslaughter or even murder. At the very least, I'd have had my P.I. ticket suspended and my gun permit pulled."

"I'd still have *my* ticket and *my* permit."

"Swell, but you're holding down the fort while I'm out chasing Indians. Anyway, I like the message it sends."

"To the cops and the D.A.'s office?"

"No. Fuck the cops and the D.A.'s office. I'm talking about who-ever sent those St. Louis bozos to splatter me. I like knowing that somewhere some asshole is wondering how I pulled that off, and is coming to the realization of just how much trouble he's in."

She frowned down at me. "What 'asshole'? This Jay Wren? Or maybe Junior Evello?"

"Or both," I said.

She slid off the desk and shook her head and the dark tresses shimmered and bounced. "You need a new hobby."

"And I bet you have a suggestion."

She nodded and gave me a look that made the *need-anything-just-whistle* one Bacall gave Bogie seem like kid stuff. She took her feline time making her way back to her desk, leaving the door be-tween us open so she could drive me crazy with those long legs.

No problem. I wasn't planning to hang around the office, anyway.

Old friends have other friends and, if the word is good, they can pass you up the line until one has something to say.

It had taken me three days and two hundred bucks to get to Marvin Stedman, a thirty-five-year-old heroin addict they called the Junkman.

Junkman was no ordinary heroin addict, if there is such a thing. Coming off twenty years of pulling down scores, and building a rep as a crook you could trust, Stedman had thrown in with Jay Wren to aid in the dope operation. So far so good, but the ex-heister made the classic dealer mistake of liking his own product too well, and he got *himself* hooked.

Within a period of less than two years, he'd been nailed by the narco squad on seven different occasions, and got retired out of the organization. He did not get a gold watch. Getting fired from the rackets often entails getting fired *at* — and the Snowbird's boys tried to liquidate him twice, not with slugs but with overdoses.

Apparently they didn't know how much immunity the Junkman had built up for himself. He'd survived both attempts and emerged with an even bigger habit. Since before he'd gone to work for Wren, Stedman had been a first-class heister, and he'd returned to his old ways. More reckless now, the Junkman still had a knack for small-scale knockovers.

The Wren outfit took him off their hit list when they found Junkman, out of desperation, overpaying for his bundle of glassine packets with two- to ten-carat chunks of jewelry lifted from show-biz personalities' hotel rooms. A junkie with this kind of initiative was rare, and he went from liability to the kind of prime customer worth keeping.

Also, the Snowbird apparently had his own uses for the Junkman's talent as a break-in artist, and kept him handy for certain delicate jobs. Junkman could plant evidence for the narcs, if a balky operator didn't like the way the game was going, or do a home invasion that was in reality a mission, Junkman checking out anybody Wren thought might be trying to work the territory.

Sweetest of all, Junkman's services came cheap. All they had to do was cut off his supply, and he was ready to do whatever it took to climb back on the Horse.

I did it the other way around.

He was hurting when I found him, and I made sure he got his fix—at least enough of one to calm him down and set me up as an all-right guy. But he was going to need more and fast, and knowing how tight the stuff was on the street, Junkman was grateful for the jolt that eased the big hurt that had him on a bare, ancient mattress, cramped up against the headboard of a metal bed in the crummy old hotel.

Funny. Around the turn of the century, these walls and halls had been filled with wealthy wastrels of the Stanford White and Harry Thaw variety, a luxurious hideaway for monied marital cheaters and other high-hat sinners. But neighborhoods change and shift, and the old hotel had long ago decayed into a way station for transients and junkies and other dwellers on the fringes of society.

I had walked a hall where paint peeled and occasional bare bulbs gave off halfhearted yellow light. You could smell the disinfectant but also the urine, mingled with the smell of cheap canned food getting heated up. The fate of the old dump might be a hot plate with a frayed cord causing a fire, or a slumlord with a can of gasoline doing the same. Either way, the terrible promise of hellish flames hung over everything.

Now I was sitting in a creaky, scarred-up wooden chair next to the Junkman's bed, as if I were visiting a patient at the world's worst hospital.

Skinny, pale, sunken-chested, Marvin Stedman was a little man made smaller by life, his face an oval of deep-grooved flesh, his thin gray matted hair as long as any hippie kid on the street, but not a fashion statement or a social protest. He wore frayed, faded long johns and no shoes—the needle marks between his toes were as obvious as on the track-marked forearm that he used to wipe his nose.

"Thanks, man," he said. His voice was a rasp crossed with a wheeze. "I was dying, man. I was really no shit dying." A shudder racked him again, and when it passed, he looked at me with blood-shot eyes, his tobacco-stained teeth clamped tightly together under gums with nasty sores. "Ain't been that close in a *long* time, my friend."

"Pretty bad, huh?"

"Bad don't cover it. What's your name, buddy?"

"Hammer."

"Where'd you score, man? Ain't *nothin'* out there. Them streets are naked as shit."

"A buddy of mine was holding a spare."

He worked at studying my face. "You don't look like no junkie, man."

"I'm not."

"And I . . . don't make you no narco, neither."

"Right again."

A little light seeped into the rheumy eyes that radiated pure fear. "What do you want from me?"

There had been no questions before. No questions when a stranger in a trench coat showed up at his door with a glassine bag of powder for him. Just snatch it up and find the spoon and heat it up and slam it home.

Now he had questions.

"You want to *know* something," he said, "don't you?"

"Everybody wants to know something, Junkman."

"Ain't nothin' free. You're gonna *hold* me here . . . until it hits again . . . and then you figure I'll talk."

"Nope. I'm just going to walk out."

He sat up. The metal bed groaned. So did Junkman. "Look, man, you *gotta* tell me where you *scored!*"

"I don't gotta do nothing," I said.

"Man, I'll *die!*" He pushed away from the headboard and half collapsed on the filthy mattress. "You don't know how it *is,* man. I can't *make* it by myself."

He dropped his head in an attitude of pure pathos, staring blankly at his hands. They weren't trembling. Thanks to me, he'd shot up not long ago. But they were empty—as empty as his prospects.

"Man, man, I didn't know I wanted to keep on *living* so bad. Used to be . . . I thought dying was nice . . . only come to find, it's *worse*'n livin'."

"They got treatment centers, Junkman."

The shake of his head was barely discernible. "Forget it. Wouldn't do nohow. Ain't nothin' for me but this." His smile was a death mask. "You're lookin' at a real, hardcore head, Mr. Hammer. You see . . . I *like* it. Mother's milk. Nectar of the gods. Only thing worth livin' for."

"But you're killing yourself, Junkman."

"Yeah, man, but slow. Like *real* slow . . . *floating,* man. . . ."

"Only when you aren't floating, Junkman, you're hurting—hurting all the way. Is it worth it?"

"Well . . . that . . . that's . . . the *bad* part. I admit it. Look, Mr. Hammer, I appreciate what you done for me. But you know I am gonna need another fix, and soon. I am *really* gonna need another fix. You think maybe you could help me out again?"

"We can talk about that after."

"After what, Mr. Hammer?" He was mellow now.

"After you answer some questions."

107

"I was right . . . I was *right* about you. . . ."

"You said it yourself—the street has dried up. Who's holding back the stuff, Junkman? What the hell is shaking out there? A price war on?"

"Might be a war coming."

"Oh?"

"Snowbird and the Syndicate."

"I thought they worked together?"

"Snowbird . . . he has ambitions."

"So he's holding back?"

"No! No . . . no . . . too much heat . . . cops got lucky couple times, and now . . . no stuff. Not for ages, not for ever. Everybody's waitin' . . . dying inside and waitin' . . ."

"Till the Snowbird comes through?"

"That . . . that bastard don't care about nothin' or nobody. *He* ain't no user. *He* ain't dying. He don't know how it feels to have your guts churn up inside you like they was tryin' to crawl out."

I shifted and the chair complained. "Junkman, businesses can't let their customers die. Otherwise there won't *be* a business."

"Sure, sure, and it *is* comin' in. It *is* comin'."

"Who says?"

"The street. Word on the street."

"Who's spreading that word?"

"Snowbird's boys. Only . . . I can't *wait* two more weeks, Mr. Hammer. Man, I'm carryin' one heavy fuckin' monkey, you know? I got King Fuckin' Kong on my back! I don't need it next *week*! I need it right *now*!"

"What happens next week?"

He got his head up and his eyes had more of a shine in them. "Mr. Hammer, that's just the word that's out. I told you. I don't know from nothin'."

"Where's the new shipment coming from?"

"I don't give a shit, understand? I just know I'm gonna *need* it. . . ."

"Junkman," I told him, "I can tap a couple of sources, but whatever those guys can spare, you won't be off the hook for more than today. I'm sorry, man, but that's all I can manage. It's tighter outside for me than it is for you. I have my contacts, my sources, but this is your world."

And welcome to it.

"Yeah, Mr. Hammer, I hear you, but you got *bread,* man. I ain't even been able to hustle a tie clip since the heat went on."

"A week is a long time," I reminded him. "If you know who I can hit, to get the stuff, you better give me the word. And maybe I can score you some."

His cheeks seemed to sink in even further and he fell back against the headboard again. "Just the Snowbird and his boys. That's the only ones I know."

I shrugged. "Then I can't help you."

He smiled weakly. "So, then, it's dying time, man, right? If it ain't on the street . . ."

"The Snowbird's cupboards are bare? I figured he was just doling out a supply."

"What supply? *He's* waitin', too."

"Who's his source?"

It was another slow span of time before he spoke again. "You're asking too small a fry, man. All I know is . . . it all . . . comes down the line."

"Who's in line ahead of Snowbird?"

The Junkman rolled his palms up helplessly. "You said it, Mr. Hammer . . . the Syndicate. The Evello Family, working their middlemen . . . the receivers."

"No names?"

"No names, no faces, nothin', man. They're just *there,* and if they don't come through *fast* . . . man, this town's gonna be really strung out, like you never seen."

"You know Russell Frazer?"

His voice was a harsh whisper: "I know the fuckin' fink."

"He bought it," I said.

"Bastard tried to O.D. me, once." His eyes came up and peered at me through the mental haze. "Come around saying he felt sorry for me. Do me a favor, for old times, fink Frazer. Gimme a hot shot. Tried to boil me out." Somehow he managed a skull-with-skin grin. "Sent me flyin', but I fooled him—man, I came down. Who's he think he's *dealin'* with? Bastard fink."

Then my words finally sank in and he squinted, trying to get me in focus. "Bought it? You mean . . . he bad-tripped out?"

"Naw. Knife job."

The Junkman nodded approvingly. "Good. Good fuckin' riddance. Now he won't be hittin' no more school kids. That's the new way, Mr. Hammer—screw the old trade . . . hook the straights. Suck the money kids." He shook his head. "That bastard was due."

He took a breath, then fumbled in the ashtray for a broken cigarette butt.

I gave him a fresh Lucky and held a match out to the tip. He drew on it till the tip burned red, but then just held it without smoking.

"Who . . . who carved his ass?"

"The cops said it was a mugging."

His dry lips stretched humorlessly across the bad teeth. "Not *that* fink. He just made too many . . . too many bad runs."

There was more I wanted to ask him, but it would have to be another time. The Junkman's eyes weren't all the way closed, but he was off in happy land.

I took the burning cigarette from fingers already scarred from hot tips, and squashed it out. No need to let the hellish flames take this old hotel, and Junkman, sooner than necessary.

But the old junkie had told me something.

I wasn't sure just exactly what it was, but something had been fed into the computer between my ears, and was sitting there waiting for other bits and pieces of information that would finally read out an answer.

Who was I kidding? I didn't know what the *question* was—though I was pretty sure it had something to do with why bringing in guns from St. Louis to kill Mike Hammer was a good business move.

For somebody.

Chapter Seven

FROM A WINDOW BOOTH at Marco's Bar and Grill, I watched
Velda get out of the cab, those long sleek legs unmistakably
announcing her. She was in a cream-colored silk blouse and a
dark brown tight skirt, simple fare that she made sexier than
a bikini on any other woman.

She strode in, purse tucked under her arm, and I came up to
take her elbow and guide her to a back booth, where we ordered a
couple of drinks. She glanced around the place, taking in the lone
hardhat gouging his way into a huge hero sandwich, determined to
finish it on a ten-minute break, and the pair of gay lovers nuzzling
at the bar. The counterman was watching a late-afternoon soap
opera, ignoring the real thing a few feet away.

Velda shoved a sealed envelope at me after the drinks came, and
held a match up to my cigarette.

"This far uptown," she said, "you're as out of place as a Van
Gogh on Coney Island."

"Says who?" I said. "I've seen plenty of guys with one ear out there." I ripped open the flap and shook out the file cards with the photos stapled to them. "Have any trouble getting the stuff?"

"Nope. Bud Tiller is still paying back for the help you gave him with the Hanley case."

"I thought I owed *him* one."

"Maybe, but that Hanley deal would've cost him his license, if you hadn't waded in." Her dark eyes were reassuring. "Being an ex-FBI type, Bud's contacts are solid."

I was looking at mug shots of the hit men who'd tried to take me out in my apartment-building lobby.

She said, "Even the papers haven't got those."

The pair of police photos had been taken over ten years ago. Despite the occasion, both faces had an expression of unconcealed arrogance. Louis "Frenchy" Tallman had been booked on attempted assault, the case later dismissed because the victim refused to press charges, and Gerald Kopf on car theft. Kopf was convicted, sentenced, but put on probation for a year because it was his first offense. No other charges were registered, although the two were rumored to be open for contract kills, and had been questioned several times about various murders in several states.

"What interests me most," Velda said, "is their background."

"Yeah. Me, too."

They were originally New York boys—specifically, Brooklynites. They'd met in reform school and, although that part of their package was sealed, the name of the street gang they'd been in was mentioned.

"The Jackers," I said. "Short for 'hijackers'—those kids were the farm team for the Evello mob."

"So we have an interesting connection, despite the out-of-town tag."

I moved on to the other photos.

The pic of Russell Frazer was taken on a slab in the morgue, and he looked like he was asleep. Well, he was—he just wasn't waking up.

The one of the guy who had supposedly knifed Frazer had been grabbed by a newspaper photog and showed a surly, half-bald joker getting hauled out of a hotel entrance by a couple of uniformed cops. Behind him was a sullen whore with a boxer's nose, a delicate flower with twenty-eight previous arrests going for her. This was the first New York bust for the guy—or maybe I should say fall guy—who was registered at the Stearman Hotel as Edwin Brooke.

I let my eyes run over the picture again, picking up the background. "Isn't this Broadway?" I asked her.

"The Stearman Hotel is next to that cafeteria where all the junkies hang out."

I frowned. "Hell, that's two blocks from the Avondale, where Frazer lived in his salad days."

Velda nodded, then caught up with me and said, "You think Brooke might have *known* Russell Frazer?"

"It's the same neighborhood."

She made a face—on her, it looked good. "Every building's a neighborhood in that area. There's at least twenty flophouses calling themselves hotels within six blocks. Besides, Frazer moved out of the Avondale a long time ago."

"It stinks," I said.

"Sure it does," Velda told me. "And it won't smell any better until you stop horsing around fighting windmills."

"Why would I want to stop, with a Sancho Panza that has your shape?"

I tore the photos off the file cards and stuck them in my pocket, letting Velda put the rest back in her handbag. I took a sip of the watered drink, grimaced and put it down. "How about the other thing?"

She reached over and flicked the ash of my cigarette off with a fingernail. "Your friend Tiller says not to quote him, but there's talk of promotions going around the narco squad."

"Oh?"

"The D.A.'s office is filled with people sporting shit-eating grins, and Washington has sent up two top men from the Treasury Department to confer with the NYPD inspector who handled all the recent narcotics busts."

"Pat claims both local and federal agencies have put a big dent in the traffic. *How* big a one, I wonder?"

"Big enough for the Syndicate's Commission to call for a general meeting—the six New York families and factions from all over America and Europe, too."

"You're kidding."

"No. Biggest one since Appalachia in '57. Inside sources say one is due and there's going to be some head-rolling."

I grinned at her. "Pussycat, you are just bursting with news."

"Naw—Bud Tiller was just playing secret agent again, trying to impress you. Maybe he thinks you need a partner."

"I already have one, kitten."

She paused, let out a warm chuckle, and said, "Getting back to business—the law-enforcement agencies, federal and local, are keeping all this under wraps, officially, anyway."

I gaped at her. "Why aren't they bragging?"

Her expression grew sly and even more catlike than usual. "Nobody seems to want to mention the fact that it wasn't superior police investigation that put such a kink in the Syndicate's drug operation."

When she paused, I said, "Do I make a wild guess?"

"Try it."

"I dunno. Anonymous phone calls?"

"You joking?"

"You aren't laughing."

Her forehead frowned and her mouth smiled. "How the hell can you always be so damn right, then?"

I could feel the scowl start between my eyes and run down into my fingertips. "Are *you* joking now? These arrests are due to anonymous damn *tips?*"

"No joke. The various agencies got calls that stated places and times, and they would have dismissed the first one as a gag if it hadn't been so accurately detailed. It was too big *not* to follow up . . . and everything proved out."

I gave a low whistle. "Somebody's spilling from the inside, all right. And that kind of a leak will get plugged up in a hurry."

"Right. Which is why the feds and the cops aren't taking public bows—their success story could be all too temporary."

"It may explain all the attention I'm getting from Assistant D.A. Traynor."

An eyebrow arched. "There's something else, Mike."

"Like what?"

"After the first call? The other calls were taped."

"Then they have a voiceprint of their tipster!"

But she shook her head. "The lab boys tried taking a voiceprint, but everything came out scrambled. It would be impossible to identify the caller from those tapes . . . even if they knew who it was."

"Shit," I said.

"That's your comment? 'Shit'?"

I thought about it. "So now we have an electronics expert figure it out," I told her. "For us."

"Who's better than the federal people?"

"Remember Vincent Rector?"

Her eyes widened. Of course she remembered Vincent Rector—the electronics genius who had revolutionized the hi-fi industry and developed the first videotape. Who had semi-retired to happy puttering only to have his young wife try to frame him for a divorce action. I'd put aside my usual prejudice against divorce cases, and proved that Rector had been drugged and photos of him with a hooker staged, and also got my own shots of the wife in bed with the photographer.

Velda said, "There's nothing Rector wouldn't do for you."

"I'll talk to Pat and get a copy of one of those tapes, and you talk to Vincent. Maybe he can tell us how you can scramble a tape so a voiceprint doesn't come through."

"You got it."

I took a last drag on the butt and let it fizzle out in the remains of my drink. "And tell Bud Tiller thanks. All favors are now officially paid back—strictly cash-and-carry from now on."

Her expression was odd. "Mike . . ."

"What?"

"You got me all jumpy inside."

"Hell of a time to discuss our love life, kitten."

She folded her arms to her chest and shivered. "I *wish* it were that kind of jumpy."

"What other kind of jumpy you mean?"

"The in-over-your-head kind. Like . . . you can't land a white shark on a twelve-ounce line."

I looked at her and let a slow grin spread across my face.

"You can," I said, "if you use a hand grenade for bait."

"Really?" she asked. "And whose dead meat are you going to wrap it in?"

If you didn't decide to go to the movies, you wouldn't have walked past the construction site where they dropped a brick on your head.

Or if the doll you wound up marrying had never taken the wrong turn down that hall, she would never have met you.

That's coincidence.

You hook up with a whore, screw her silly, and catch the clap.

That's *not* coincidence.

I cut in to save a working kid's ass from three punks and two of them get killed and another hospitalized because I happen to have a client at a building where the shit went down. *That's* coincidence.

A bastard tries to knife me in the back and two hit men wait for me in my own lobby to blow my brains out. That's *not* coincidence.

But the trouble was conceived in coincidence, incubated in curiosity, and given birth with inquiry—all uptown in a strange backyard where the bridge and the park and the towers of Manhattan loomed behind me like the disinterested spectators they were.

The last customers at the Village Ceramics Shoppe were having their packages wrapped while a pudgy, balding, tired-looking middle-aged man waited impatiently by the door to lock up when I edged in. He had the weary expression of minor managerial authority, so I supposed he was Mr. Elmain and said to him, "Just have to give Miss Vought a message," and brushed on past.

There were no green smudges this time, no smock or dusty hands, just a lovely, shapely blonde in a navy blue suit topped by a pert little hat and a ready smile.

I said, "Be a shame to get that smart outfit dirty."

"It's suppertime, Mr. Hammer," she said. Her eyes did that little dance again. "You *do* eat, don't you?"

"I'm a card-carrying carnivore. Maybe we could do it together?"

"Do what together?"

"Eat. Let's make it my treat."

"What makes you think I don't already *have* a date?"

"I'd be surprised if you didn't. I was hoping you'd cancel."

That made her laugh—a nice throaty one. "And I was hoping you'd ask. Date accepted."

She excused herself and went off to use a phone at the rear of the workshop/storeroom. I couldn't hear the conversation, but it didn't last long, and soon she was returning, her smile turned up at the corners.

She tilted her head, pulling on her coat. "I'll try not to act frightened by your rather . . . unconventional appearance."

"Nobody ever accused me of being a pretty boy."

"I think you'll do quite nicely," she said.

Another Neanderthal-lover.

"Now," she said, "where do you intend to take me?"

I shrugged and grinned at her. "This isn't my turf, ma'am. Suppose you pick the spot."

She tinkled a laugh at me and nodded. "Okay, we'll try a little French place I know. It's chic, secluded, and the food is delicious. It's quite expensive, but I didn't promise to be a cheap date."

"No, you didn't."

She shrugged and blonde tresses bounced. "Anyway, between courses you can interrogate me."

"Why would I want to do that?"

"Because it's too early to do anything else."

"It's never *that* early," I said.

"No, I don't suppose it would be," she told me, with an appraising look. "Not for you, Mr. Hammer."

I ushered her through the curtained portals from the back room into the shop, where the presumed Mr. Elmain opened the door with a smile and closed it behind us without one.

"That's the boss?" I asked.

"That's the boss. He's really very sweet."

"I'll take your word for it."

Le Petite wasn't quite what I had expected. It was in an odd little corner of the city that I wasn't familiar with. A half-dozen chauffeur-driven limousines lined the curb, the drivers clustered in a group, most of them smoking, some eating sandwiches from home, all of them talking in low tones.

The uniformed doorman greeted Shirley Vought by name and

held the door open for us. Inside, the maitre d' repeated the performance and personally escorted us to a finely carved oaken booth as though my date owned the place. The captain was equally solicitous, hovering over us as if attending a queen.

I didn't miss the glances we got from several other tables, including a couple of envious looks from a pair of national television personalities. My mug was well-known enough to garner that kind of reaction, at least in some quarters, but I could tell the scrutiny wasn't for me . . . unless it was respectable folk wondering what was a nice girl like her doing with a face like this?

When my drink and her white wine came, she lifted her glass and asked, "Curious, Mr. Hammer?"

I tasted my tall rye with ginger, put it down, and lit a Lucky. "You caught me off base, baby, and let's keep it on a first-name basis, okay?"

"Certainly, Mike. Now back to your question."

"I didn't ask one, Shirley."

"You were about to. Let's see—how would you phrase it? Why is a working girl like me getting all this attention at such an exclusive bistro?"

"That's a good start."

Her smile poked fun at me a moment, then: "Don't let my occupation throw you. I happen to be independently wealthy."

"Yeah?"

She shrugged. "A small matter of a large inheritance. Ceramics is a hobby I've always enjoyed, and rather than be the playgirl type, I stay up to my elbows in clay and paint. I'm one of those many people who find the hobby quite therapeutic, and very rewarding."

"So is marriage, some would say."

Another shrug. "I tried it once. That's why I need the therapy. Incidentally, have you checked out my address?"

"Nope."

"No automatic background check?"

"Nope."

"Well, just in case you're telling the truth—it's a penthouse affair in the East Fifties."

I let some smoke out. "We're practically neighbors—except I live halfway downstairs with the rest of the riffraff."

"Hell to be poor, isn't it?"

"I get by on my character," I grinned.

"Which leads us into your next question," she said.

"Clue me."

But she waited until the waiter had brought our main course, and watched me try to fathom an odd taste—that's what I hate about French food, "sauces" that aren't anything but weird gravy.

Then she said, "I'm not sure exactly what your next question would be . . . just that it would have something to do with Russell Frazer, Billy Blue, or Dr. Harrin."

I looked up from what was supposed to be veal, and waited.

Her mouth smiled but her brown eyes were dead serious. "All roads lead to Rome, as they say. Frazer, Billy, the good doctor . . . they all had some connection with the shop, and you had a connection with them, Mike. How am I doing so far?"

"Right on the track, sugar."

"Right in the *middle*, wouldn't you say?"

"Not exactly . . ."

"Then start your interrogation." She was still smiling impertinently, something of the little girl in her showing through. Spoiled rich kids have a cocky attitude that can endear or irritate, depending on the context. I was endeared . . . so far.

"Okay," I said. "How did Frazer get the job there?"

She mulled a second, her fork poised over her plate—she was having the Dover sole, and I wished I was.

"Russell came in about a year ago," she said. "He had been making deliveries for another company in the area—paper supplies, shipping materials—and we were one of his stops. He seemed to be genuinely interested in ceramics, and when the shop expanded, Mr. Elmain asked him if he'd like to work there. Russell grabbed at the chance."

"You ever see his apartment?"

"No. I told you, Mike, we weren't close."

"Regular lover-boy bachelor pad, and a closet full of Carnaby Street. Trust me, he spent a lot more than he made with you."

She shrugged noncommittally. "Maybe he had a sideline."

I shook my head. "I think the ceramics shop was the sideline."

Now she frowned, interested, confused. "Sideline for . . . what?"

"Beats me," I lied.

Shirley studied her plate a few seconds, as if looking for permission there, then looked up. "I don't know if you've run across this in your investigations, Mike, but you know, Russell . . . he liked to gamble."

"Didn't know that. Care to elaborate?"

"Well, I know he played the numbers. Could he have hit one, from time to time?"

I shook my head. "Daily players don't lay out that much, so the take couldn't have accounted for his assets."

She sat forward, the brown eyes alert. "But that isn't all—I heard him call in horses occasionally. Supposing he parlayed one chunk of money into something *really* big?"

"It's possible," I agreed, "but luck rarely runs like that. For the guys who make a profession of gambling, maybe. For small-timers like Frazer likely was, it's generally a washout."

Her eyes tensed. "Then . . . where would he get that kind of cash?"

"That's one of the things I'm going to find out."

"Mike . . ."

"What?"

123

"You told me that . . . that Russell tried to *kill* you."

I nodded and filled her in on most of it. The rest involving the drifter Brooke, she had read in the papers. Now she watched me, frowning. Finally she asked, "Are you *sure* Russell tried to kill you?"

"Take it from an old soldier, doll. He made a damned good try at it. If I hadn't had my mind on other things, I would've known it wasn't some punk trying to mug me."

Her eyes squinted up and she cocked her head. "Mike—you said we're practically neighbors."

"Uh-huh."

"Two men were killed in the lobby of—"

"My building. Nothing to do with you, sugar. Maybe nothing to do with me, either."

Her tongue dampened her lips and she laced her fingers together, not able to take her eyes from mine. For an instant there, she was looking at me as if I were something that just crawled out of a hole. It was a look I'd seen before.

I wasn't about to louse up my story, so I said, "Last week there was a mob killing down on the corner. Two days later, the bank a block away was hit. Who knows what's going to happen anymore? This is big bad New York, honey."

The cloud left her eyes and she shrugged. "I guess you're right, Mike. But it *is* kind of frightening, isn't it?"

"Especially when you see it for the first time. To me, it's everyday stuff. I only get bugged when it's *my* ass somebody is after."

For some reason, that made her smile. Then I figured it out, and said, "I get it—you're *used* to having guys after your ass."

She didn't blush or pretend to be shocked. She just said, "Like you said, Mike—everyday stuff."

For a few minutes we ate in silence, then her eyes drifted upward again. "Why do you do it, Mike? Put yourself at risk, I mean. There must be safer jobs."

"Safer, but not as satisfying. Anyway, day in day out, my work is routine. Recovering lost property, finding missing kids, looking into insurance claims. But it does have its moments."

"I know. I've read about some of them. . . ."

"Don't believe everything you read in the papers."

"Oh?"

"Some of it is worse."

She managed a tiny smile, then asked, "Does it bother you to kill somebody? Or is there a . . . rush of some kind?"

I thought about it, then felt around for an answer. "There's no thrill to it, if that's what you mean. If you're in a firefight, sure there's a rush. But killing *itself*. . . . If it has to be done, all I can say is that I don't feel any remorse afterward."

Her expression was blank but somewhere behind it, she was disturbed. "How do you justify killing somebody?"

"No sense in trying."

"No . . . remorse?"

"It's either you or them. When it comes to survival, I want to be on the breathing end. Remorse doesn't enter in."

She shuddered, just a little. "I would think killing someone would always bring remorse to somebody."

I shrugged. "Sometimes it brings relief to the survivors."

Shirley shook her head slowly. She was getting a crash course in the cost of being attracted to Neanderthals. "What about Dr. Harrin's son? He took that awfully hard."

"Grief and remorse are related, but not the same animal." I was lighting up another smoke. "It hit the doc hard because that kid died too young, too early. Did you know the boy?"

She nodded. "He came in the store a few times, to pick up some things for the hospital. Twice the doctor was with him . . . and when he came back, after his son died? I couldn't get over how Dr. Harrin had changed. He looked ten years older."

"I didn't know him before, so I've got no basis for comparison."

"Well, trust me on this, he was a vital older man, very upbeat, very jovial . . . clowned around with everybody, and had a real interest in the ceramics project he had going in the children's ward. After his son died, though, he seemed to lose interest. Oh, he kept things going with the program, but he didn't have that personal involvement anymore. Billy Blue managed everything for him."

"Billy's a good kid."

"Very," she agreed, "and the doctor really took him under his wing, I understand. But there's no substituting for flesh and blood, is there? David, Jr. — Davy — was an outstanding young man. A very good student, I understand, excelled at athletics — and practically the image of his father."

"I thought you only saw him a few times."

"True, but Davy Harrin was pretty much a local institution . . . especially among the girls. He dated one who used to work after school at the shop, for us. She was forever showing clippings from the *Weekly Home News* about her great love."

"*Weekly Home News*?" I asked her. I hadn't even heard of it. "What's that, a supermarket rag?"

Shirley smiled and shook her head in mock disgust. "You downtowners forget that Manhattan Island is more than Times Square and Central Park. The *News* is a twelve-page tabloid of local news only. No comics, but an easy crossword puzzle." She smiled in open amusement. "Would you like a subscription? I can get half off mine, if I get a friend to sign up."

"No thanks. But if you have Girl Scout cookies for sale, I'll think about it."

The waiter was heading over to see if we had a dessert order.

"End of interrogation, Mike?"

"Almost. Tell me about your manager."

We decided to share crème brûlée, and then returned to the topic.

"Mr. Elmain?" she asked.

I nodded.

Shirley propped her chin on her hands and looked at me across the table. "You saw him as we exited the shop. A nice gentleman in his late fifties, widowed at an early age, remarried and has two chubby teenage daughters. His father had a porcelain business in Holland, and Mr. Elmain took up ceramics over here. He used to have a place in Brooklyn that made only inexpensive restaurant pieces. He sold that and set up the Village Ceramics Shoppe."

"How is business?"

She beamed. "Absolutely terrific. You'd be surprised how many bored people there are looking to express themselves in an art form. It's within their capabilities, doesn't cost much, and they always have something concrete to show off or give away."

"What you sell," I said, "is generated by students in classes?"

"Some of it. And we produce the more professional items ourselves. Four of us on staff are trained in the craft, the art."

"I see."

"Most of our income is the street trade of people, tourists mostly, looking for interesting gift objects. There aren't too many ceramics shops in the city, so we get the trade from all over, including mail orders."

"And Elmain?"

Her smile was warm. "As for Mr. Elmain, I'd say he was very well off, a conservative fussbudget, and as innocuous as they come. I like him. We all do."

The dessert came, with coffee, and we set the dish between us and went after it with our spoons—an intimate arrangement for a first date.

I asked, "How did the boss get along with Frazer?"

"Russell did his job," she said, and licked creamy stuff off her lips. "That was all Mr. Elmain ever asked of him."

"Susie Moore told me Frazer had some odd friends that drove black limos."

She smirked at the thought. "I think Russell was more talk than action."

"I told you—you should see his *Playboy* pad."

"I'd rather see yours," she said impishly.

My eyes swept the place deliberately and there was a caustic note in my voice when I said, "I'm not convinced I'm your type, Shirley."

"Still waters may run deep," she said, "but a rough current is a lot more fun to surf in." She had that funny smile going again. "Please don't typecast me, Mike."

Like she wasn't me?

"Okay," I said, and put my spoon down. "Let's get back to Frazer. He ever give you a hard time at all? Too sexually frisky, maybe, or argumentative or . . . anything?"

She thought a moment and shook her head. "I can't come up with anything, Mike."

"Let's put it this way—has there *ever* been any trouble at the shop?"

This time the response was instant: "Well, we had the front window smashed by some drunk one time . . . then about six months later, somebody broke in the back door, smashed up some greenware, and pried open the files. But we never keep any money on hand, and nothing was missing."

"What about the cash register?"

"The drawer is always left open and empty at night. Mr. Elmain makes a night deposit right after we close up, and takes home enough to open the register with the next day. Apparently the burglars thought the cash was in the files and forced them open. We had to buy all new drawers the next day."

"That's the extent of it? No other trouble?"

"Oh, we get occasional shoplifting, but that's usually around the holidays."

"What *was* in the files?"

"Invoices, receipts, correspondence from customers and suppliers. The usual sort of thing."

I nodded. "What kind of a locking device did the file cabinets have?"

She fished in her handbag, took out a ring of keys, and handed me two simple flat steel jobs about two inches long. "One for each file of four drawers each," she said.

"Hell, any amateur could handle that kind of deal without even busting the drawers."

"A screwdriver is just as easy," she admitted. "I had to do it once myself, when I lost my keys."

I handed the ring back and snubbed out my cigarette. "How about letting me take a look at those files?"

Her tongue wet her lips down and they slipped into a pretty smile. "Okay, but there are more interesting things you could examine."

"Women's Lib is ruining this country," I said. "Don't you know it's the male of the species who's supposed to be the aggressor?"

She rolled her pretty brown eyes. "Not with all the competition around these days, brother. Hey, a woman needs every advantage she can grab."

"What makes you think I'm up for grabs?"

Her smile got even more provocative. "Up *for* . . . or up *to*?"

"Don't make my working hours so hard, baby."

"Maybe I like the idea."

"Of what?"

"Of making it hard for you."

I let out a little laugh and waved the waiter over to bring me the check. I put it all on my credit card, like shelling out this way for food was an everyday occurrence, and reminding myself never to come back here again. I folded the receipt into my wallet and took Shirley Vought outside to a cab.

The way she held on to me, I might get my money's worth yet.

The files in the back room were simple gray steel affairs, powdered lightly with ceramic dust. Two oversize figurines and a collection of painted chess pieces were stacked on their tops beside a box of color charts.

Each drawer held alphabetically filed folders with the exception being the lower left-hand one, where a bag of hair curlers, a can of spray, and a comb and brush were tucked away. Most of the filing related to domestic business, but two drawers were given over to the foreign accounts, suppliers of certain paints and European-oriented molds.

I asked her, "Would any of this stuff be of value to competitors?"

"I can't see how," she said, eyes narrowed, brow furrowed. "Everybody has access to those firms. It's an open market—it isn't as if the business had any great financial or social significance."

Just to be sure, I riffled through the files one more time, picked out the one labeled SAXONY HOSPITAL, and looked over the purchase orders signed by Dr. Harrin. Practically all of them were for novelty items from ashtrays to toy banks along with paint, stains, and equipment to decorate them.

Before I could ask her, Shirley said, "The hospital has a kiln in the basement that a wealthy patient donated. They bake their own pieces."

I put the folder back and slid the door shut with disgust. I said, "Damnit," and Shirley shrugged.

"I told you there was nothing to look at."

"Maybe I should have taken you up on your first offer," I said. She came into my arms, her face tilted up toward mine. She

130

might have been just a little tipsy from several glasses of wine. Lifting herself on her toes, hands behind my head pulling me closer, she ran her tongue like a little firebrand across my lips.

"It still isn't too late," she said.

"I should just take you home," I told her.

But I didn't count on the little alcove dressing room with the soft pink light and the big overstuffed chair. She was out of the designer dress as quick as a jump cut in a movie, and although I was trying to swear off those wild oats Velda had said to get sown, I was human—that curvy body with the dramatic tan lines and the puffy, hard-tipped areolas against stark white flesh and the dark pubic triangle against that same startling white was mine for the asking, *without* asking, and she began by falling to her knees to worship the part of me that seemed to be in charge. Soon I was lost in sweet-smelling flesh and hair and caught up with the incredible agility of a woman who loved the unusual, whose curious sounds of total enjoyment were like thunderous applause.

A long time later she said, "Thank you. You're nice. *Now* you can take me home."

Chapter Eight

TO EVERYTHING THERE is a season, and in every season
there is rain. Spring downpours that hit hard, then leave the
sky blue and sunny and rainbow-streaked. Light summer
showers you can walk in with your best girl, and fall storms
that drone steady and turn the leaves soggy. The winter kind that
can turn on you, raindrops freezing to pellets, or switching to snow
with thunder and lightning making a crazy mix.

Then there's a New York rain, a rain that is apart from seasons.
It settles like a big gray blanket over the city and grumbles a while
and just when you figure the threat is an empty one, the stuff
sheets down, slicking the streets, fogging the windows, and prom-
ising nothing but a slate-gray sky when it's done.

I managed to beat both the rain and Velda to the office—the latter a rare feat. She arrived four minutes after me, with her hooded
black raincoat dripping, and she shook it out in the hall before she
hung it in the closet—no coat tree in these modern digs.

I was seated at her desk, with coffee in plastic cups waiting, plus an unfrosted doughnut for calorie-counting her and two frosted ones for who-gives-a-shit me.

She frowned, immediately suspicious. "Who did you kill this time?"

Close, I thought, *but no cigar.*

"Can't a guy just be nice?" I asked innocently.

She shook her head. A little water had gotten on the dark tresses despite her best efforts, and droplets flicked me in the face.

I got out of her chair and she took it. She started in on the coffee and doughnut, and I sat on the edge of her desk, munching my second frosted. The sky rumbled and the blinds rattled.

"I tried to call you last night," she said. "You must have got home late."

"I was working," I said.

"At what?"

"Talking to this Shirley Vought, who works at the Village Ceramics Shoppe."

Her eyes narrowed. She swallowed a bite of doughnut politely, then impolitely asked, "What color is her hair, how old is she, and how much does she weigh?"

"You think I had the chance to weigh her?"

"Did you just develop a speech impediment?"

I shrugged it off, casual. "She's blonde. Mid-twenties. You know I prefer brunettes, kitten."

Thunder rattled the windows and she said, "Any port in a storm."

I slid off the desk, took my coffee and the *Daily News* with me—the doughnuts were gone—and said, "You're impossible before you've had your first cup of coffee."

"This is my second."

"Fine. Take your time drinking it, then bring your pad in, when you're in the mood to work."

I was halfway through the funnies when she came in with her

pad and no attitude, and took the client's chair. "You want me to check up on her?"

I put the paper aside. "The Vought girl?"

She nodded.

"That's a good idea," I said. "She claims to be a rich kid, but it doesn't hurt to be sure. Says she works in that ceramics shop for therapy. And based on the French restaurant she made me take her to—and the looks she got from everybody from the doorman on up—she may well have a Park Avenue pedigree."

Velda was jotting that down. "Anything else?"

"Yeah, she mentioned a little neighborhood tabloid, the *Weekly Home News*—familiar with it?"

She nodded again. "Just what you'd think—local squibs, lots of want ads and personals. Kind of like the *Village Voice* without the sex ads and politics. Why?"

"I want you to go over there, after this weather clears up, and see if they have a morgue or maybe microfilm files. I want you to go back several years, checking for stories about Davy Harrin."

"You mean Dr. David Harrin?"

"No—his *kid*. David, Jr. Davy."

Her mouth made an O. "The one who died? Young and tragic, the athlete?"

"Right. Miss Vought says that tabloid covers the area high school scene. Anything that strikes you as interesting, either make notes or if it's one of those microfilm machines that print copies out, do that."

She frowned. "Okay, Mike . . . but why the interest in the doctor's dead son?"

"Not sure. Call it a hunch."

The frown became a smile. "All right. I can't claim that your hunches don't occasionally pay off. That it?"

"No. Pull in Bud Tiller again, or somebody else at another agency that we can trust." She arched an eyebrow at me and I added: "It's part of the same hunch. Both Junior Evello and Jay Wren, the Snowbird himself, wound up at Saxony Hospital under Doc Harrin's care."

"Is that suspicious?"

"It's got me thinking. Both were minor automobile accident victims—one got clipped by a lady driver, the other by a truck. Two big-shot crooks involved in the dope trade, and each winds up in the hospital under similar circumstances? That doesn't pass the smell test."

"I've heard you say it," she said, head cocked. "Coincidences do happen."

"Yeah. But so do fake insurance claims. Do I have to tell you that there are guys out there who know how to walk in front of a car or a truck, and get hurt just bad enough to make a claim?"

She was ahead of me. "Just like there are guys who can drive a car or a truck, and are expert at making non-fatal accidents happen for the same purpose."

Nodding, I said, "Bud does lots of insurance-claim work. He might know who we should be talking to."

She was taking that down as she asked, "We're obviously not talking about insurance scams here. We're talking about somebody hiring drivers to put somebody else in the hospital, non-fatally . . . but out of commission for a while."

"Roger that."

She sat forward, the lovely face taut with thought. "But, Mike—why would somebody take Evello and Wren out of the action, temporarily?"

"Maybe somebody new on the stage. Somebody trying to cut into the Lower Manhattan drug scene, or possibly bigger, with citywide ambitions. Hell, the Evello mob is a conduit for the whole damn country."

The dark eyes stared unblinkingly at me. "Somebody out there's trying to take over from Wren and Evello? *Who?*"

I waved her off. "No, sugar, it's too crazy to share. Some hunches you don't take out and show around like something you're proud of. Some hunches you have to let play out."

She didn't press me. But she did say, "Well, maybe I have another piece of the puzzle for you. A little piece of information came in yesterday afternoon—that's why I was trying to get ahold of you last night."

"Yeah?"

"Remember Edwin Brooke? The guy who supposedly came along and took advantage of you incapacitating Russell Frazer . . . and conveniently mugged and killed him? Pat called to say those two *did* know each other—in fact, they were booked on mugging charges on three occasions. Four or five years ago, when they were kids, but—"

"Booked on mugging charges," I said, blinking at her. "*Together?*"

"Yeah." She shrugged. "They were a team."

This was the kind of rainy day where you don't bother getting your car out of the building's parking garage. This was a day for taking cabs, and I slid in the back seat of one and asked the driver to take me to Bellevue.

He grinned at me in the mirror, a wiseass with a Brooklyn accent: "The mental ward?"

"Yeah, I'm fighting my urge to strangle cabbies."

That took the funny out of him, and I sat looking out at cars whooshing by with their lights on in the daytime and rain coming down so damn straight, you had to admire God's aim if not His sense of humor.

Bellevue is the oldest hospital in New York, maybe in the country. It's a free hospital and the city won't let anybody be turned away, which is probably why the cops often stick their sick or wounded suspects there. Anyway, that's where the county morgue is, so sometimes it saves a trip.

I could remember when old Bellevue was a nest of mid-Victorian buildings as gray as this rainy day. It had a nasty reputation, too, but that was a long time ago. The brick-and-stone buildings were put up in the late '30s and still seemed modern.

Norman Brix really rated. He had a private room and a uniformed cop seated outside. If you break the law in New York and get hurt doing it, try to get almost killed if you want the best in medical attention.

The young cop recognized me, scrambling to his feet and saying, "Morning, Mr. Hammer," and his little metal nametag allowed me to say, "Morning, Officer Wilson," as if I knew who the hell *he* was, too.

I nodded toward the closed door. "I need to pay the patient a visit."

He had dark hair, blue eyes, and a boyish look, like he'd gone right from the Cub Scouts to the NYPD. "I can't let you do that, Mr. Hammer. There's no visitors."

"It's official business, son. You can check with Captain Chambers."

"Well, I can't leave my post. . . ."

"Damn." I put on disappointment, not irritation. "That means I wasted a trip. And I know Captain Chambers wanted me to see what I could get out of this clown. He *is* awake, isn't he?"

"Oh, he's awake, all right. He isn't very talkative, though."

I figured I could change that. "How about it, son?"

Officer Wilson looked right and looked left, like he was checking to see if maybe the police commissioner was among the doctors, nurses, and patients walking the corridor. "I guess . . . I guess it would be all right, Mr. Hammer."

The kid even opened the door for me.

Feeling just a little guilty, I said, "I'll put in the good word for you with Captain Chambers."

"Thanks, Mr. Hammer!"

The kid would need it.

They had given Brix a butch haircut, possibly to attend better to his minor head injuries, and he was hooked up to a hanging plastic bag of clear liquid. He was as pale as death, but he was breathing, all right, a skinny, battered-looking guy in a blue gown with the covers pulled way up. He was watching a game show on a wall-mounted TV, and I went over and clicked the remote on his bed stand.

He gave me a half-lidded look of non-recognition. His enunciation not up to snuff, thanks to the wired jaw, he demanded, "Who the hell are you?"

"The guy who de-balled you."

Now the eyes popped wide. They were dark blue and bloodshot and scared as hell. He reached for the little white doohickey with the button that called for the nurse, but I got there first, and dropped the thing to the floor, letting it dangle on its cord.

His consonants were sketchy, and his vowels droned, but the wired jaw didn't keep the hate in: "You . . . *Hammer* . . . you bastard . . . you *bastard*. . . . You castrated me!"

"Yeah, that's what de-balled means. Hey, you've still got your prick, at least. It'll still work, stand up and say howdy and everything. Where you're going, being able to make babies is kind of a moot point."

"Get out of here! I'll *scream* bloody—"

I clamped my hand over his steel-reinforced mouth and his eyes bulged. "That's no way to talk, Norm. I come around to pay my respects, and you treat me like this? I'm just here to ask you a few questions, pal. Then I'll leave you to enjoy whatever kind of junk they're pumping into you. Got it?"

Under my hand, he nodded, though the eyes remained big and terrified.

I let go of him. "Why did you and your buddies jump Billy Blue? The truth, Norm."

He didn't scream, I'll give him that.

And he had the balls, metaphorically speaking, to say, "Go *fuck* yourself, Hammer."

I nodded toward the hanging plastic bag of clear liquid hooked into his arm. "What is this? Methadone? Morphine? Good shit, Norm? How's the staff here at Bellevue—they get it right? Or do they sometimes have a screwup?" I clutched the bag and squeezed it. "I suppose even the tightest ship has the occasional O.D., huh?"

"Don't! Shit! *Don't!*"

I let go of it. "Billy Blue, Norm. What's the score? The real one."

He shook his head. With his hippie hair sheared off, he looked like a boot-camp recruit, the type that would wash out the first day.

"Herm and me, we knew Billy from years ago, from school. If he wanted to, he could get us stuff from the hospital—Saxony? And they got a pretty decent supply at that medical college, too."

"Why fool with such piddling product, Norm?"

"Man, ain't you heard, the streets are bone dry. We needed some kind of shit, something to tide us over. Our customers are climbing the walls, and I mean, *really* climbing. And Billy, selfish goddamn son-of-a-bitch bastard, wouldn't help . . . so we figured, teach the little pussy a lesson."

"You were going after him with a bicycle chain, Norm. That could've killed his ass. What kind of 'lesson' is that?"

He shook his head. "We wasn't gonna kill him. But after how he reacted, when we hit him up for a source? We didn't figure, no matter *what* we did, he'd *ever* play along. There's others at that hospital who might, though . . . and, you know, if they saw what could happen to somebody who messed with me and Herm, then they'd think twice about saying no to us."

I asked, "No other reason for the takedown?"

"No! What other reason could there *be?*"

"Word could have come down from the Snowbird to—"

"*Hell* no! The Snowbird don't know Billy Blue from Little *Boy* Blue."

I believed him. I wished I didn't, I wished I'd got a new lead here, but this sick kid wasn't lying. He was too scared and too stupid.

I pressed on, anyway. "Whose idea was it?"

"What idea?"

"Teaching Billy this lesson."

"It was *Herm's* idea, strictly Herm. This is all his damn fault. I'd like to wring his stupid neck."

"When you get out," I said, "why don't you dig him up and do that?"

He was stupid, but not stupid enough to reply. He just lay there, mute, watching me go, praying for me to go, and I did.

The uniformed cop got to his feet. "Everything okay, Mr. Hammer?"

"Yeah. Swell."

"Get what you needed?"

I nodded to him, and the kid called after me, "Don't forget to put in a good word with Captain Chambers!"

"You bet," I said, knowing it would probably be, *Don't fire the little twerp on my account, buddy.*

The Village serves up a pizza slice of Little Italy, south of Washington Square and all the way to Spring Street. At the pushcart market on Bleecker between Sixth and Seventh Avenues, you can get the best fruits and vegetables in the city—all the usual suspects from peppers to bananas, but also more exotic items like zucchini and finocchio. Locals mingle with tourists, who dig the occasional street fairs with their singing and dancing, and their ices and candies.

What the tourists *really* want to see are the Mafiosi. And the many cafés and restaurants offer plenty of opportunities for that kind of negative star-gazing, though the mobsters dress like businessmen and are only identifiable by their bodyguards, who also dress Madison Avenue but physically run to type.

Also, some of the bigger bosses avoid the times of day when out-of-towners come around asking who got shot at what table.

Which is why I didn't go to Salvatore's—a brick-fronted street-level *ristorante*—until after two o'clock. With the rain still tommy-gunning down, the place should be free of tourists, and the guy I wanted to see might have taken an earlier lunch, knowing that.

But I figured Carlo "Junior" Evello would stick to his pattern. The Evellos of the world have a keener sense than most of the random, chaotic nature of things, and they seek solace in habit, in a self-designed structure that gives them a false sense of security. The joke, of course, is such behavior makes them prey to police and federal surveillance, not to mention prone to getting dropped in their spaghetti sauce by business rivals.

I came in and got out of my trench coat and left it on a hook just inside the door. I hung on to my hat, after shaking the rain off it, and moved into the dark, chilly restaurant. Over at the left, in a black vest, white shirt, and black bow tie, a bartender—whose bullnecked build tagged him as doing double duty as the bouncer—was doing zero business. I bought a glass of Pabst on tap from him, just to make him feel wanted.

The place was so empty it might have been closed for cleaning. The carpet was red, the tables black, the booths red. The yellow stucco walls had the typical gilt-framed Sicilian landscapes—oils not prints. The lighting was subdued and made more so by the lack of sunlight through the street windows onto the day's gloom. The deeper into the narrow restaurant you walked, the darker it got.

And the only customers were three businessmen in a booth.

Two were big and greasy-haired and could have been twins but for the slightly smaller one's pockmarks. They were not eating—they didn't even have drinks. Between the big guys, seated in the booth with his back to the wall, was the only one of the trio eating.

And all he had was a bowl of what looked to be chicken soup. Water and no wine, not even coffee.

Carlo Evello was about as threatening-looking as a seventh-grade English teacher, his importance suggested only by the gray Brooks Brothers suit and the darker gray silk tie. He had small, dark, sad eyes in pouches of fat that didn't go with the rest of his fairly slender frame. His eyebrows were slashes of black and his hair was gray and his well-lined face had a funeral-parlor pallor.

When I walked up to the booth, the bookend bodyguards got halfway out of their seats, their tiny eyes flaring even as their tinier minds crawled into action.

"Why don't you tell your goons you'd already be dead," I said to Evello, "if that's what I was here for."

He made a calming motion with one hand and the two settled back down, the pockmarked one frowning. The idiot didn't like being called a goon.

"Join me, Mr. Hammer," Evello said with a smooth voice that didn't go with the diamond-hard beady eyes. "The kitchen is closed till four, but I'm sure for a guest of your . . . renown . . . an exception can be made."

"That's okay. I already ate at Fortunio's. They serve a mean manicotti."

He shrugged and pushed his dish away. He frowned at the half-eaten soup. "Chicken broth and tortellini, Mr. Hammer. I suffer the curse of today's busy executive—an ulcer."

"Having a hole in your stomach *can* be painful." I nodded one at a time at the two greasy-haired watchdogs. "Can you dismiss Heckle and Jeckle? They don't have to leave the room. I just want us old friends to share some privacy."

143

He studied me for a moment, nodded once per bodyguard, and they frowned and shifted but stayed put.

The smooth-cheeked, slightly bigger one said, "At least he should let us take his gun, Mr. Evello."

I gave the guy more attention than he deserved. "Why, are you girls going to give me yours?"

Evello frowned and waved that off, and finally the two thugs slid out of the booth and took a table halfway across the otherwise empty restaurant, where they sat and pouted.

Their boss smiled and laughed to himself, though no sound came out. "Bearding the lion in his den, Mr. Hammer?"

I put my hat on the table, set my beer and myself down, got comfy. "You and I both know, Carlo, that the feds staking you out saw me come in, and they'll expect to see me come out."

He shrugged. He was getting something out of his suit-coat pocket—a silver cigarette case. He removed a small brown smoke and I gave him a light with my Zippo, then fired up a Lucky. I had an ankle on a knee and was casual as hell. We were old friends, though we'd never spoken before.

"I know, generally," Evello said, and painted an abstract picture in the air with a hand that bore a couple gold-and-diamond rings, "why you're here. But let *me* start."

"Like the man said—shoot."

That made him smile again, and he shook his head, as if saying, *That Mike Hammer—what a card.*

Then his face went somber, suddenly as hard as the eyes. "I was not responsible for what those two former employees of mine did outside that Chinese restaurant, some weeks ago. They had been drinking, I understand. They knew the stories about you having . . . having a hand in my uncle's death. They thought they could please me by taking you on, and out. They were fools. I didn't desire it, and they weren't capable of it."

"It's all right. They're as dead as your uncle now."

He waved that off, exhaling blue smoke. "As well they deserve to be. My understanding is that you were badly wounded, and that it required a trip out of town to recover, and . . . well, I apologize for the inconvenience."

"Yeah?"

"Yeah. Wherever this discussion goes, that's behind us. Ancient history."

I gave him a guarded grin. "What about your uncle?"

Half a smile twitched the gray face. "No one knows precisely what happened to my uncle. There were marks on his neck, as if someone had tried to strangle him . . . but he was killed by a knife belonging to one of his own men."

"I didn't kill him," I said.

And I hadn't. He had tied me to a bed and let his men work me over, but I hadn't killed him. I'd gotten loose and I'd squeezed his throat so hard, his eyes almost popped out of their sockets, but I hadn't killed him. I'd watched his head roll back and his tongue loll out, but I hadn't killed him. He was still breathing when I tied him to the bed in my position in the darkened room and called for his guy to come in and finish the job. I hadn't killed him—his own knife-wielding thug had.

Of course, *him* I killed.

"The truth, Mr. Hammer, is that I never much liked my uncle. He was a cold man, selfish and innately cruel. But he was a successful man, with a considerable reputation, and my physical resemblance to him aided me in my . . . climb. I rather resent the nickname this earned me—Junior—and I notice you pay me the respect of calling me Carlo, and I do appreciate that."

"I find grown men don't take to being called Junior."

This time you could hear the chuckle. "Absolutely right, Mr. Hammer. You are a keen observer of human foibles."

"But the word on the street has always been that you blamed me for your uncle's death."

145

Blue smoke exited his nostrils, dragon-style. "Simply a face-saving gesture. It is expected of me to speak ill of the man responsible for my 'beloved' uncle's death. At any rate, I'm not suggesting that you and I are destined for a great friendship, Mr. Hammer—just that we are not, today at least, adversaries. Now—what brings you to Little Italy . . . besides Fortunio's."

I sipped beer. My tone would have fit right in with discussing sports scores. "Did you read about the two St. Louie guys who got in a shootout in the lobby of my apartment building? One was playing dress-up, pretending to be a doorman."

He stiffened. "Mr. Hammer, that also was *not* my doing. . . ."

"Louis 'Frenchy' Tallman?" I said. "Gerald Kopf? Out-of-town talent with ties to the Evellos. Graduates of the Jackers, the street gang who even today make up the Evello Family junior auxiliary. . . ."

He was holding up both hands as if in surrender. "Mr. Hammer, that attempt on your life had nothing to do with me or any of my . . . immediate associates."

"How about your *not* immediate associates?"

He shrugged with his eyebrows, sucked on his little brown cigarette or cigar or whatever-the-hell, then asked, "Aren't my connections, nationally and internationally, extensive enough to secure gunmen who would not be so immediately traceable to me?"

"Are you suggesting somebody wanted me to make that jump? Knowing my history with the Evello Family?"

He turned a hand over. "Isn't that more likely? More logical?"

"Who?"

He sipped his water. Smiled again, but there was no amusement in the tiny hard eyes. "You've been nosing around, Mr. Hammer, as is your wont. You have a rather well-known nose."

"When something stinks, I know it."

"Admirable. You recently came to the aid of a young man who was set upon by two of Jay Wren's people—the Snowbird?"

146

"That's right. Billy Blue. You *know* Billy, Carlo. He mailed a letter for you once."

"Did he?"

I sat forward. "If that's what this is about—if you think that kid saw something he shouldn't have, remembered a name he shouldn't have—then here's your one warning: Back the hell off. I talked to that kid, and he doesn't remember a damn thing about—"

Through most of that he'd been shaking his head, and now the surrender palms were up again. "Mr. Hammer, Mr. Hammer—I swear on my mother's grave that I have no memory of what that letter was. He's a nice boy. He ran some harmless errands for me—nothing sinister—while I was hospitalized."

I settled back. Had a sip of beer. "I spoke to the Brix kid—one of the two attackers—today, at Bellevue. He swears they jumped Billy just because he turned them down on some petty drug-pilfering scheme at Saxony."

He let smoke out, lifted a shoulder. "That sounds credible to me."

"What you said before—about no 'immediate' associates. Would that include the Snowbird? Where does Jay Wren rate with you?"

One of the black eyebrows rose. "He is an ambitious young man who has done an excellent job for me. But, as you well know, Mr. Hammer—ambition has its pitfalls."

"You're suggesting the Snowbird hired those two St. Louis torpedoes."

His faint smile spoke volumes.

"And that Wren did so," I went on, "intending to leave a trail to you?"

He sighed. Sipped his water again. "Mr. Hammer, Jay Wren has, for reasons unknown to me, apparently singled you out as a threat to him. Perhaps he envisions a scenario in which you and I take each other out of the picture. Who can say?"

"But he's just a glorified dealer, right? An underling."

"From time immemorial," he said, "underlings have had a way of . . . getting ideas."

I wasn't buying it. "And he did all this from Miami, I suppose?"

The tiny eyes under the dark slashes of brow blinked a couple times, then he said, "I don't believe so. Wren has been back in town for several days. Since before this incident with the Blue boy even went down."

"I had police information otherwise."

That got more than a chuckle out of him. "Yes, well, Mr. Hammer . . . we all know how reliable police intelligence is."

I grinned at him. "Police intel says a big shipment of H is coming in. How reliable is that, Carlo? A shipment that will turn this dry spell into streets awash with junk."

No smile, now. Just eyes as dead as his Uncle Carl's, if not bulging. "I don't think that's an area we should get into. You are, Mr. Hammer, in your unique way, a policeman yourself. You may or may not have killed my uncle, all those years ago, but you definitely cost him, and my family, a rather major shipment of a certain commodity. And I have no reason to think that your . . . unique views on how to solve what the do-gooders call 'the narcotics problem' have radically changed over those years."

"What do you call it, if it's not a problem?"

The brown cigarillo was between the fingers of the hand he waved, and it made little gray-blue trails. "It's a personal choice, Mr. Hammer. We are in an era of young people who are expanding their reach, their minds, who seek entertainment in ways forbidden to our more stodgy generation. I'm a capitalist in this Marxist world, and am happy to supply freethinkers of all ages with their entertainment needs."

"What a load of horseshit," I said.

And what a load of horse.

Then something came together in my mind. I sat forward again. "This super shipment, should it exist—are you implying the Snowbird has his eye on it? That he might try to hijack it, steal it from you, and set out on his own?"

Evello let out an appreciative grunt. Then he took a small pill-box from his pocket and selected two capsules and popped them with his water. "Goddamned ulcer—we *all* have our drugs, don't we, Mr. Hammer?"

"Yeah." I finished the beer. "I suppose we do. Thanks for the talk. You were frank, and you get brownie points for that."

"Thank you."

"But don't get confused. We're not on the same side. Not even close. No matter how the Snowbird tries to stage-manage this little show. The shit you deal in, it's the plague, Carlo. And the best way to deal with a plague is to wipe out as many rats as possible."

This seemed to amuse him, dryly. "Understood."

I got up, put on my hat, then turned back to him. "Oh, I almost forgot. This Dr. Harrin, who took care of you at Saxony. What's your take on the guy?"

"Why, he's a brilliant man. He's treated rare diseases with such boldness and inspired thinking that you can't help but admire him. And he was very kind to me, very generous with his time and his talent."

"He does seem like a good man."

I nodded to Evello, smirked at his boys, got my trench coat, and went on outside. The rain had finally let up, delivering on its promise of a slate sky, leaving a damp chill to remember it by.

As I flagged down a cab, I was thinking . . . Was I imagining it, or did Evello's little speech about Dr. Harrin sound rehearsed?

And why the hell would he do that?

Chapter Nine

THE RAIN HAD SCOOTED, and morning sun was slanting in the side window of my inner office through blinds that were half shut.

Pat tossed a manila envelope onto my desk and it landed with a clunk. Hat pushed back, he hadn't sat down yet, and was looking at me with a narrow-eyed skepticism I knew all too well.

"There's your latest favor," he said.

I didn't have to open the envelope to feel the spool of tape within. "Thanks, buddy."

"Never mind the soft soap. Now I want some information."

I gestured to the client's chair. I realized he preferred to tower over me and do his cop intimidation number—like that would work with me. He made a sour face and tossed his hat on the desk and plopped down.

"What do you want to know, Pat?"

He sat forward, eyes hard and sparking. "What the hell were you doing going around to Little Italy yesterday and confronting Junior Evello?"

So the feds and the NYPD were cooperating today.

I said, "Who says I confronted him? Salvatore's is a public place. A restaurant open for business."

"Can it, Mike. What went down?"

I shrugged. "We had a polite chat. No guns were drawn, no saps or brass knuckles came into play. Just a quiet little powwow between two factions."

"What do you mean, two factions?"

"Good and evil, buddy. Aren't you paying attention?"

He smirked. "Yeah, which are you?"

I ignored that crack and filled him in, telling him about Evello denying any part in the attacks on me or Billy Blue, and how the mobster all but confirmed that a big shipment of H really was due any day now.

Pat was frowning. "Tell me something I don't know."

"Okay. The Snowbird is back in town. Has been for some time."

He shifted in the chair, vaguely embarrassed. "Well, I *knew* that . . . but I admit I just found it out. The feds down Miami way say he slipped out by private plane maybe a week ago. I don't see how that's pertinent."

I shrugged. "Maybe it isn't. And a guy like Jay Wren can pull strings from Miami easy enough. But somehow, with all that's been happening, it makes sense that he's been right here in the thick of it."

Pat's forehead tensed. "You think Wren's behind all of this? Not Evello?"

"I'm not sure. Evello has a smooth line, so it's hard to say. But I tend to believe the son of a bitch. And Wren is tied to Billy's attackers—Brix, Felton, and Haver."

Pat half climbed out of the chair, shaking a finger at me. "Speaking of Brix—goddamnit, I almost forgot, over this Evello thing. . . .

What's the idea going over to Bellevue and scaring the shit out of my prisoner?"

"Why, are they short bedpans?"

"You go in half-cocked and hand that rookie on the door a load of crap about 'Captain Chambers,' when all you had to do was *ask*, and I'd have arranged it."

"Would you?"

"Well. Maybe." He gave me the RCA-Victor-dog head tilt. "So . . . you get anything out of the creep?"

"He swears up and down that jumping Billy was strictly over the hospital supply-room pilferage dispute. Nothing bigger or more far-reaching than just trying to stave off this shortage on the street."

Pat shook his head. "Then why the hell these attempted hits on you, Mike? If all you did was break up a couple junkies ripping off a decent kid, why send Russell Frazer after you? Or those St. Louis boys?"

"That's what keeps me up nights." I sat up. "Look, Pat—about Wren."

"Yeah?"

"See what kind of surveillance photos the feds and Miami PD have on the Snowbird's recent recuperation visit."

"Why should I?"

"Because it gives me another thread."

"Are you making a sweater, or unraveling one?"

I grinned. "Do me the favor and find out."

"Fuck you, Mike. Really. I mean it. Fuck you, anyway."

"I love you, too, buddy. Now . . . tell me the big news."

He frowned. "What?"

"How long have I known you?" I tapped the manila envelope. "You could have had this messengered over. Captains of Homicide don't play delivery boy. And you got the expression of a constipated billy goat. What's happened?"

His face turned blank. He dropped the phony theatrics, cut the comedy completely, and said, "Edwin Brooke."

"Guy who robbed and supposedly offed Russell Frazer. Right. What about him?"

Pat sighed. "He got a taste of his own medicine last night, and I don't mean cocaine—somebody shivved him in the shower at the Tombs."

I leaned forward. "What kind of condition is he in?"

"Cold," Pat said. "The kind of cold you get when they file you away in a drawer at the morgue."

"Shit," I said.

"You're trying to gather threads, but somebody else is going around picking them up and getting rid of 'em."

"Shit."

"You said that."

I frowned at him. "The shiv artist? In custody?"

Pat shook his head. "It's stir, Mike. Guys get shivved. And nobody rats."

"Shit."

"Some vocabulary you got."

Then I gave him a look that made him uncomfortable—the slit-eyed, half-smiling look that told him things would get worse before they got better.

"Mike . . ."

"What if there's somebody new on the scene, Pat? What if somebody is moving in on not just the Snowbird but Evello?"

Confusion lined his forehead. "Isn't the Snowbird moving in on Evello enough?"

"Should be. But what if there's another player in this game? Like two people are playing chess, then they get distracted and a third party slips in and makes a move that neither of them catches."

His eyes were tight. "Who?"

"Not sure, old buddy. Don't know."

"Don't hold out on me, Mike. . . ."

"I'm not." I leaned back and pretended to change the subject. "Say, I haven't remembered to compliment you and your pals in Treasury."

"About what?"

"That solid police work you've been doing. These brilliant efforts you've made, working as a team, interdepartmental cooperation and all. Really cracking down on the illegal drugs, rolling up your sleeves and getting those streets dried up."

"Well, uh, thanks, I guess."

"In a pig's ass." I gave him the horse laugh. "Your entire effort is based on anonymous phone tips! You just go running after the leads some voice on the phone hands you. . . ." And I tapped the envelope that bore the tape.

"I didn't deny we'd had phone tips, Mike."

"No. But you didn't tell me those tips were the whole megillah. Ever consider that somebody inside the organization—somebody trying to take over from Evello—might be playing you john laws like a kazoo?"

He didn't deny it, just asked, "Wren, maybe?"

"Maybe, but it sounds to me like the Snowbird and his people are suffering the street shortage right alongside Evello."

Pat chewed on that, then he plucked his hat off my desk and got to his feet. "It's a theory. I'll share it with Treasury."

"Do that."

The sound of Pat shutting the outer office door preceded Velda shutting the inner one. She was wearing a copper-colored silk blouse and a darker brown tight skirt that ended just above her knees.

She came over and sat on the edge of my desk. When she did that, crossing her bare legs, I wanted to get up, use an arm to sweep everything but her off the desk, and hike that skirt up and take her right there.

But I was just too damn professional for that.

"Sounds like things got a little heated," Velda said.

"You know Pat. Whenever I'm doing most of his work for him, he starts making noise like a ruptured walrus, thinking nobody will notice he's a washout."

She picked up the envelope with the plastic spool in it. "This is the tipster tape? I'll get it over to Vincent Rector. Messenger okay, or hand-delivered?"

"Hand-deliver it, doll. Take your .32."

She nodded. "Pat had a funny look, going in. And a funny look, going out, now that I think of it. What's up?"

"Edwin Brooke got stuck in the showers at the Tombs."

"Like that's news."

"I'm talking about with a knife, kitten."

"Oh." Her eyes went big. "Somebody's cleaning up."

"That's what you do in the shower. Anything on the Vought dame?"

She nodded. "Shirley Vought did have rich parents. Her father was Mr. Vought Chemical, and she was an only child. So she should have inherited big-time."

"*Should* have?"

"*May* have." Velda shrugged. "It's not public knowledge, how much she wound up with."

"Or didn't wind up with?"

"Or didn't."

I grunted. "Why wouldn't she have?"

Velda shrugged and nice things happened with her hair and breasts. "She had a rather public falling-out with her father about five years ago, couple years before his death. Seems she dropped out of college in the first year, and she was a regular wild child—attracted to dangerous men, I gather."

"You don't mean *mob* guys?"

"No! Celebrity types—actors, rock musicians, some of the jet-set party boys, too. Making the Manhattan club scene, up all night drinking and dancing. Could just be a girl feeling her oats. You know about feeling your oats, Mike, right?"

I didn't take the bait. "So can we confirm whether she's independently wealthy, as she says?"

She raised both eyebrows. "Well, I have a line in to a P.I. agency we've worked with a couple times—one that deals with financial stuff . . . the kind of bank-records research that verges on industrial espionage, which isn't usually our bag. It's expensive, Mike. Could cost a couple grand, and we don't have a client."

"Sure we do, sugar."

"Yeah, who?"

"Me. I hired us to find out why so many people want me dead."

She chuckled, and slid off the desk, and her tight skirt hiked halfway up her thighs. "Hard to imagine, a sweet-tempered soul like you, Mike . . . making enemies."

And she hip-swayed out, taking her time pulling the dress down.

"With friends like you, baby," I told her, "who needs 'em?"

At Dorchester Medical College, I went looking for Billy Blue and was directed to Dr. Harrin's modest office, where I found the boy straightening and cleaning up in anticipation of the doctor's imminent return.

The kid, in a light blue T-shirt and jeans and white tennies, was in the process of pounding a nail into the wall, and didn't hear me come in.

"Mr. Hammer!" he said with a jump. "Good to see you."

"You seem pretty well recovered," I said. "So when's the doc get back?"

"Couple days," Billy said. He displayed a minor limp when he went over to rest the hammer on top of a file cabinet, then leaned down to pick up a framed plaque, propped against the wall—the *Caveat emptor* one—and hung it on the new nail.

"Dr. Harrin sure gets a kick out of these crazy plaques," Billy said as he went around making them hang straight. "What do a bunch of stupid slogans do for a smart guy like Dr. Harrin, you suppose?"

I helped myself to the chair behind the doctor's desk. "They just distill his philosophy, I guess, into little pills you can swallow. He said some of them remind him of past incidents in his life."

"Oh, sure. He told me about that 'Let 'em eat cake' deal, when he was in the war. Were you in that war, Mr. Hammer?"

"Yeah. Harrin was in Europe, though. I was in the Pacific theater."

"Really? Where?"

"The jungle. A crappy little island nobody's interested in anymore. We left enough blood behind on both sides to irrigate that godforsaken chunk of real estate, and yet it's still worthless."

Billy took a break and pulled up the chair opposite me. "I just got my draft card. A lot of guys I know are getting called up. Vietnam."

I studied his face and smiled. "You don't want to go, do you, son?"

"No. I won't burn my card or anything, or go to Canada, either. I'll go if I have to. But the doctor is helping me."

"Yeah?"

He beamed. "Dr. Harrin, he's a great guy. I mean, he's a great *man*, great *doctor*, but also a great guy. He's set up a college fund for me."

"So you'll get a deferment."

"I should. And then when I *do* go, I'll have a skill."

"You want to be a doctor, son?"

"No. I'm not that smart, Mr. Hammer. But I am interested in medicine. I want to go to nursing school."

I nodded. "Always a need for male nurses. And when you get called up, you'll be Medical Corps."

"That's what I'm hoping. I really don't think I'm up for the killing . . . but if I could help guys in trouble, that would be different." The kid looked young for his age, but his voice had a weary quality that surprised me. "I hope I'm not taking advantage."

"Advantage?"

"Of Dr. Harrin." He shrugged, his expression glum. "Look, I know the score. I'm filling in for Davy. I'm a surrogate son, that's the term, right? So taking the doc's money for college, does that make me a leech?"

"No. You knew Davy? In school?"

"Yeah. He was ahead of me, though."

And that seemed to be all Billy had to say on the subject.

"Mr. Hammer, what brings you around? Were you looking for me?"

"Yeah, Billy. Couple of loose threads. Listen, I spoke to Junior Evello about you yesterday."

He frowned. "Really? About me?"

"Do you remember telling me you mailed a letter for him? You said you ran errands for Evello, when he was in the celebrity suite, and one of them was mailing a letter . . . ?"

"Sure."

"What *was* that letter?"

He shrugged. "I dunno."

"You really don't?"

"No. Why? Is it important?"

"Billy, I need you to be straight with me. If you saw an address on that letter, it might be the reason you got jumped by—"

"Mr. Hammer, I mind my own business. I just mailed that letter for Mr. Evello that time. And as far as why I got jumped, you *know* why—because I wouldn't be a supplier for Brix and those creeps."

I nodded. "I believe you. And I believe you're right."

That was the thing about threads. Sometimes you pull them and you get a little piece of string and you toss it. Sometimes you pull them and half a sweater comes off.

Billy stood. "It's nice to see you, Mr. Hammer. But I've got the doctor's office pretty well spruced up. And I have some storeroom stuff to do, so—"

"One last thing, Bill."

"Sure."

I gestured to the desk. "Where are the family pictures?"

"Huh?"

"Dr. Harrin lost his son. He loved his son. The loss was devastating. And yet . . . nowhere in this office is there any trace of the boy. Not a single picture. Not a framed sports letter or trophy the boy won, zip. Nothing on the wall, just those slogans. And on the desk . . . nothing."

Billy was obviously uncomfortable. "Well . . . I don't know why. . . . Maybe the doc's so upset, he doesn't want to be reminded."

"Of the son he adored? Bill, you said you *knew* Davy. What kind of kid was he?"

"He was . . . a great athlete."

"Yeah, right. So I heard. What else?"

"He was . . . real popular."

I leaned forward and put an edge in my voice. "Bill, goddamnit, level with me. What kind of boy was Davy Harrin?"

He swallowed. "Not perfect, okay? Look, there were things about Davy the doc wasn't happy with, all right? It's not my place to say, Mr. Hammer."

"Bill . . . Billy . . ."

But he was at the door. "I have to get back to work, Mr. Hammer. Nice seeing you."

And Billy Blue, who wouldn't fink out another kid even if that kid was dead and buried, was gone.

• • •

Bud Tiller almost never wore ties.

If he had a court appearance, sure. If he was meeting the president of a major corporation, maybe. The broad-shouldered, blond bulldog had been in the FBI for so many years, where a tie was standard issue just like .38 revolvers, that when he quit to go into business for himself, he swore off neckties except in extreme circumstances.

What he almost always did wear was a selection from his extensive collection of Hawaiian aloha shirts, gaudy paint-factory explosions that could brighten a sunny day into something blinding. He could even brighten up a back booth at Marco's Bar and Grill.

"Tell me you don't go undercover in those things," I said, after a sip of Pabst.

He sipped his own glass of beer, then grinned at me with foam on his face. "I don't go undercover anymore. That's for the youngsters. And when I go out talking to people, I like to get their attention."

"No kidding. So what do you have for me?"

A jukebox was playing Sinatra singing "Luck Be a Lady," reminding me of my debt to the old girl.

He wiped the foam off with the back of a hand. "Mike, this is going to be vague."

"I ask for intel, and I get vague?"

His expression was grave. "It has to be. I'm lucky I got anybody to talk to me about this at all. Think about it. Killing somebody like Junior Evello or Jay Wren is one thing—hitting them with a vehicle and *not* killing them is a whole other deal."

"Somebody takes on that job," I said, "and if it ever catches up with them, more than a car would hit them."

"Exactly. These are insurance scammers, who are well outside mob circles. But they know the possible consequences, plying their talent on big-time criminals like the Snowbird and Junior."

"Which is why one driver was a gal in a car, and the other a guy in a truck."

"Right," Bud said, nodding vigorously. "Guys like Wren and Evello, they're going to look hard at *any* accident, to see if it really *is* an accident."

"And in these cases, it wasn't."

"They were not accidents, no. But the cops accepted them as such, and more important, so did the victims, Evello and Wren."

"Who was the client?"

His eyes went wide and he shook his head. "No. That info's *not* available."

"You lead me to your contact, and I'll make it available."

"I know you would, Mike. But I have to protect my sources. I do a lot of insurance work. More than you. All I can do is confirm that somebody had the kind of money that could make these scammers take on the very risky job of playing hit-and-run with a goddamn Mafia boss."

I swirled my beer, looking into it like I expected tea leaves to read. "Wealthy client, then."

"Fair to say."

"Not another mob guy?"

Bud shook his head again. "I would say not. This I just gathered, Mike. More gut than intel, okay? But I would say a straight john hired this done. Somebody way out of the loop."

"And yet somebody who was somehow able to get to these scammers. Who would have that kind of inside info?"

"I don't know. An insurance investigator like me, maybe? Possibly a medic?" He gave up an eloquent shrug. "Afraid I'm going to have to charge you for this one, Mike."

"I know."

"Don't choke when you see my bill. It's gonna be over a grand."

"I'm hip. But why don't you buy the fuckin' beers, at least?"

Bud's bulldog puss split in a grin, and he said, "My treat, amigo," and stopped at the bar and paid up, on his way out.

I just sat there with my Pabst, wishing my mind weren't taking me where it was, when I looked up and two guys who were definitely not in Hawaiian shirts were standing there, looming over me, like ads in *Esquire* come to life.

One was tall and thin and in a dark gray tailored suit with a black necktie. The other was short and thin and in a dark gray tailored suit with a gray-and-black necktie. They had hair cut short but left long enough to run a comb through, and the kind of pale complexions you get in casinos or in a coma or maybe on surveillance.

"FBI?" I asked. "Or T-men?"

They slid in the booth opposite me, the shorter one first. The tall one, who had blue eyes as faded as the ass of an old pair of jeans, seemed to be in charge.

"Treasury," he said. His voice was baritone with no inflection to speak of. "Would you like to see ID?"

"Why not?"

They both showed me their plastic cards with photo identification. The shorter guy had brown eyes, but otherwise these two were peas in the same federal pod.

"Agent Radley," I said to the tall one. "Agent Dawson."

"Make it 'mister,' Mr. Hammer," Radley said. "We don't advertise our status as agents."

Like hell they didn't.

"I appreciate the trouble you've gone to," I said. "Normally my tax refund just comes in the mail."

Radley smiled but it was small and a real effort. "I know your reputation, Mr. Hammer. And you might be interested to know that there are those of us, in government circles, who appreciate your methods. Even . . . envy them."

"Thanks. Maybe you can be a character witness the next time I'm up on charges."

He smiled again and with less effort. "Your friend Captain Chambers speaks highly of you."

Not to me, he didn't.

The smaller T-man piped in: "And he suggested that we make contact with you directly."

"Swell. What can I do you for?"

"Mr. Hammer," Radley said, "you and Captain Chambers recently discussed the rumored shipment of heroin that is, right now, about the only thing heroin-related on these streets. The notion that this so-called super shipment might be a myth or a ruse, either on our side or the . . . other side? We want to disabuse you of that notion."

Dawson said, "It's very real, Mr. Hammer. Hundreds of pounds of pure heroin, about to hit these shores."

"When?" I asked.

"That," Radley said, "we do not know. We believe it to be . . . imminent."

"Define 'imminent.'"

"As soon as a day or two. No longer than five or six."

"Okay. Narrowing it down like that means we're right on top of nothing at all."

Radley exchanged blank glances with Dawson. Then he said, "We're aware, of course, that you are deeply embroiled in this affair, starting with the attempted robbery of William Blue. That there have been attempts on your life, and that you have been in touch with many of the major players."

"Yeah, I know all this. I was there."

Dawson said, "Captain Chambers told us about your theory."

"What theory is that?"

"That a third party, someone new in the equation, may be attempting to take possession of this shipment . . . possibly as part of an effort to overthrow Evello and Wren. That this third party may be using you to play Evello off Wren, and vice versa."

I shrugged. "Just piecing things together, boys."

"Well, it's an interesting theory, Mr. Hammer. And one we had not contemplated."

Radley asked me, "Whom do you suspect?"

"Someone inside."

"Inside the Syndicate drug operation, you mean?"

"Not Radio City Music Hall."

"Who, Mr. Hammer?"

"No idea." Actually, I was starting to have an idea, but I wasn't ready to share it.

I gave them a grin that was only a little threatening. "Fellas, I don't mean to cut in on your action. But this is personal. When people try to knife me or shoot me, I take an interest."

Radley held up a hand, a stop motion, but a gentle one. "We are not asking you to stop investigating, Mr. Hammer. Quite the opposite. You have ways and means not available to the Treasury Department. You have access to people and places that we do not, and *cannot*, without raising suspicion and undue questions."

"And?"

"And," Radley said, "we ask only that you keep us abreast of your efforts."

Dawson handed me a card. It had four phone numbers on it and no names and no agency designation.

"You hear anything about the shipment," Radley said, "whether solid information about the time and date and delivery, or just a rumor . . . you let us know."

They gave me curt smiles and matching nods, and slid out of the booth and vanished like your money in government hands.

I finished the beer and put their card in my wallet. So—Uncle Sam was on my side.

But was that a good thing?

Chapter Ten

VELDA MET ME for lunch at the Blue Ribbon Restaurant. I got there first, and picked up a stein of Prior's dark beer at the bar and went to my table, tucked in a corner where I wouldn't be bothered. And it was *my* table—all it took was a phone call half an hour out to keep anybody else from claiming it, including the mayor and any of the celebrities in the framed signed photos hanging around me.

Velda was in a white cotton blouse with a little tan jacket over it—it was getting cooler—and a tight black skirt with black pumps. Simple attire on any other dame, grounds for an indecent-exposure arrest on her. She had the big black purse under her arm, big enough for all her girl garbage plus the .32 auto and anything else she might need to tuck away.

Halfway over to me, she was already getting into the bag, plucking out a fat manila folder to deposit in front of me like an oversize summons she was serving.

She took her chair, and I called, "George! Coffee regular, over here," got a nod from the headwaiter who co-owned the place, and smiled at my secretary.

"You could smuggle state secrets in that thing," I said, nodding to the big purse, which she rested on an otherwise vacant chair at our table for four.

"No secrets," she said. "Public knowledge, for anybody who wants to spend four hours traipsing through microfilm of that fascinating publication, the *Weekly Home News*."

"A real kick, huh?"

She grunted a little laugh. "Yeah, if high school football scores and amateur concerts and church bazaars jingle your chain."

"Then why the smile?"

And she did have one going—the kind that turns up at the corners in that cat-munching-a-canary way.

"I'll order first," she said.

"Tease," I said.

"Look who's talking."

I got the knockwurst again and she had a corned beef sandwich, requesting the fat be trimmed, which ought to be criminal in the state of New York. Her coffee came, with cream and sugar just how she liked it (courtesy of George), and she sipped it, then nodded to the manila folder.

"Those are crummy copies," she said. "You know how those microfilm machines are."

They were crummy, all right—gray and smeary, the stuff coming off on your fingers. But the content was worth the trouble. As I thumbed through the pages, Velda did a running commentary.

"Davy Harrin was the top athlete everybody said he was," she said. "But there are interesting wrinkles. His sophomore year, he sat out two games on disciplinary action."

"Does it say for what?"

"No. But the clerk at the *News* was a little guy who'd been in school with Davy, and he helped me read between the lines. His sophomore year, Davy was arrested for drunk and disorderly, along with half a dozen other kids, at an all-night party. You won't find any records on that, because he was a juvenile."

"Plus, his pop was a prominent doctor."

"Right." She pointed at the gray copy I was perusing. "The *News* gives four pages over every week to the local high school—it's apparently in lieu of a school paper. The articles are by the students, including a kind of gossip column. Again, I got some help from the clerk, who seemed to like me for some reason . . ."

"Imagine."

". . . and the jokey, coy copy written by various giddy girls makes it clear that Davy was a legendary bad boy around campus . . . very popular, but linked with just about every pretty girl in school, from cheerleaders to Honor Society, and known to be a real 'party animal.' That phrase even gets into the gossip column, more than once."

I had a drink of beer. "We know Davy was into booze when he was probably only, what, fifteen? What else was he into? Your clerk pal say?"

"No, just that Davy was 'wild' and also 'kind of a jerk.' But I don't think my pal and the Harrin kid ran in the same circles. Davy was your most-likely-to-succeed type, and Between the Lines was treasurer of the chess club."

I was still flipping through the pages. She was watching me, that catlike smile going again—only I was no canary she was stalking. A mouse maybe, or a rat.

Then I came to the piece of cheese she had for me—a page dominated by a picture of three girls and two boys, facing the camera with big smiles, the pair of guys in the center holding up a plaque together—the cut line said, DEBATE CLUB WINS DIVISION. One of the guys was Davy.

"The other one," Velda said, "is Jay Wren."

My mouth dropped and my eyes rose. "Davy Harrin and the Snowbird were in school together?"

"Yup. And not just classmates, but teammates, on the debate club. Davy was a freshman, Jay a senior. Could be innocent. A guy I went to school with became a United States senator, and that doesn't make me a crook."

Our food came, and we ate in silence.

Then I said, "I need to talk to Wren. Time we met."

"I doubt he's in the book."

"No ideas?"

She thought. "I did some checking. Word is, Wren is a silent partner backing that new club in the Village—the Pigeon?"

"That club was a favorite hangout of Russell Frazer's, according to Susie, our little supermarket chick."

"Makes sense." She shrugged. "I could try calling over there, but they don't even open for business till ten-thirty at night."

"Try till you get somebody. For now, I'm heading over for another Dorchester Medical College visit. There's somebody I want to talk to again, who'll either be there or at Saxony Hospital."

"Billy?"

"No. No use talking to him again. He's a good kid, and straight as they come. But he won't fink on other kids. That's the code."

Velda shook her head. "He gets jumped by these freaks, and still feels loyalty to them?"

"That's not it. We're over thirty, kitten. We can't be trusted."

She smirked at me. "You couldn't be trusted at twenty."

This time I found Dr. Alan Sprague at Saxony Hospital. It took a little doing, because he was in surgery, and I sat around for an hour reading year-old *Life* magazines.

When I finally caught up with him, the round little doc was sitting on a bench with a blood-spattered smock on and his surgical mask hanging loose, like a stagecoach robber who'd been foiled.

The doctors' locker room might have been in a YMCA or attached to a high school gym, an aquamarine chamber with metal hallway-type lockers and communal showers. Twenty or more could have used the locker room at once, but Sprague was alone, sitting slumped, dejected, smoking a cigarette. Or anyway he had a cigarette between the fingers of a hand draped over one leg as ashes drifted to the tile floor.

The mood was somber enough that I took off my hat and said, "Excuse me, Dr. Sprague—this may be a bad moment. . . ."

The little man glanced up, glazed-looking, and it took a couple of seconds for him to recognize me. Since I have one of the more easily made maps in New York, this demonstrated how deep in the dumps he was.

"Mr. Hammer," he said. "No, please. Sit down." The humidity and sweat from his recent surgical effort had conspired to flatten down his bristly gray hair. "You'll have to excuse my appearance. . . ." He gestured to the bloodstained smock.

"I have the same problem sometimes," I said.

I sat next to him, but giving him some space. "Lose one?"

"Yeah."

"It happens."

"A child. Mere child. Not even ten." He remembered his smoke and had a drag. "It's not easy to lose *any* patient, but surgeons learn to cope with that early on, or they don't last. Still, when a life gets cut off before it's had a chance to really *begin*. . . ."

"What about a teenager who makes a bad choice, doc?"

That question pulled him back from where he'd been and he turned to look at me, curiously. "What do you mean?"

"When do they have to take responsibility? We're in a do-your-own-thing world right now. If a sixteen-year-old, a seventeen-year-old goes the wrong way, is it the parents' fault? Or society's?"

"Did you drop by for a philosophical discussion, Mr. Hammer? Or perhaps you're taking a sociological survey."

I grinned at him, got out my deck of Luckies, and shook one free. "I'm just asking. I really don't know. I was a stupid kid once. I started smoking at fifteen—Christ, I'd like to kick this habit some-day."

"That makes two of us," Sprague said, making a disgusted face. He dropped his smoke to the tile and crushed it with a heel. "What are you *really* asking me, Mr. Hammer?"

I fired up the Lucky with my Zippo, then snapped it shut, a sound that bounced off the ceramic-tile walls. "I know you and Dr. Harrin are tight. I know you're good friends. . . ."

"He's my *best* friend," Sprague said. "He could be my brother."

"How about his kid—Davy? Was he like a nephew, then?"

Sprague's eyes tensed and they turned away from my gaze. "I wasn't really close to Davy. When he was a little boy, yes . . . but later on, no. He was a gifted youth. It's a tragedy, of course. So many scholarship offers, so much potential, and to . . . to die like that."

"To die like what?"

He swallowed. "After that track meet. Exerted himself. Heart attack. Surely you know the story."

"I know the story. I'm after the truth."

He gave me something that was supposed to be a smile but played as a grimace. "Mr. Hammer, if you don't mind, I need to have a shower."

I wasn't going anywhere. "Be my guest."

We spoke as he got out of the clothes. I'll skip the details—this was not a striptease worth recording.

"I think Davy was a druggie," I said. "A user. And maybe even a pusher at school."

"Why do you make these assumptions?"

"Just from digging. He was pals with Jay Wren—the Snow-bird, remember him? Maybe that's why you were so familiar with Wren—your surrogate nephew was tight with him. Wren was an upperclassman, and might have set Davy up in business. Maybe Davy was Wren's high school connection."

172

The fat little man, naked now, tromped into the nearby showers. I stayed put on the bench a while. He was in there, clouded in steam, and the sound of water needles discouraged conversation. But not me.

I got up, leaned a hand against the wall where it opened into the shower room, and called out, "The kid was gifted! He was a good athlete, maybe a great one—but not a great *kid*."

"You don't know that!" His voice echoed, rising above the driving spray.

"Davy died of an overdose, didn't he?"

Nothing but spray now, and the doc soaping himself.

"What was it, Dr. Sprague—heroin? He started out early on the daddy of gateway drugs—booze. Arrested for drunk and disorderly at a tender age, right?"

He came trundling out, feet slapping against the wet tiles. I had a towel ready for him. Thoughtful of me, but also I prefer naked fat men to cover up.

I gave him room while he toweled off. And I said nothing as he got into shorts and T-shirt and socks. Then I asked, "Who are you protecting? A kid who died stupid?"

He turned to me with such speed, the water on his bristly hair flecked me. Anger turned to regret, and then to full-bore sadness. Still in his skivvies, he sat heavily on the bench, his back to the shower, head bowed and almost bumping his locker.

"Talent unbridled," he said, "can be a dangerous thing in a boy. He was an only child, and his mother spoiled him terribly, and his father . . . his father was a doctor, and doctors are around for everybody who needs them, except their families."

"So he turned into an arrogant little prick."

He swallowed, turned to me with a ghastly expression, and said, "A . . . very arrogant little prick. But such potential. He might have grown out of it. Only, he . . . he wasn't as smart as his father, was he?"

"You tell me."

"He wasn't. He had charm, which he got from his mother, and his father had been a high school and college athlete, as well— baseball. But Davy was merely an average student, and he didn't try hard at all. Of course, the teachers passed him, padded his grades—he was the star player, you know, football, basketball, track."

"I suppose he started out on speed. Most athletes do."

Sprague said, "Do we have to belabor this?"

"Was he a pusher, Doc?"

"I . . . I don't know. I wouldn't be surprised."

"Does his father know all this?"

"Certainly."

"Have you ever discussed it?"

"Never." Then he added, "Not directly."

I let him get his suit on—he deserved to gather a little dignity. Two more doctors entered during this phase, and when he was dressed, Sprague said, "Let's have some coffee in the doctors' lounge."

Soon we were seated quietly at a table near a window.

"There's something else we should discuss," he said.

"Okay."

He was putting a third sugar packet into his coffee. What would his doctor say about that?

"The last time we spoke," he said, "I expressed my frustration with the way Dr. Harrin has fraternized with the likes of Wren and Evello."

"Graduates of your celebrity suite."

"Indeed. I have a suspicion, Mr. Hammer. It is based on observation, and is not ungrounded . . . but I caution you that it is a suspicion only."

"All right."

Very quietly, glancing to make sure we weren't being overheard

174

in the good-sized but near-empty lounge, he said, "Do you know what a 'Dr. Feelgood' is, Mr. Hammer?"

"Sure. A medic who prescribes drugs to patients without regard to actual need—essentially, a pusher with a medical degree, dispensing illegal recreation, not required medication."

He smiled faintly. "Very well put, sir. Would it shock you to hear that I think my colleague, my trusted friend, has become just such a practitioner . . . and to the most unsavory clientele imaginable?"

"Little shocks me, Doc." I frowned at him, though, as if trying to pull him back into focus. "You're saying Dr. Harrin has become a Dr. Feelgood to the Syndicate?"

"I am."

I thought it over. "We'd be talking Evello, not Wren. The Snowbird is close enough to the street action to use his own product, if he's so inclined. A guy like Junior Evello, though, has layers of protection—he insulates himself from the nastier aspects of his business. Syndicate guys like him don't dare use street product."

"Why not, Mr. Hammer?"

I shrugged. "Their lives are too carefully watched."

"But why would David do it? He hardly needs the money. David Harrin is one of the wealthiest doctors in Manhattan."

"Yeah?"

Sprague nodded. "You're aware he's a rare-diseases specialist. He's heavily involved in research and testing, and has been for years. He was on Salk's polio vaccine team, and had a hand in the development of half a dozen other vital vaccines. He's done a great deal of public good, certainly, but also has amassed something of a fortune doing it."

I was still frowning. "So he doesn't exactly *need* to play Dr. Feelgood to anybody."

"No! And why would he befriend the likes of Evello and this Snowbird character? These men were indirectly responsible for his son's death!"

I didn't bother responding. Dr. Sprague was in the business of saving lives. But I worked the other end of that equation. I came in when a victim was beyond help, and the only thing even approaching a remedy was taking vengeance.

Was Dr. Harrin ingratiating himself with Evello and Wren, to get close enough to take them out?

But those two slobs had been under Harrin's care at the hospital—he'd had the perfect opportunity to murder them in some medically undetectable fashion.

Dr. Sprague said, "Perhaps I should apologize, Mr. Hammer. I may be sending you down a blind alley. And the notion that Dr. David Harrin could have any affiliation with the likes of Junior Evello and Jay Wren, why . . . it defies credulity."

"That's okay, Doc," I said. I put on my hat and got up. "I've had my credulity defied before."

In the hospital lobby, I used a phone booth to check in with Velda. I figured she deserved to know that her hours at the *Weekly Home News* had paid off, Sprague confirming that Davy Harrin had been a user and possibly a pusher.

But I hadn't started getting my news out before she blurted hers: "I *got* him!"

"Who, kitten?"

"Jay Wren—I got through to him at the Pigeon. He has an office there. And he was very nice, gracious even. Wanted very much to speak with you."

"Great. I can head over there now. . . ."

"No, he has meetings. He said he'd be glad to see you at the club tonight. He'll have a table reserved for us."

"Us?"

"Yeah . . . I think I deserve a night out. Come on, Mike—the Pigeon is the latest thing. The new 'in' spot. Throw a girl a crumb."

"Crumbs don't throw crumbs," I said, but she stayed at it and I finally said yes.

Somebody called it the City That Never Sleeps.

And although plenty of honest working folk snooze away in the dusk-till-dawn hours, nightlife has been a part of New York since not long after the Dutch screwed over the Indians.

Vices and passions too troubling for daylight flourish in a smoky nocturnal realm where the things respectable people pretend to believe by day are eclipsed by casual carnality at night. Here, social barriers are banished, and one-night stands encouraged between fashion models and bikers, debutantes and delivery boys, gangsters and housewives.

Some niteries, like the Copacabana and Stork Club, have been around since dry days, but Harlem's Cotton Club lives only in memory, like a sax solo fondly but dimly recalled. Lately El Morocco had been transformed into a discotheque called Arthur—an all-night party for the Broadway and Hollywood crowd opened out of revenge by Sybil Burton after hubby Dick dumped her for Liz Taylor.

It was a loud new scene, and a blast in its brash way, even if I'd rather be squeezed in at a tiny table at Jules Podell's Copa, listening to Nat King Cole or Bobby Darin out in front of a big band. But those days were fading fast, and even now, my columnist buddy Hy Gardner at the *Herald Tribune* was preparing to gather his loot and head into the happy sunset.

How long would it be, I wondered, *before I didn't recognize my own damn town?*

It was eleven when we got to the old warehouse on a side street in the East Village. This was an establishment that went to no great shakes announcing itself, almost like something out of speakeasy days. The only indication that the building wasn't abandoned was a small glowing white neon outline of a bird—a pigeon, apparently—that stuck out above the door, next to which stood a bouncer type in a white shirt, black tie, and black leather pants.

This guy eyeballed everybody who entered, and turned some away. His criteria did not seem to be a matter of dress code, since a straight in a nice suit and tie was half of a rejected couple ahead of us.

Velda had been working all day and hadn't had time to change— she was still in the white blouse, tan jacket, and black skirt. But a tall dark-haired beauty like her, even if she was a decade older than the kids standing around the sidewalk smoking, was not about to be turned away anywhere. Even accompanied by a charm-school reject like me.

Within, the senses were immediately assaulted, starting with a smokiness that suggested a fire, and music so loud it took a while to discern it as more than white noise. Passing through a crowded, fairly narrow holding area off of which was the coat check to one side and MEN'S and LADIES' to the other, we entered a high-ceilinged near-darkness that the black light only magnified.

The warehouse interior had not been remodeled much, except for varicolored Day-Glo spatter on the walls that I guessed was meant to suggest pigeon droppings. A thatched-roof tiki-hut bar would shoot you either left or right into a sea of tables, many abandoned for the dance floor beyond. More tables were at left, tucked under facing balconies that had stairs at either end, and most of these were filled, amber cigarette eyes staring out, the sweet smell of weed wafting through the tobacco stench.

An unpretentious open stage had been put in against the back wall and a band of shaggy fake Beatles were doing what I now could tell was a Chuck Berry song with a British accent, using huge black and chrome amplifiers whose collective sound wasn't any louder than a 747 taking off. The drummer was up on a platform of his own, trying to break his cymbals. In Plexiglas cages suspended over the left and right of the stage, girls with long straight swinging hair wore fringe but not much else as they go-go-goed.

And on the wall above and behind the band, right onto the bricks, a bizarre film was playing, a nonsensical, stitched-together thing that combined still images ranging from the beautiful (bright flowers) to the horrific (decomposing animals) with clips from old silent films and newsreels, even World War Two footage from the Pacific, my jungle memories jarringly intercut with a Woody Woodpecker cartoon.

Colored lights were flashing, and now and then a strobe effect kicked in. Weirdly, a ceiling-suspended mirrored ball, right out of a ballroom for squares, was rotating and catching and throwing around those lights, the dance floor near the stage arrayed with teenagers and adults in their twenties and thirties and forties, all flapping their hands, winglike, and bobbing their heads. A pigeon dance? I didn't know and I didn't care.

Velda was smiling, though, getting a kick out of it. She always stayed simple with her fashion choices, but I saw her taking in with interest the miniskirts—polka dots and stripes and geometric shapes—while I took in the legs beneath.

We were still stranded toward the back of the big chamber, getting our bearings. A blonde wearing a mini comprised of small yellow plastic discs seemed to be the hostess—she had a short, jagged haircut that looked like an accident. We got lucky, because right when the blonde approached us, the band took its break, and we had just long enough, before the disc jockey took over, to tell her who we were and that we were expected.

We were shown up carpeted stairs to a balcony where we seemed to be above the sound system speakers enough for us to be able to hold something like a conversation. The blonde seated us at a standard-issue round black bar table near an iron railing over the dance floor, and a girl in a pink mini-dress with very tall platinum hair and exaggerated makeup worthy of a transvestite came and took our drink order.

I asked for a Pabst and Velda requested a Tab, and they arrived sooner than I expected. I went to pay and the little tall-hair honey waved "no"—it was on the house.

The balcony was fairly empty. You could tell the tables were occupied from the jackets on chairs and the drinks left behind by dancers on the floor below. The guy spinning platters talked to the crowd over the P.A., building momentum and doing the personality bit like a radio DJ. I was thinking about lighting up a Lucky and then decided with all the smoke in the air, it would be redundant.

A tall slender man in a powder-blue suit cut in the mod style with lacy collar and cuffs approached us with a smile and a decided limp. His clean shoulder-length hair was shades of brown and golden blond, a combination unknown to nature but familiar to hairdressers, and he was deeply tan. His smile was big and toothy, his face handsome with high cheekbones but very lined for his age, and he wore sunglasses whose lenses were the same light blue as his suit. The need for sunglasses in this dark club was not great, unless maybe you had a medical condition requiring protection from the flashing and strobing lights.

He extended a bony hand and I stood and shook it, then sat back down.

"Welcome, Mr. Hammer," he said, in a midrange voice easily heard above the music. He didn't even seem to be trying that hard. How did he do that?

"Mr. Wren," I acknowledged with a nod. Making him was no problem: he wore the same big smile as in that debate-club photo. "Hopping joint."

"Thank you." He beamed at Velda. "And your lovely companion . . . ?"

He was using a phony English accent. Not overdoing it, but from a guy born in Queens, it was a little much.

"My secretary," I said. "Miss Sterling."

"Yes, we spoke on the phone," he said, and took her hand as if about to kiss it. But he didn't.

He sat next to me, opposite Velda. Wren had a good two inches on me, but I had shoes that weighed more. I wondered if he partook of his own product, like Russell Frazer and the Junkman. Or maybe he just had the metabolism of a pigeon.

"I was pleased," he said, "hearing you wanted to meet with me."

"Really?" I was almost shouting.

"I considered approaching you, but . . . what with your colorful reputation . . . I decided against it. Let's begin with me assuring you that I had nothing to do with the attempts on your life."

"Good to hear." Hell, it was good to hear anything.

He raised a forefinger. The DJ was spinning an instrumental with a distorted guitar solo, and even Wren had to work to get up over it. "I also did not sanction that unprovoked attack on William Blue."

"Those were your people."

His smile continued, but the teeth disappeared. He gave me that one-man-of-the-world-to-another look. "Certain of my employees are not of the caliber I'd like. Aspects of my business require taking on help that can be less than . . . wholly reliable. And, anyway, all of my people—like me—are really Junior *Evello's* people."

I gave him the hairy eyeball. "You're saying Evello's behind the bungled Billy Blue rip-off? And the flubbed hits on me?"

The Snowbird shrugged elaborately. "He can reach out and make things happen, Evello. You *know* that, Mr. Hammer."

"He denies any responsibility."

Wren was smiling again. "And you believe him?"

"I'm reserving my judgment." I gave him some teeth. "Hearing your denial, Mr. Wren, I'm still reserving it."

Another shrug. "I can understand that. But you and I have *no* argument, while—"

"I have history with the Evello Family, yeah . . . but Junior doesn't really have cause to go after me."

And yet another shrug. "Maybe he *thought* he did."

"Go on." I wondered if I'd shout when I talked for the next few days till I noticed I was doing it.

He upraised a palm. "You were at the scene when William Blue was attacked. Then you went around talking to Dr. Harrin. You *have* been known to . . . look into things that aren't entirely your business. Meaning no offense at all."

"So I talked to Harrin—so what?"

He worked surprise into the smile. "Mr. Hammer, don't you *know* who Dr. Harrin is to Junior Evello? That he is Evello's personal physician?"

I notched it up one: "His Dr. Feelgood, you mean?"

That pleased him and the smile returned. "Precisely. I'm impressed, Mr. Hammer. You really do have a way of digging things out."

"It's a gift."

He turned over a hand. "As for why Evello would try to remove you from the scene, consider—Dr. Harrin is a confidant of Evello's, a valued and trusted associate. You sniffing around the doctor, after the Blue assault, might well make Evello nervous. *Very* nervous."

I didn't deny that.

He leaned back. "Now, Mr. Hammer, I'm going to reach into my inside coat pocket. Please don't interpret it as a threat."

"Fine. But first I'll reach inside mine." I did. "Feel free to interpret that any fucking way you like."

For the first time, the big toothy smile grew nervous. I had my hand around the .45's butt and he damn well knew it. But Wren reached inside his coat anyway, slowly and with care, and withdrew a folded-over envelope. He handed it to Velda.

She looked it over, hefted it, then said to me, "Sealed. Feels like cash."

"That," Wren said, "is because it *is* cash. Four thousand dollars in hundreds." He jabbed a finger at the air. "I want you to give that to Billy Blue. He has college plans, I hear."

"Why so generous?"

"Consider it a settlement. I didn't order it to happen, but either my people took this upon themselves, to jump the Blue kid, for their own petty reasons . . . or Evello reached out to them. Either way, they're my people, and I take full responsibility."

Velda gave me a look and I shrugged. She stuffed the envelope in that big purse of hers.

"In the meantime," Wren said, getting up, "you're guests of the house. The bar serves cold sandwiches until two A.M. And thank you for stopping by. How do you like the club?"

"I dig it. It's handy having the idiots all in one place."

That wiped the smile off him.

I got up and so did Velda.

I said, "For now, I'm taking you at your word. But if I find out you sent Russell Frazer to shiv me, and then those St. Louie boys to bat cleanup? I'll start with rebreaking your goddamn leg, then see where inspiration takes me."

I took Velda by the arm and guided her away, though she did smile back pleasantly at him and say, "I wish I could tell you he's all talk. . . ."

Chapter Eleven

VELDA HAD BEAT ME to the office and was standing at her desk threading tape into our old Ampex reel-to-reel, the one that used to catch messages before we replaced it with a new cassette recorder.

It was raining again, so I'd shaken the moisture off my hat and coat out in the hall, and now hung them up in the closet. I had a paper sack of Danish, figuring Velda would probably have coffee ready.

Without looking at me, she said, "Vincent Rector dropped this off personally this morning. You just missed him. Coffee's made—get us a couple cups, would you?"

I did, and she was saying, "Rector said he was able to improve the signal-to-noise ratio—his company is working on a system for the recording industry, to improve dynamic range. . . ."

"I'll pretend that means something to me," I said.

"What it *means* is, these are advanced techniques not in general use by government or law enforcement yet."

"That I can follow." I handed her a cup of coffee and sipped my own as she hit the switch.

The tape rolled through its predetermined path and she said, "Our former client claims this should greatly improve the chance that Pat can get a workable voiceprint analysis of the tipster."

The caller was male, and the exchanges between the emergency operator and the anonymous tipster were short and sweet.

"*Tell the Narco Division,*" each call began, followed by the time and place of a shipment.

Though these calls came into the NYPD, not every location had been here in the city—several tips told of bundles set to come in over the Mexican border, while the local shipments that got tagged were not at point of entry, but drops where a supplier was turning over a sizable quantity of cocaine or heroin to some major dealer.

"Never allowed time for a trace," I said, after we'd gone through half a dozen of the calls.

Her head bobbed in agreement. "Shall I get this over to Pat? For voiceprint analysis?"

I was perched on the edge of her desk now, nibbling a Danish. I'd had time to get used to something I'd realized from the first few words of the first tipster call we listened to.

"Nope," I said.

"We're sitting on this? Why?"

"Dr. Harrin gets back from Paris this morning."

Her eyes tightened. Her head cocked. "How is that an answer to my question?"

I nodded to the tape recorder, where the spools were now motionless. "That's the doc's voice, kitten. I don't need voiceprint analysis to make it."

"Dr. *Harrin* is the anonymous tipster?"

"Yup. Junior Evello's Dr. Feelgood himself—the mob insider who spilled just enough dope on the dope racket to dry up New

York. And who got half a dozen key lowlifes tossed in the Tombs and various federal pens."

Her eyes widened, her mouth dropped, and she didn't seem able to even form a question.

That was okay. I wasn't sure I had any answers.

I just knew I wanted to get to Dr. David Harrin before I let the NYPD and the Treasury Department in on it.

If Harrin was the new self-appointed kingpin moving in on both Evello and the Snowbird, I might have a more direct way of dealing with the problem than Captain Chambers or those T-men, Radley and Dawson.

"Call Dorchester Medical College," I said, sliding off her desk, "and leave word I want to see Dr. Harrin today. I'll be available this afternoon or this evening, at his convenience."

"Where are you off to now?" she asked, seeing me head for the closet.

"Suddenly remembered," I said.

"Remembered what?"

"Time for my arts and crafts class."

The rain had let up, but behind its glowering gray face, the sky was clearing its throat, threatening any second now to spit its derision at the humans below, pitiful creatures presumptuous enough to think they were in charge. The air was chilly and damp with that dark promise, and tourists were scarce in Greenwich Village, no one at all browsing in the Village Ceramics Shoppe.

Shirley Vought was out front this morning, beyond the aisles of plates and art pieces and behind the counter, with no sounds of activity coming from back of the curtained archway.

"Dead today," she said with a little smile. The lovely blonde could still do a lot for a simple powder-blue smock, and those brown eyes were searching my face like treasure was buried there. No psychedelic green streak on her cheek this time, though.

"Rain's coming," I said.

"It already rained."

"It's going to get worse. You alone here?"

"Yes. No classes this morning, either." She gave me a half-smile. "After the other night, I was *hoping* I might . . . hear from you."

"Yeah, that was a blast. But it's dangerous being next to me right now, honey. You might catch something, and I don't mean a cold."

My arm was resting on the glass top of the counter. She touched my hand, gazed up at me with coyly half-lidded orbs. "I could hang a closed sign on the door. . . . That dressing room is still available. . . ."

I patted her hand. "Rain check, doll. I'm working."

Her expression fell, and she drew the hand away, but she said, "I understand, Mike." She worked up a smile. "So—what brings you here on a beautiful morning like this? You're not looking for decorative ware, I'm guessing."

"I'm looking for what I'm always looking for—straight answers."

Those big eyes got smaller. She sensed a vague accusation in my words, and she was right.

I said, "You told me you'd only met Davy Harrin a couple of times, but seemed awfully knowledgeable about him."

"I told you," she said carefully, "he was well-known around this part of town. Star athlete."

"Right. What else was he known for?"

"He was an outstanding student—"

"I heard different. I heard they padded his grades to keep him eligible."

Shirley's eyes dropped from mine. She folded her hands on the glass top. "I didn't . . . lie to you, Mike. Not really."

"I know. Sin of omission, though. Davy was into drugs, wasn't he?"

She swallowed and nodded. "Yes. Not everybody knew that, and I really *didn't* know him very well . . . but we had mutual friends."

"Like Russell Frazer?"

She shrugged, nodded. "'Friends' is too strong a word. But I *was* aware Russ and Davy knew each other."

"They would have shared a mutual friend in Jay Wren."

She shook her head, blonde hair flouncing. "Him I don't know. I mean, I know *who* he is—he's involved with that new club, the Pigeon? But I've never met him."

"Davy and Wren were in high school together."

She smiled and shrugged again. "Sorry. I went to a private school."

I grinned. "I forgot. Poor little rich girl. Was it common knowledge around this part of town that Davy Harrin was a pusher? That he was his high school's Boy Most Likely to Get You High?"

She was avoiding my eyes again. "Actually . . . I did know. Not firsthand knowledge, Mike . . . but I heard the rumors. Most people knew, at least anybody under thirty in the Village did. I think he dealt in pills and pot, not the hard stuff."

"But you didn't tell me."

"No." She leaned her head to one side and the big brown eyes were moist and her expression was clenched with regret. "I just didn't want to sully the name of a dead boy. Can you understand that? His father is a very nice, a very respectable, *important* man, who was crushed by his son's death. I didn't want to hurt Dr. Harrin any more than he already had been."

"You don't think the doc knew about Davy?"

That seemed to confuse her. "Well . . . I didn't *think* he did. . . ."

"His boy died of an overdose. Davy may not have sold the hard stuff, but he had access to it."

"The papers said heart failure." She was shaking her head. "But if Davy had died that way, wouldn't Dr. Harrin have done something about it? Gone to the police or the newspapers or . . . something?"

"Maybe *he* didn't want his son's memory sullied, either." I shifted weight, and subjects. "Shirley, I'd like to speak to your boss—Mr. Elmain. When would be good?"

She blinked a few times. "He should be here this afternoon, by one or so. Why?"

"I wanted to ask him about that robbery you had."

Her eyes widened and the blinking halted. "*Please,* don't. I shouldn't have *told* you about that."

"Why not?"

Her words came out in a rush: "It's just nobody's business, he didn't report the robbery to the police, and he'd want to know what in God's name I thought I was doing, telling somebody about it. Could you blame him?"

I shrugged. "I guess not. Maybe I don't need to talk to him, then."

Her smile seemed forced. "There's no reason why you shouldn't, just . . . not about that robbery, which was a big nothing, anyway. Please, Mike—don't make me look bad."

I gave her another grin. "Independently wealthy lass like you? What do you care? You could just buy the old boy out."

Her expression turned serious, almost comically so, a child playing grownup. "I like it here. Please don't spoil it for me."

"All right," I said with a shrug.

She licked her lips, the red lipstick shimmering. "So, Mike . . ."

"Yeah?"

"*Was* that just a one-night stand? Or will you ever *really* call me?"

"It was fun. We'll have to do it again."

That was just enough to satisfy her, and to give me a graceful exit.

The rain roared all afternoon, but by early evening had dissipated to a gentle drizzle, making hazy halos around streetlights. This halfhearted mist wasn't enough to stop Greenwich Village from coming alive, as windows glowed and neon signs pulsed while taxis disgorged curious tourists, suburban refugees, and the occasional celebrity to feed the waiting maws of coffeehouses, restaurants, nightclubs, and gin mills, to trade some dough for food, drink, and laughter.

By midnight it would get rough out here, when the whores and junkies and predators got more brazen. But this time of night, it was a playground for grownups, and about as dangerous as Disneyland.

Of course, some people actually lived in the Village. On a side street off MacDougal, I found the brownstone that matched the address Dr. Harrin gave to Velda over the phone. This weather-beaten structure was the kind of three-story walkup that might have been a wealthy family's home, turn of the century. Some unknown decades ago, it had been converted to studio apartments for writers and artists, and would-be writers and artists, and what one of the city's wealthiest doctors was doing in these unpretentious if decent digs was a mystery I hadn't yet solved.

But inside the foyer, down the list of names under the mailboxes, there he was: HARRIN.

I went up to the third floor and he answered on my first knock. The tall, slender, white-haired doctor with the narrow cadaverous face, dark eyebrows, and washed-out blue eyes behind wire-framed glasses wore a tan pullover sweater and darker tan chinos and brown leather sandals with white socks. He seemed more professor than physician, but of course he was both.

He extended a hand and smiled warmly, as if we were old friends reunited, when we'd really only ever spent a few hours together.

Either he was a hell of an actor, or I was really on the wrong track. The .45 under my left shoulder was loaded, safety off, in case I needed to kill him. But I wanted to talk to him first. He needed to hear my story, and I needed to hear his.

Anyway, I shook his hand, and he gestured for me to come in, saying, "Good to see you, Mr. Hammer. I gather you've been a busy man while I was away."

I went down a short narrow hall that opened into a living room that was as spare as a monk's bunk. There was a fireplace, and a bookcase that included a shelf for a turntable and speakers, with a stack of classical LPs, though nothing was playing. No picture was above the mantel, and no other framed prints or paintings or even family pictures were displayed on the dark-wood-trimmed pale plaster walls. The framed quotations that characterized his office at Dorchester Medical College were not in evidence, either.

The few furnishings, however, were not cheap—brown leather sofa, two brown leather armchairs, and a glass coffee table with several art books—Dali, Miró—on a small Oriental carpet on the hardwood floor.

"I'm guessing you didn't raise your family here," I said, prowling the spartan space. He had taken my trench coat and porkpie hat, and was hanging them in the entry-hall closet.

"No," the doc admitted, "we had a bigger place, and all to ourselves."

At the bookcase I noted medical tomes, some heavy-duty philosophy running to Kierkegaard and Nietzsche, and doorstop classic novels by Russian writers. The doc didn't exactly come home to Harold Robbins or Irving Wallace, and no TV set was in sight.

Harrin continued: "After my wife, and then my son, were gone, I just didn't want to kick around in that big old place. Figured a bachelor pad was more in order."

As bachelor pads went, this wasn't exactly the Russell Frazer variety. There was, however, a small wet bar in one corner, trimmed out in the same brown leather, and he was heading over there, asking if I'd like a drink.

"Rye and ginger," I said.

He got me that, and—not caring to be medicated in any other way—I watched him do it; then he built himself a tumbler of Scotch. His expression was friendly as he gestured toward the furnishings that faced the fireplace. He took one of the easy chairs and I settled on the couch.

"So how was Paris, Doc? Pick up any new tricks at the conference?"

"Meeting with one's peers is always . . . instructive," he said. "A lot of new information on hand, fresh research."

I sipped the drink, then set it on the glass coffee table next to the Dali book with a melting clock on the cover. "I wonder, if I hired a guy I know in Paris, to look into it? How many of those conference sessions you actually attended."

He sipped the Scotch, savored it, and his eyes remained cold as he gave me what was supposed to be a warm smile. "I attended enough of them to make a convincing case of it. Should some ambitious civil servant, or paid gumshoe, decide to check up on me, I'd come out smelling of roses. Or maybe disinfectant."

"People I work with, Doc? They can dig deeper than that."

He hiked his eyebrows, which were as black as his head of hair was white. "What *do* you think I was up to over there, Mr. Hammer?"

I didn't answer directly. I looked around the room, at living quarters that were little more than a cozy cage. "You don't exactly throw your money around, do you, Doc? Not what I'd call a hedonistic lifestyle."

"I'm comfortable."

"There's what, a kitchen here? A bedroom and bath? And that's it?"

He nodded, swirled his drink in one hand, looking down into the liquid like a fortuneteller studying a crystal ball. "I'm not sure I see your point, Mr. Hammer." He looked up sharply. "And why the tone, the undercurrent anyway, of hostility? What have I done

193

to deserve that? You asked to see me, and I invited you to my home. . . ."

But this wasn't his home. This was his cell. And that was seriously screwing up what I'd been thinking.

I tried anyway: "You've been conserving your money, haven't you, Doc? Because you had a big purchase to make, a big score."

Only one black eyebrow hiked this time. "Really? And how did you arrive at that conclusion, Mr. Hammer?"

"I'm like a physician in my way, too, only my remedies run a little radical. I study certain diseases, unfortunately not so rare as the ones you study, and come up with diagnoses, based on not just fact, but psychology."

"Sounds very scientific."

"Not really. It's more an art."

He gestured toward the window and the street beyond, and smiled. "Then you should be at home here in the Village, Mr. Hammer. Everyone here is an artist."

"You have your artistic side, too, Doc. It starts with your son, doesn't it?"

His smile faded.

"Davy was a gifted kid. I'm guessing he started out a good student as well as a natural athlete, but the academics fell by the wayside, when sports kicked in. Sports and all the fun and popularity that come with it, that can swell a kid's head. He was a party animal, your son, and he was into booze and it took him to pills and a lot harder stuff, possibly courtesy of a rough crowd he got in with—Russell Frazer, Jay Wren, maybe the Brix kid and his cronies, too. That I'm not sure about."

"*Mr. Hammer*," he said, and his words cut like a scalpel. "My son was a victim of both his own weaknesses, and mine. I do not blame him, not wholly, for the sad trajectory of his short life." The faded blue eyes stared at the fireplace, as if flames were licking there, which they weren't. "My wife spoiled him terribly—he was a brat from the time he could talk, but he was beautiful and gifted and she spoiled him."

"You didn't?"

"I was . . . complicit." The blue eyes went to half-mast, and they studied the swirling liquid again. "I have been, in my lifetime, a driven man. A man caught up in himself, and his own goals and grandiose aspirations."

"My understanding," I said, "is you've contributed to society. You've cured, or anyway helped cure, a good share of diseases."

The tiniest shrug of his head preceded words that sounded distant: "Yes. That is true. But I neglected my wife and my son, in so doing. I allowed Linda to lavish attention and praise and possessions upon our son. And he learned, early on, that nothing was to be denied him. No desire, no happiness. All was his for the asking—anything he wanted to have or to do. It became an expectation. A right."

I sat back on the couch. My jacket was open, the .45 easily accessible. "Were you aware of his drug problem?"

"No. The extent of my parental attention was to attend his sports events, when I was available . . . which was perhaps a third of the time. After Linda's death, I tried to get more involved with Davy, but for the most part he wasn't interested."

"Didn't he help you with the pottery program in the children's ward at Saxony?"

He smiled again, with genuine if rueful amusement. "That's a loaded question, isn't it, Mr. Hammer? Suppose you tell me what you know, or *think* you know, about the ceramics program at the hospital."

I shrugged. "It's not so much the program as the source of the ceramics—the Village Ceramics Shoppe. Too many of the players in this melodrama converge on that supposedly innocent little place. Russell Frazer worked there as a glorified delivery boy, and yet he dressed like Rex Harrison and lived like Sammy Davis—

must've been pulling down good bread for menial help, huh? Your son picked up packages for the hospital program there, and Brix and his pals were seen in or around the shop. Even Billy Blue was in and out, after your son died anyway, and he may have been jumped because somebody thought he knew too much."

His eyes were narrowed now. "And what does all of that add up to for you, Mr. Hammer?"

"I think it's a dope distribution center. Russell Frazer, delivery man, could be making real dough if it was junk he was delivering, not bisque dishes and statuettes. Hell, I think they bake the stuff right into their figurines, and through some chemical process, the junk comes out again ready for marketing. They don't sell to individuals—a respectable shop like that wouldn't want junkies hanging around. But boxes or even crates of supposed greenware could be shipped out of the back nationwide, and smaller orders could be dropped off locally. It's an ideal system, and an innocuous front."

His smile was wide now, and he was shaking his head in apparent admiration. His words confirmed that: "Very good, Mr. Hammer. Excellent. It was only after my son's death that I was able to determine that the unbaked ceramic forms in my son's room represented more than just a sudden, unexpected interest by Davy in the welfare of hospitalized children."

I frowned. "The program at the hospital, for those kids—that was *Davy's* idea?"

"Oh yes. He took advantage, after Linda was gone, of my need to get closer to him, and suggested the therapeutic value of such a program in the children's ward. It was the perfect cover for the pieces to be in his room at home, or in a box in his car. You see, he really did have brains, my Davy."

I grunted a laugh. "So do you, Doc. You had the inspired notion of getting both Junior Evello and the Snowbird himself, your son's old friend Jay Wren, into your personal care at Saxony."

"I arranged that, did I?"

"Oh yeah. I was able to dig out the fact that those two 'auto accidents' were staged by insurance scammers hired by someone, but *not* someone from Syndicate circles—a wealthy straight. You, Doc."

"And why would I do that, Mr. Hammer?"

"Because Junior and the Snowbird were at your mercy, even if they didn't realize it." I grinned. "What did you use, Doc? Sodium pentothal? *Some* drug that would loosen their tongues, without their knowing about it. You found out all sorts of good stuff from those two, key information that you passed along to the cops as an anonymous phone tipster."

This genuinely surprised him. His head rocked back and he smiled in amazement. "How could you know that? My voice was scrambled electronically beyond recognition."

"I have friends in high and low places, Doc. I also have the unscrambled tape, and can turn it over to the NYPD and feds any time I please."

He was frowning now. "Go on, Mr. Hammer. . . ."

"I'm not sure when you found out about the big shipment—whether that came first, and you used the tips to dry up the streets. Or if after you made those calls, the streets dried up, and the big bang became a Syndicate necessity. Chicken or the egg, huh? Anyway, you saw your way clear to get even with the bastards who caused your son's death. You could take their business away from them, knowing that in their circles, screwing up like that doesn't get you a gold watch. More like cement shoes."

His face was crinkled with amusement now. "And then what, Mr. Hammer? Become the top drug lord myself? A gangster? A Syndicate man?"

"You already were a Syndicate man. You wormed your way in as their Dr. Feelgood—that gave you access to your patients, even after the automobile accidents you arranged had been recovered from. You could continue giving them the truth-serum treatments, and tipping off the cops and feds." I shook my head. "You know, I'm starting to think that hypocritical oath you took must've had some loopholes."

His expression had a dazed quality now. "You . . . you know about all *that,* too? Mr. Hammer, I am impressed. I had no doubt that you were a remarkable man, but this . . . this is truly impressive."

"Meanwhile, back at the ceramics shop, you're needing some details that the big fish, Evello and Wren, didn't keep in their craniums. The kind of stuff middle management files away—and I'm figuring this character Elmain is the conduit here. Product is coming into that innocent little tourist trap, and going out again, so there's information in his file cabinet, about people he does business with, that might not be as routine and innocuous as you'd think."

"Impressive indeed. . . ."

"That's why you maintained the ceramics program at the hospital, after Davy's death—so you could maintain contact with the shop, legitimize hanging around the place, actually casing the joint . . . because *you* pulled that robbery there. You got into the files, to fill in the rest of the names you needed for your trip to Europe."

"You're doing fine, Mr. Hammer. You're doing fine."

"You've purchased the big shipment. You've come up with some new way to ship the stuff in, doing an end run around Evello and Wren that your football-playing son would be proud of. You've set yourself up as the new kingpin." I shook my head. "But that's what I don't get, Doc—why would you want to take over a business that you despise? A traffic in death that cost your son his life, and that's taken the lives of so many others?"

His mouth twitched a smile. "Any ideas?"

"Just one. When we spoke about the drug problem, you said it was a 'vicious circle, impossible to break.' Perhaps you intended to punish Evello and Wren, denying them their business, and planned to use the money you made from this junk for good—maybe plow it into cancer research or something. How am I doing, Doc? Close?"

"Close, Mr. Hammer. Close." He sat forward. "May I ask you something?"

"Shoot."

He laughed, once. "Actually, *that's* my question—did you come here to shoot me? You're an avenger, Mr. Hammer, a well-known proponent of frontier justice. Is that your prescription for this illness? To kill me?"

I got out the .45, thumbed back the hammer—the click was sharp and loud in the enclosed space. "How would you put it, Doc? It's one possible avenue of treatment."

He seemed not at all fazed by the weapon. He said, "What if I asked you to trust me?"

"What?"

He sat forward, his manner, his tone, both conciliatory and confidential. "What if I told you that I have a . . . *treatment* in mind . . . that may well break that vicious circle. That my intent here is not to become a criminal 'kingpin,' but to cripple their organization, perhaps even *end* it."

"How in hell?"

He shook his head. "That's why I must ask you to trust me. The burden of what I have conceived must be mine alone. It's a responsibility, even a guilt, that I alone must bear."

"I'm not following you. . . ."

He frowned. "Well, *try*. Because it shouldn't be hard for you. How many times have you faced killers down, Mr. Hammer, with that very gun in your hand? How many times have you made some monster stare down its barrel and see death coming out to claim him, or her?"

"Who's counting?"

His smile was razor thin. "For you, such a choice comes naturally. No soul-searching needed. Perhaps few if any sleepless nights." One black eyebrow arched. "But let me ask you this— would you dream of asking anyone else to *join* you in shouldering the responsibility, the guilt, the burden? Would you ask any other person on earth to squeeze the trigger on that weapon? Or must it be you alone? You, the judge, the jury, the executioner?"

My mouth felt dry.

Not even Velda, I thought.

Finally I said, "I wouldn't ask anybody to take any of it on. Like somebody said once, vengeance is mine."

"Right." His voice took on a quiet urgency. "And I ask you, Mr. Hammer, to believe me when I say that I am on a course of action that I *must* be allowed to complete. It will avenge my son, oh yes, but it will do so much more. So very much more."

"What are you asking?"

"For one week."

"One week?"

"One week."

"And what then, Doc?"

His shrug spoke volumes. "Then I will answer any question you have for me. Pay whatever price. I will accompany you to the police or the federal people or whomever you like. Or I will stand before you and that gun of yours and allow you to play judge and jury and executioner yet again. Without expectation of pity. With no complaint. One week."

I didn't know what to say.

"Otherwise," he said, and he flicked a finger at the .45, then did a trigger-pulling gesture, "you can get it over with right here. Life has little meaning to me now, other than a desire to carry out my last, my most radical therapy."

I didn't know what the hell he was talking about. Maybe he was nuts. Maybe *I* was nuts. But one thing was certain—I no longer thought the point of all this was for Dr. David Harrin to become top hoodlum in the narcotics racket.

"Shit," I said, and eased the hammer down. "I hate dealing with people smarter than me."

I put the gun away, safety on.

Then I stood and said, "You want a week, Doc? Well, I need a day to think about your week. How's that for a compromise?"

He rose and nodded. "Fair enough."

We shook on it.

"Here," he said, almost gently, as he got my things from the closet, "I'll walk you out."

I shrugged into the trench coat, shoved the hat on my head, and we exited the spartan apartment, which he did not lock behind him.

Soon we were on the front stoop of the building. The rain was over, even the mist gone, though water pooled and glimmered where time had made impressions in the stone steps. The residential street was quiet, the wildness and weirdness of MacDougal Street a block and a half up.

He put a hand on my shoulder, looming over me, a good three inches, anyway. His expression was serene.

"Please understand, Mr. Hammer. I cannot tell you precisely what my intentions are. It's not so much that you might disagree with my approach, and try to stop me—"

"If I did, Doc, I would."

"I know. . . . It's more that I do not want you to be implicated, because what I have in mind has far-reaching implications, legally and ethically."

"Legalities and ethics, Doc, don't always enter in with me."

His smile turned gentle, almost wistful. "You never know, Mr.

Hammer. You never know. Perhaps one day . . . you'll see the light."
Half turning, he was about to go back in when he added, "Maybe
you *will* see the light."

*Which, as fate would have it, was exactly when light washed over
his face, headlights, and the serene look was overtaken by wide-eyed
alarm, and the doc stepped in front of me, pushing me down, and the
night exploded with gunfire and three slugs stitched their way across
his sweater, forming black periods that welled into red commas, and
his expression was blank-eyed and slack-jawed as he thumped back
against the door, and slid down, leaving three smeary trails on the
wood.*

I was in a crouch when I fired at the vehicle, which had slowed
initially but now screamed into the night, and I took the seven
steps to the street in two bounds and was out in the slick black
pavement firing at the car, a late-model green Buick. The rear
windshield shattered and the car swerved over to the left and just
missed a parked car to go up over the curb and into the side of a
brick building.

A horn blared in loud monotony and I ran almost a block, coat
flapping, losing my hat along the way, until I got to the vehicle.
The driver was a longhaired kid who had taken one of my .45 slugs
in the back of the head, the windshield dripping with gray and red
and white material that had exploded out his forehead.

The shorter-haired rider—in T-shirt and jeans, who'd done the
shooting—had broken his forearm against the dashboard, on impact, and I could see jutting white bone glistening with decorative red against brown skin. He was a Puerto Rican kid, and was
swearing or praying or something, and I'd have spared him if he
hadn't gone one-handed scrambling for the nine millimeter that
had fallen in his lap. The .45 slug entered his right temple, splat-
tered blood and brains onto the dead driver, and shut off the rider's
chatter like a switch.

People were yelling and screaming, but I ignored that and, not even stopping to retrieve my hat, ran back to the brownstone, where a hippie girl up on the stoop was holding Dr. Harrin in her arms like the *Pietà,* and wailing, "Somebody *help* him!"

But even if a doctor as good as Harrin had been around, it wouldn't have helped. Nobody had ever found a cure for his condition.

Chapter Twelve

THERE WAS NO ducking it.

No sneaking over to Velda's and avoiding the mess and the time and the trouble, and playing the Little Man Who Wasn't There. Harrin had died next to me, pushing me down to safety, taking three bullets likely intended for me, and maybe that oath he took a long time ago about protecting others from harm had still held some sway over him.

The only thing that went fast was how long it took for Pat Chambers to get there. He beat the lab boys to the scene, and I met him as he climbed from the rider's side of the unmarked that pulled up in the street, siren blaring and cherry top painting the already shell-shocked bystanders a shade of red rivaling the blood they'd been gawking at.

"Man," I said, "that's service."

"Normally," he grumbled, "I'd have left this to the night-tour boys. But I have standing orders that when Mike Hammer's name comes up, I get a call."

"I'll take that as a compliment."

He had a rumpled, got-dressed-in-a-hurry look, and something smudgy red under his ear.

"What's this?" I said, and worked my thumb on the smear. "Looks like Helen DiVay's shade."

He grinned and damn near blushed and said, "Cut it, man. This is serious."

"I'll say. You dog."

That was as light as the banter got for the next six hours. We were at the scene for the first two, and the rest were at Central Headquarters. Pat had gotten the scoop on the street, but of course at HQ, I had to go through chapter and verse for Assistant D.A. Traynor.

The sharply dressed, sharp-eyed Traynor deposited himself behind Pat's desk again, while its rightful occupant sat behind the same mousy stenog, his arms folded, chin on his chest, possibly half asleep. Helen must have given him a real workout.

The closest Traynor got to anything significant was when he pressed about why I'd been at Harrin's: "He's been out of the country for a week, Mr. Hammer. And the first day he's back, barely unpacked, he invites *you* over for the evening?"

"I told you before. He's taken that boy Billy Blue under his wing. He wanted an update on my investigation into the kid getting jumped."

"Why, was Harrin your client?"

"No. Just an interested party. Anyway, my investigation didn't stem from that attack on the Blue kid, which I believe was strictly those freaks getting back at Billy for refusing to be a drug supplier."

Traynor frowned. "Then what *did* it stem from, Mr. Hammer?"

"From Russell Frazer trying to mug and maybe kill me, and then getting killed himself. And from those hit men showing up in my lobby."

He gaped at me. "You're admitting that was your handiwork?"

"I'm admitting to known professional killers showing up from out of town, to die in my apartment-house lobby. I thought you said that coincidences bothered you, Mr. Traynor?"

That went on for over two hours, and got absolutely nowhere. I didn't lie to the guy, I just wasn't forthcoming. What Dr. Harrin and I had discussed, I planned to keep to myself. Other aspects of my inquiries—like Harrin being their inside-the-Syndicate tipster—were in that same column, for now, anyway. Let them do their own damn work.

Finally Traynor gave up, and Pat accompanied me to the break room, where we had coffee and vending-machine sandwiches, which added up to cruel and unusual punishment as far as I was concerned.

But Pat didn't grill me, not exactly. He seemed genuinely concerned.

"That's the third try, Mike," he said, meaning the third murder attempt on me. His gray eyes were melancholy. "You're in over your head, buddy."

"I learned to swim a long time ago."

"Not in this river of blood. Years ago, as a young buck, you went up against the old Evello mob, and even then were lucky to come out alive. If the aftermath hadn't been a shakeup between rival Syndicate factions, back then, somebody would've come after you."

"What makes these slobs any different? The old pistoleros were tougher."

"Tougher maybe. Not more ruthless. There's so much at stake now—it's going worldwide, with these drug cartels, violence on a scale even you can't picture. It's big business, Mike."

"What was booze in Prohibition?"

"A fucking cottage industry by way of comparison."

Pat rarely swore, so that got my attention.

I wasn't joking when I said, "I appreciate it, pal. I really do. I'll watch my ass."

"You better. I can't do it for you. Can't keep up with you in these circles. Best I can do is come in and tell the photographer what to shoot and the morgue wagon boys who to fit for a rubber shroud. And I can't even cover for you on *my* end, not anymore."

"Why not?"

He grimaced. "Because this dope racket is federal—Narcotics Division of the Treasury Department. And you can't go home yet because two of their boys are coming over."

What Pat didn't know was, it was old home week—Agents Radley and Dawson in their gray tailored suits and black neckties. Tall, thin Radley didn't just take over Pat's chair, he took over the whole damn office and threw the captain of Homicide politely out. This was confidential, between the Treasury Department and a loyal taxpayer.

I was sitting opposite Radley, with the shorter but just as skinny Dawson standing just behind and to one side of him, like a shadow with clothes on. They weren't unfriendly, just heart-attack serious, giving me stares so unblinking and cold I almost busted out laughing. Almost.

"Is there any possibility," Radley asked, "that Dr. Harrin was the target?"

"I don't think so," I said, and I didn't.

I supposed it was possible that the Syndicate found out the doc had been using sodium pentothal to go fishing for info, but I figured they'd pull him in and question and maybe torture him, before any rubout. Not just order up a drive-by assassination.

Of course, I didn't share these thoughts with the T-men.

"Mr. Hammer," Radley said, "we have solid intel that Dr. Harrin was friendly with Syndicate leaders. That he had been a source of narcotics via prescription for select Mafia customers."

I shrugged. "Evello and maybe Wren. I heard that."

"Did you discuss it with the doctor?"

"I might have. Why?"

208

Radley and Dawson traded tight glances.

Then Dawson spoke for the first time tonight: "Harrin just returned from Europe."

"Yeah, France. That's in Europe."

Dawson paused, as if selecting words from invisible file cards. "We have reason to believe that Dr. Harrin may have been involved with a certain major shipment of contraband."

"The big shipment of H, you mean?"

He drew in a breath, let it out. "Yes, the, uh, big shipment we discussed. In Paris, Harrin was observed talking to individuals who may be part of the French faction that is believed to have supplied the American Syndicate in the past."

"Okay. And what do you make of that?"

Radley picked back up: "There's the possibility that Harrin was acting as an intermediary for Junior Evello—or possibly for Jay Wren, who we think is hoping to either take over from Evello's old guard, or eclipse them."

"In a bloody war?"

"Perhaps just by controlling the product. And then there's *your* theory to consider."

"My theory? Remind me."

Dawson twitched a smile. "That a third party may be attempting to assert himself in this illegal trafficking. That a new drug kingpin, or let's say someone who aspires to that position, may have inserted himself into the picture."

"And you think that was Harrin?"

Radley said, "Again, Harrin may only have been playing intermediary for a party we've not yet identified—it can be very useful to criminal types to engage a respected citizen as a front." His eyebrows rose. "Or Harrin could indeed have been setting himself up for a power play."

I shifted in the chair; it creaked, or maybe that was my bones. "And you think the doc got himself shot for that?"

Radley lifted a shoulder. "Possibly. Of course, the previous attempts on your life would seem to make *you* the logical target, Mr. Hammer."

I let out a short laugh. "You're forgetting something, fellas. Doesn't matter whether we're talking the Evello bunch or Wren's up-and-comers. Unless they already know the specifics of the shipment, its arrival date and place and the nature of the smuggling scheme? Then killing Harrin makes no sense."

Radley and Dawson frowned at each other.

"No, somebody tried to hit me, boys, and if I hadn't killed their asses, their boss probably would have, for the stupidity of missing me and hitting the doc. You don't kill the Golden Goose, and that's what Harrin potentially was."

Radley stayed silent for a while, then in an overly measured fashion said, "We can't know what you and Dr. Harrin discussed. Unfortunately, we did not have his apartment wired for surveillance—a day or two later, and . . . well. No use bemoaning what wasn't." He gave me the Uncle Sam pointing finger. "But if by some chance, for whatever reason, he shared with you any *information* about that shipment . . ."

"Like what day it's coming in, you mean, and at what pier?"

The eyes on the two T-men popped; it was comical, like one of those rubber dolls you squeeze.

Radley, a tremor in his voice, asked, "What do you *know*, Mr. Hammer?"

"Not a damn thing."

Radley's voice grew hushed and it grew tight. "Listen to me. We've been patient with you. We've not subjected you to a recitation of your record with its alarming number of killings."

"Justifiable homicides, you mean."

"Self-defense cannot excuse the outrageous number of vigilante actions you've taken . . . *yes*, vigilante actions, Mr. Hammer, and we will not suffer such foolishness, not in a situation so dire, so critical."

I grinned. "Few days ago, you guys were encouraging me to keep investigating. You were saying how I could go places and get away with things you couldn't. Why is my fan club turning on me?"

Radley ignored that. "Never in history has a shipment of this magnitude been in the offing. We can save lives, and we can put a real dent in the Syndicate with this one. It's *important*. If you learn anything, anything at all, you need to share it with us. It's your patriotic duty, Mr. Hammer."

Whenever they start talking to me about my patriotic duty, I check my wallet.

"I served in the Pacific," I said. "Draft somebody younger." I stood. "Is that all, gentlemen? I like to get in bed before sunup— otherwise I have trouble nodding off."

Radley swallowed thickly. "You know where to reach us. If you learn anything, bring the information to us. Do not take it upon yourself to deal with this situation, Mr. Hammer. You really are in over your head on this one."

Second time I'd been told that tonight.

"Then I better go home," I said, "and put on my water wings."

On my way out through the bullpen, Pat came up and took me by the arm. With his back to the rest of the room, he carefully slipped me a manila folder. "I could get my ass in a wringer, helping you."

"Sounds like a safe bet. What are these?"

"The Jay Wren surveillance shots you asked for, courtesy of the Miami PD. Nothing from the feds, but maybe these'll tell you something."

"Thanks, buddy."

I didn't look at the photos till I got to my car. They showed Wren in the walled-in pool area of a fancy Spanish stucco villa with the expected palm trees. The angle was high, from one of those palms maybe or an adjacent house.

In the earlier dated photos, Wren started out with his leg in a cast, and then after it came off, he was just another skinny tanned dude lounging by his pool. Nothing remarkable about it, except the blonde in the bikini, who was only in some of the shots. In two, she was giving the Snowbird mouth-to-mouth resuscitation, below the belt. Mostly she just worked on her tan.

It was a tan I was familiar with—I'd even seen the white flesh and dark snatch under the skimpy two-piece.

Jay Wren's bikini babe was Shirley Vought.

I didn't make it in till midmorning. I'd phoned Velda a couple times the night before, from Central Headquarters, so she knew what I was in for and that I'd drag in late. I came in without a coat because the day was sunny, and Velda gave me a wide-eyed look and bobbed her head to her left, at the couch where clients waited when business was really good.

Seated there, on the edge of a cushion like an expectant father waiting for the word, was Dr. Alan Sprague, Harrin's round little gray-haired, bespectacled colleague. He wore a brown suit and red bow tie and a constipated expression. On the floor next to him, leaning against the couch, was an oblong butcher-paper-wrapped package, not thick at all.

On seeing me, Sprague shot to his feet. "I don't have an appointment, Mr. Hammer. I do apologize."

"No problem," I said, gesturing to the door of my inner office, and he scurried ahead of me and let himself in.

I followed and shrugged at Velda and gave her a what-the-hell look, and she shrugged at me and did the same. She started to get up, reaching for her pad, but I shoved a palm at her and shook my head. She sat back down, and I closed myself in with my guest.

Sprague was already in the client's chair. His eyes were spider-webbed red, his bristly hair even bristlier than usual, and he had a rumpled, haphazard look.

I got behind the desk and asked, "How can I help you, Doctor?"

"I don't know if you can." He had the awkward butcher-paper package on his lap, held with two hands like some weird musical instrument. "From what I understand, what I read and hear, you . . . you were *there* last night."

"Yes," I said. "You have my condolences, sir. I know you and Dr. Harrin were close."

His shell-shocked expression was pretty pitiful. "Yes . . . yes, he was my closest friend. And yet sometimes I feel that I didn't know him at all." He placed the package on the desk. "I had instructions from Dr. Harrin—he asked me, yesterday afternoon, right after he got back, to give this to you, should anything . . . *unexpected* . . . happen to him."

"Only then?"

His eyes widened, then returned to normal—bloodshot normal, anyway. "Well, I suppose he meant, he'd give it to you himself, otherwise."

"Are you saying he anticipated something might happen to him?"

Sprague shook his head, shrugged, a frustrated mess. "I don't know. I really don't. There's so much I don't understand. Perhaps . . . would you mind opening it, before I go?"

"You haven't seen it?"

"No." He pointed a tentative finger at the package. "He left it for me . . . for you . . . wrapped like that."

I could feel through the paper what it was—there was no box, and the wood and the glass of it were apparent: one of his framed sayings. I tore the paper off, and the fancy lettering on parchment-style paper said: *"At the darkest moment comes the light."* The attribution was to Joseph Campbell.

"I don't know him," I said, pointing to the name under the saying. "What is he, the soup guy?"

"No. He's an author David admired."

"What does it mean?"

"That it's darkest before the storm, I suppose. That eventually light will follow. I don't know. I really don't."

I leaned forward. "Would you like something to drink, Doctor? Some coffee? Some water, maybe?"

"No. No, thank you. I wonder if . . . no."

"What?"

"There *is* something troubling me. I don't know who to share it with. It may be nothing, nothing at all. But when I heard about this, this . . . shooting . . . for some reason, what David told me, just yesterday afternoon, came rushing back, and I felt a chill. An awful chill to my very soul. How, how very silly, how stupid that sounds. . . ."

"What did he tell you, Dr. Sprague?"

Sprague, looking every bit the absent-minded professor, flopped back in the chair, his eyes dazed behind wire-framed glasses. "He told me a story. He *said* it was just a story, anyway. A kind of fantasy of his. Purely hypothetical."

"Go on."

"He said . . . suppose there was a doctor whose son took an overdose, and that doctor became so angry over his tragic loss that he decided to go into the drug business himself. Not for profit, mind you, but . . . for revenge. Maybe . . . maybe I *will* have that water, Mr. Hammer."

I didn't call for Velda. I went out and got him a cup from the cooler myself. From her desk, Velda gave me another wide-eyed look and I gave her the palm again, and went back in, shut the door, and gave the guy his water. He sipped it greedily.

"Now go on, Doctor."

"Well. In David's story . . . the doctor goes to Europe, and he

214

acquires this huge load of heroin. The method of smuggling is strange but I would say credible. The heroin has been fashioned into molds, the kind of molds they use in ceramics. They look just like ordinary molds, for dishes, for statuettes. They would easily pass Customs. But these molds, when crushed down, would become pure heroin."

Why not? Using ceramic figurines and art pieces and dinnerware as innocent items that could be sold out of a shop and shipped around the country, that was only part of the plan. The stuff could come into the country, via that same shop, in the form of plasterlike white molds. . . .

Dr. Sprague sipped his water some more, and then resumed: "But this doctor, he was not interested in money, remember, only in vengeance. With his expertise as a research scientist and master chemist, he developed a deadly, undetectable poison that could be mixed in when the heroin went through the process of being formed into those molds. He had gone to the source of the heroin and dictated certain additives and, without anyone's knowledge but his own, he arranged for this entire shipment to be contaminated."

"Fatally so?"

He nodded several times. "Anyone who took a single shot, no matter how they diluted it, would die. Thousands would die."

"My God . . ."

He sat forward, eyes wild as the story began to take hold of him. "But the friends and families of the thousands who died would be so consumed by rage at those who sold their loved ones this poisoned poison that they would rise up as one, and they would *take down* the Mafia. They might do so through police channels, but more likely as obsessed avengers, 'Hit the Mafia, kill them all.' Possessed by grief-fueled outrage."

"Thousands . . . would die?"

"Oh yes, many thousands. The doctor reasoned that these would be chiefly hardcore addicts, because heroin is not a casually taken drug. These are people who are already lost souls, on the road to hell, the doctor has decided."

"But his son . . ."

"He mentioned his own son as a case in point. He said Davy had been lost to him long, long ago. The selfish monster his boy had become, who had used and sold hard drugs to other children, was already dead. Morally dead, spiritually dead, even before the overdose took him."

"Damn."

For a long time, Sprague said nothing.

And neither did I.

"Mr. Hammer . . . tell me—*was* it just a story? A fantasy?"

"It would have to be," I said, but I was not at all convinced.

Sprague was staring into nothing. "He was very troubled. He was sick in his heart. Bitter, of course, but a . . . a *good* man. *Could* a good man like David do something so horrific . . . so terrible?"

"No."

His gaze found mine and was so haunted I could barely maintain eye contact. "I keep hearing what he said to me, so many times . . . 'Alan, it takes dead cells to create a vaccine.' Could he have *done* such a thing, Mr. Hammer? Could he have equated the drug problem with such a . . . a *radical* treatment?"

I stood. "No. I'm sure not. You've lost a friend, and you're upset, and your imagination is getting away from you."

He rose, sighed heavily, struggled to form a small smile. "I hope so. I hope that's all it is. Thank you for the reassurance . . . it may help me to sleep tonight. It may." He nodded toward the framed saying on my desk. "I hope you'll consider giving that a place of prominence here in your office, Mr. Hammer. In memory of a great, if troubled, man."

We shook hands across the desk, then he nodded almost shyly, and was gone.

I picked up the framed piece and looked at the flowing script: *"At the darkest moment comes the light."*

I propped it against a wall, then went into the outer office, and over to the closet to grab my hat, and Velda, on her feet, said, "Hey! Where are you off to? And what was that all about?"

"You don't want to know," I said.

My plan was to find Billy Blue at Dorchester Medical College, and for him to let me into Dr. Harrin's office. But the kid made it easy for me—he was in Harrin's office already, the door ajar, seated at his late mentor's desk, slumped over with his head on his folded arms, like a napping grade-school kid. He'd been crying.

"Billy?"

He popped up. "Oh . . . hello, Mr. Hammer."

I stepped inside and shut the door behind me. I took my hat off and said, "I'm sorry, kid. I was right there, but I couldn't do anything about it."

He came out from around the desk, as if I'd caught him at something. He wasn't crying now, fresh out of tears, but their trails, both wet and dry, streaked his cheeks. With his short haircut and baby-face features, in the blue-and-white-striped T-shirt and jeans, he looked younger than his age, the wholesome kid Dr. David Harrin wished he'd had.

I motioned the boy over to a beat-up two-seater sofa between file cabinets and we sat down, the framed slogans and sayings on the walls all around and behind us.

Billy asked, "Do you know when the funeral's going to be, Mr. Hammer?"

"No. I figure Dr. Sprague's probably handling the details. Pretty tough, kid. You hanging in there?"

He swallowed and nodded. "I had a phone call this morning, from Dr. Harrin's lawyer. I'm supposed to go around and talk to him next week—about the college trust fund the doctor set up for me."

"The doc thought the world of you, son."

He was shaking his head. "What do I do now? Where do I go for advice and . . . ?"

I put a hand on his shoulder. "You take the financial help Doc Harrin left you, and you get educated, and you make the kind of life for yourself he'd have been proud of."

"I'll do my best, Mr. Hammer, but . . . God, it hurts."

"I know. I know." I squeezed the shoulder. "Look, can you give me a couple of minutes in here alone, Billy? I need to do some snooping. Wait in the hall for me, would you?"

"Will it help get the bastards who killed him?"

"Might."

"Okay," he said, nodding, and he snuffled snot and did as he'd been told.

I went over to the desk. I had only one idea, only one card to play; either I'd gotten the message from Harrin or I hadn't. I picked up the crystal lighter from the desk, with its many flat edges and its naturally abstract design. Tried to light the clunky thing several times, and got nothing.

I give David a nice new present, Sprague had bitched, on our first meeting, *and he doesn't even bother to put fluid in it.*

Turning the lighter over revealed a metal plate that would allow me to get inside and change the flint and put in fluid, if that was what I had in mind.

It wasn't.

But I took off that plate, anyway, hoping I'd seen the light like Harrin asked . . . and found an envelope, rolled up like a fat little scroll. I withdrew it, flattened it out on the desk. The envelope was blank and unsealed. Its contents consisted of several sheets. One page, under Harrin's letterhead, was addressed to me.

For Mike Hammer, it began, followed (with no further preamble or explanation) by two lines—one, tomorrow's date and a time;

218

and the other, the street address and number of a certain Port of New York pier.

Also included was a carbon copy of a bill of lading, with a handwritten sheet of stationery paper-clipped to it:

On behalf of the Evello Family, Jerome Elmain of the Village Ceramics Shoppe will be present for pickup at this time and date; he will have his own copy of the bill of lading. Jay Wren has been attempting to discover the time and date of the shipment in order to intercept it. I do not believe he has had any success.

If you are reading this, I am no longer in a position to carry out my plans. You will only need this bill of lading should you wish, for whatever reason, to intercept the shipment.

I ask that you honor my intentions, but cannot insist that you do so. In fact, some shred of doubt about the sanity of my actions has compelled me to share this burden with you. I do apologize. But the decision, Mr. Hammer, will now be yours.

D.H.

This was obviously the much-awaited big shipment of heroin. But was it in fact fatally toxic? Or had what Dr. Sprague heard from his tortured friend been a fantastic fantasy of revenge?

If so, it was an incredibly elaborate one. . . .

And the tone, the words, of the message seemed to confirm the story Harrin told Sprague as no parable, nothing at all hypothetical. Ask any junkie in New York out there, from the Junkman to the freaked-out kids Davy Harrin hooked, they would all say they were dying for dope. Maybe they didn't know how right they were.

If a huge supply of fatally contaminated heroin hit these hungry New York streets, the overnight death toll would be staggering.

And the Syndicate would take the rap, and the public outcry for

219

justice would be loud and harsh and relentless. Harrin had envisioned the families and friends of victims rising up with guns and knives and clubs and anything they could get their hands on, to take bloody vengeance like villagers with torches storming Frankenstein's castle.

Would there be riots, vigilante action, if such a thing happened? Very possibly. But certainly the shared tragedy would create a new and undeniable demand that law enforcement grow itself a spine, and make the war on crime a real one, not just a slogan.

Could the Mafia really be brought down by such a demented scheme?

No way, I thought, shaking my head.

Then my eyes caught one of the framed sayings: *"The man who says it can't be done is interrupted by the man who did it."*

Others spoke to me, too: *"Keep Cool and Obey Orders," "The king can do no wrong," "Let Them Eat Cake," "Caveat emptor"* . . .

"Jesus," I said to the empty office. "You really *did* it, didn't you?"

And the clever, even foolproof ceramics delivery system, from molds to pottery, was in place to do the late Harrin's bidding. Had Harrin played intermediary for Evello, or had he been attempting to overturn the longtime mob boss? And in either case, would the good doctor have invested his ill-gotten gains in charity or medical research or perhaps even to buy and contaminate another cash crop of junk, to feed the rest of the country his deadly vaccine?

I could never know.

But I did know where and when the poisoned shipment would hit the docks.

I stuffed the sheets back in the envelope, sealed it, and went out in the hall and handed it to Billy.

"Messenger this over to my office, kid."

"Sure, but I can get you a stamp—there's a mail slot on this floor, Mr. Hammer."

"No, deliver it personally to my secretary and have her put it in the safe." I handed a five toward him.

He raised surrender-like palms. "Hey, you don't need to do that, Mr. Hammer. . . ."

"Kid, everybody's got to make a living. Take it and go."

He took it and went.

With the cops and the Treasury Department breathing down my neck, I didn't want to risk carrying that packet on my person. I had several things to do this afternoon, including call on Shirley Vought and inquire about her good friend Jay Wren, and didn't want those papers on me.

Good thing, too, because I was just to my car in the parking lot when the van rolled in and three guys in jumpsuits, faces distorted by nylon-stocking masks, leaped from the vehicle. I was clawing for the .45 when the chloroform found my face and my last memory was them dragging me.

Chapter Thirteen

I CAME AWAKE SLOWLY, the first sensation one of dizziness, then a grogginess quickly took over, only to be cut by a sudden headache—nothing blinding or pounding, just a dull steady ache.

I was in my shirt with my tie loosened, my shoulder holster empty of course, and they'd left me my pants but taken my shoes. I'd been plopped down in a comfortable chair, an overstuffed easy chair.

Across from me was Jay Wren, smiling amiably, seated in his own comfy but mismatching chair. We were in an area underneath a balcony at the Pigeon, his trendsetting discotheque, where low-slung square plastic-topped tables were surrounded by purposely dissimilar seating straight out of secondhand shops.

The shabbiness was supposed to be hip or clever or something, and maybe that worked in the dark. But the lights were up in the Pigeon, in off hours—this was presumably still the afternoon, I hadn't been out *that* long—and, like any nightclub, the reconverted warehouse looked pretty seedy, the Day-Glo paint spatters on the brick walls un-enhanced by black light and looking like kindergartners had done the decor.

The regular seating beyond, surrounding the dance floor, had its chairs up on tabletops, and the functional platform of the stage revealed itself as what you might see in a high school gymnasium set up for a concert. The smell of disinfectant mingled with the spilled beer and stale smoke common to any club, between closing and opening hours, and the thatch-hatted tiki-hut bar, designed for serving on all sides, looked pretty shabby by day.

Not that the illumination was intense. The house lights were meager, and the windows were high up and blacked out. The dimness preserved a fraction of the club's nighttime appeal, though the size of the chamber, with its two facing balconies and high ceiling, was the only aspect of the club that was more impressive after hours.

The Snowbird again wore a mod-cut suit, this one lime green, and a white shirt including the trademark lacy collar and cuffs. With his long blond hair and golden tan, he looked like a Breck Girl who'd had a hard life. By male standards, he was almost handsome, though like the club, better lighting did not improve him, his cheeks revealing pockmarks and stressing the artificiality of his hair color.

His sunglasses were the same lime green as the suit and his smile was, as before, generously wide and with more teeth than absolutely necessary. Maybe I could do something about that.

I moved my arms, my hands.

He waved a cigarillo like a magic wand, and the smile shifted sideways.

"No, Mr. Hammer," he said, in that light yet still phony British accent. "You are *not* bound. You are our guest, not our prisoner. But I do insist you maintain a certain . . . decorum."

His eyes lifted to right and left, and I glanced behind me. I'd been too groggy to even sense their presence, but standing over my

224

shoulders were two big boys, one a black guy with a shaved skull in a black muscle shirt and black chinos, the other a shovel-jawed hardcase with a Marine haircut, a pale yellow T-shirt, and camouflage trousers. Together they weighed maybe four hundred fifty pounds, ten of it fat.

I glanced at the gyrene-type hardcase and said, "Almost didn't see you there, pal. In those pantaloons, you damn near disappear."

He ignored that, like I was a tourist and he was a Buckingham Palace guard.

"I do apologize," Wren said, exhaling smoke through his nostrils, "for the rude invitation."

"You mean the kidnapping?"

He fluttered a dismissive hand. "We needed to talk, and I had reason to believe you might harbor ill feelings toward me."

I shrugged, settled back in the comfy chair. "Why, because you sent Russell Frazer to stab me? Or hired those St. Louis clowns to ambush me at home, thinking I'd blame Evello if I squirmed out of it? Maybe you mean last night, when you sent those freaks around to splatter me, and got Doc Harrin instead."

The cigarillo slanted out of his thin lips, which when the teeth weren't showing formed a wide, never-healing cut in his tanned face. "I won't deny it. If we're going to have an honest conversation, Mr. Hammer, I have to be frank with you. Ah . . . *here's* someone you know."

Coming over from the tiki bar, with a tray, was a good-looking blonde in tight black slacks and a frilly white blouse that might have been the stuff Wren's cuffs and collars were cut from. She was halfway over before I realized it was Shirley Vought.

On the tray, she carried several coffee cups, a tiny pitcher of cream, a little dish of cubed sugar, and a gleaming silver coffee pot.

"Hi, Mike," she said.

"Hiya."

She was pouring coffee for Wren. "Not surprised to see me?"

"Nope."

She poured me some, smiled faintly. "Why not? What gave me away?"

"The surveillance photos of you going down on Jaybird here." I made a clicking sound in one cheek. "I'm a trained detective—give me something like that, and I can put two and two together."

That threw her a little. But she managed, "You take cream and sugar, don't you?"

"I'll doctor it myself, thanks."

She put the stuff on the table, then pulled up her own comfy chair and joined us. Wren was already drinking from his cup, so the java wasn't spiked.

I took a couple sugars and poured in some cream and said, "Ain't we a cozy bunch? So, Mr. Wren—why isn't one of us dead by now? What do we have to talk about?"

He sipped coffee, then set his cup down on the plastic tabletop, where an ashtray held his cigarillo, its smoke swirling upward in almost a question mark. "This entire affair, Mr. Hammer, is unfortunate. A study in false assumptions on my part and yours. Strictly a comedy of errors."

"You might want to get more specific than that."

He shrugged and his long blond hair bounced off his shoulders—that hair looked better on Veronica Lake. "When you took an interest in the little incident, involving that messenger boy— including getting next to Dr. Harrin—well, I jumped to some . . . unfortunate conclusions."

"I didn't get next to Harrin. I just talked to him one afternoon."

He sighed cigarillo smoke. "Yes, well, you have a rather notorious reputation, Mr. Hammer. And you have a history with the Evello Family, with whom I've frequently done business. I thought you had taken it upon yourself to cause me problems. So I took preventative measures."

"You had Frazer try to shiv me."

He raised both hands in surrender. "As I say, I jumped to conclusions, and I overreacted. And things began to spiral out of control."

"You mean, you kept trying to have me killed."

His smile was embarrassed. "I know . . . I know. It does call my judgment into question."

What the hell could I say to that?

He leaned forward, his expression laughably earnest. "Mr. Hammer, you stumbled into my business at a most inopportune moment, and I reacted badly. What I am trying to do is see if we can negotiate a truce, and perhaps a peace. I believe we may have mutual interests."

"This I gotta hear."

"As I said, you have long been a thorn in the side of the Evello Family, and they have caused you a certain amount of grief over the years, themselves. Weren't you until recently in Florida, recuperating from one such attack?"

"Yeah. We must have been down there at the same time." I grinned at Shirley, whose big brown eyes couldn't seem to meet mine. "Too bad we couldn't have got together, and started our friendship sooner."

Forcing herself, Shirley looked at me. "Mike, you don't understand—this situation is a delicate one, and very dangerous."

"I kind of think I do understand." I grinned some more, but nastier. "It's delicate, because you're the Snowbird here's girlfriend, and you work for Mr. Elmain, who is in Evello's pocket. That makes you a kind of spy, right? And as for dangerous, I'm going to cite the corpses piling up, as evidence."

She was avoiding my gaze again, pouring herself some coffee. She stirred cream in.

"Mr. Hammer," Wren said, "we are at the birth of a new era, a new golden age of entertainment. My club here is a harbinger of things to come. The pharmaceuticals I dispense, without a prescription I grant you, are merely one wing of that entertainment."

I gaped at him. "Heroin is entertainment?"

He winced, as if I shouldn't bring up such unpleasantness. "That's at the far extreme of things, and I engage in that business only because there's a market, a market well established before I came onto the scene. But the world of drugs is changing—marijuana is already commonplace among the young, and cocaine is a favorite among well-moneyed grownups."

I turned to Shirley. "That's where you fit in, isn't it, baby? You didn't *get* your inheritance, did you? But you still have friends among the jet set, and you became Evello's connection to that market, and now the Snowbird's. Right?"

She gave Wren a nervous glance, but he only smiled and raised a palm in stop fashion. "As I've gathered, Mr. Hammer, you are very astute. *You* understand. As a small businessman yourself, and man of unconventional tastes, you grasp that I am merely another capitalist, serving willing, even eager customers. After all, one cannot legislate morality."

"What's that supposed to mean?"

He frowned, waved as if to a departing child. "I'm not talking thievery or murder. I'm talking about adultery, and sex acts considered perverse by some, and obviously recreational drugs—hallucinogens are already the rage on college campuses—and such old standbys as gambling and prostitution."

"You're saying gambling and prostitution aren't illegal? What planet do you live on?"

"I'm a neighborhood boy, Mr. Hammer, raised in and around the Village—and my earliest memories are of whores, junkies, and queers . . . don't misunderstand, many of my best friends and certainly business associates fall into one or more of those unflattering categories . . . and among those early memories are the tourists and New Yorkers from beyond the neighborhood, who came to the Village for some naughty good fun."

I suppose I could have asked how a neighborhood kid got the British accent, but I just didn't give a shit.

"No, Mr. Hammer, I'm saying making things illegal that people want and crave does no one any good, not individuals or society at large. It doesn't stop a single customer from wanting to buy, and in fact creates a nicely wicked atmosphere in which customers are not only willing to buy forbidden goods, but to pay premium prices."

"Yeah, all right. I get that."

"*You* do, but the Evellos of the world do not. They are locked in Old World ways, antiquated thinking. It will take a visionary to take full advantage of the opportunities of the new freedom."

"And you're the guy. You're the visionary."

"With no false modesty, I would have to say yes." He sat forward. "I am making alliances that the old Mafia families, with their inbreeding and prejudice, could never conceive, much less execute. I have business associations overseas that will transform conventional drug trafficking—forget France, Mr. Hammer. How about South America? What about Vietnam? New sources, rich sources, new alliances, *lasting* alliances."

"I don't know. I never was much of a United Nations guy myself."

"Diplomacy has its place." He gestured with an open hand, a fey gesture considering the lacy cuff. "If you and I can sit down, as representatives of our warring nations, and come to terms of peace . . . we can do business together."

"What can I do for you?"

"I need a chief of security. I need a man who understands law enforcement but who has no hesitation to do whatever is necessary to make a point, or gain an advantage. I need someone terrible. Someone ruthless. I need *you,* Mr. Hammer."

While all this talk was going on, I'd been thinking about how I was going to make my exit. The coffee pot was both metal and filled with steaming liquid, so that alone could incapacitate the muscle-bound Frick and Frack behind me. Shirley wasn't armed, except for her natural thirty-eights, and they'd already done all the damage to me they were going to. And I didn't think Wren was even armed, certainly the tight cut of his suit didn't allow for it, and that was when Shirley's face started melting.

I tried to blink it away, and looked toward Wren and he was melting, too, like one of those Dali clocks, and not just his face but all of him, mod suit, lace cuffs and all, and the plastic table between us was pulsing, as if taking breaths. I tried to stand, but the floor was rubbery, and before I could flop back down in the chair, hands were gripping me, and pulling me away from there, dragging me bodily, and my feet and legs were as long as a stilt-walking man's, but useless. The guys who were hauling me were tall and then short and then tall again, as they towed me through those tables with the chairs on top, the silver legs wiggling like Busby Berkeley gals on their backs, and for the big finish, the inside of my head exploded, splintering into a thousand multicolored fragments.

Someone said, "Hit the lights. Sound system, too. And get the projector started."

I was shoved into a hard chair and it, at least, felt solid under me. The hands on my arms turned into tentacles, tight, clutching, only they weren't tentacles but ropes, clothesline I think, and for a while the room, the world, settled down, and I knew who I was and where I was—roped into a chair on the dance floor of the discotheque.

"Settle down, Mr. Hammer," Wren said. His coat was open now and I could see my .45 stuffed in his waistband. Had it been there all along? Was it there at all?

"What the hell . . ."

The black muscle man and the maybe Marine came from behind me and fell in on either side of Wren—they both had guns stuck in their waistbands, too, the black guy a .38 revolver, the one in camouflage trousers a nine millimeter. From somewhere on the sidelines, two more bodyguard types fell in with Wren, one on either side—a big Oriental guy with a Fu Manchu beard and a red shirt and brown chinos, sporting an automatic of some kind in a shoulder rig; and a short, stocky character with shoulder-length brown hair, a yellow and orange and green geometric shirt and green bell-bottoms, a sawed-off shotgun in his hands.

"It's called LSD," Wren was saying. "Lysergic acid diethylamide. Maybe you've heard of it? Very big on campus."

"You . . . *you* drank the coffee, too. . . . And the bitch had the *cream*. . . ."

"But you dropped the sugar cubes, Mr. Hammer. Miss Vought told me when you took her to dinner how the big tough guy took sugar with his coffee."

"You're dead."

"No, Mr. Hammer. That's just another hallucination of yours. Now, we need to get to work. The cocktail I gave you is unpredictable."

"Cock . . . tail?"

"I'm not Dr. Harrin. I don't resort to simple sodium pentothal, although that's in the mix, along with horse tranquilizer and of course the dose of acid. I know a good deal more than Harrin did about narcotics—he was only a doctor, but I'm an artist, although ironically not one who partakes of my own art."

"You're dead."

"You're repeating yourself, but that's to be expected. We don't have a lot of time before you go-go-go on your trip . . . that's what they call it, Mr. Hammer, a *trip*, which you'll take inside your mind, and from which you will probably recover, despite the strength of the dose."

"What . . . what was all that bullshit . . . ?"

"Over there, at the table? Not bullshit. It's quite a sincere offer. I think you're a man of considerable talent, and as close to a violent psychopath as one can be and still make recruiting worthwhile—I feel you're socialized to a workable degree."

"Fuck you!"

"Well, there *are* rough edges we'll have to polish off. But for now, as the drugs begin their magic, you should feel compelled to answer my questions."

He wasn't melting. The walls weren't pulsing, and I was getting centered. Maybe I had hold of it.

Then the lights went down and the flashing orange and purple lights kicked in, and above me the mirrored ballroom ball was spinning and catching those lights and sending them everywhere, like that splintering multicolored effect inside my head. Music blared from the sound system, a raucous soul number with few words that could be discerned, but "Shotgun!" was one of them. That crazy stitched-together film was flickering on the brick wall over the stage, just above and in back of Wren and his men, those weird images of flowers and rotting carcasses and Buster Keaton and Guadalcanal and Woody Woodpecker and Lana Turner and Adolf Hitler and fashion models and Venus de Milo and Shirley moved in front of me, blocking Wren, and she leaned down and her voice was kind.

"Tell him what he wants to know, Mike. He won't hurt you if you cooperate. Tell him what he wants to know, and we can be together in this. You and I can be together again. The Snowbird has a lot of girls, and boys, too, and he won't mind . . . he won't mind. . . ."

It was a nice little speech but the jarring thing was that halfway through she seemed to turn into Velda, when the orange light hit her, and then back to herself on the purple, and then Velda, then Shirley, but the voice for both was slow and slurry like a 45 rpm record on 33⅓.

She moved away and Wren stepped forward. If my hands had been free, I could have grabbed his throat, or that .45 from his waistband. But my hands weren't free, they were roped behind me.

"Mr. Hammer, I have reason to believe Dr. Harrin was the middleman on the super shipment, and I suspect he was planning to hijack it, perhaps even turn it over to the feds. His son Davy was one of my people, and died of an overdose, as maybe you know . . . and I became suspicious of Harrin's solicitude, although he seems to have fooled that idiot Evello entirely."

I heard every word, but this time speeded up, the 33⅓ on 45, and his face seemed distorted, like putty that was stretching itself. And the gunmen behind him, two on either side, had disappeared to be replaced by Jesus and Satan on the one side, and Milton Berle and Pinky Lee on the other. *But they all still had guns. . . .*

"Did Dr. Harrin tell you anything about the shipment, Mr. Hammer?"

He had made a mistake telling me about the LSD, because I knew, *for now* I knew anyway, that these distorted sights and sounds were hallucinations, they were not real, I did not need to be frightened, though the reality behind them remained deadly. Jesus and Satan and Uncle Miltie and Yoo-Hoo It's Me My Name Is Pinky Lee all had guns and would kill my ass and it would not be a TV channel I could change or a dream I would wake up from.

So I told him what he wanted to hear: "Yes. He told me. The doctor told me."

The bizarre sights and sounds could be closed out by shutting my eyes, though I saw intense colors in strange patterns, like an abstract painting that moved and wiggled and slithered across the inside of my eyelids, but even so I could still hold on to some sense of sanity, some sense of *me*, and I knew something that Wren did not.

I knew that I always carried a safety-razor blade inserted in a slit in my belt for just such occasions. I'd been tied with my hands behind my back before, and more than once, but after the first time, I said never again, and ever since carried that tiny blade. But I had to hold on to my marbles long enough to get that blade out and start working on the ropes. . . .

"What do you know about the shipment?" Wren spoke softly and yet his voice seemed to echo throughout the old warehouse.

I hoped there was nobody I didn't know about behind me, no one who could see what I was up to. It was a delicate process cold sober, getting the blade out of its little hiding place, but I managed it, though I was hammered on a hallucinatory cocktail and the world was going crazy all around me and if I dropped that blade, I was finished, because I probably would spill what I knew and this fucker would kill me, that bullshit about working for or with him was bullshit, and thank God my hands were steady and I could somehow focus and I did not drop the blade and the rope was nice and soft.

"I know the date," I said.

"When?"

"Tomorrow."

"What time?"

"One o'clock."

"What pier?"

My hands were loose and I brought that safety blade around in a vicious swing that sliced the air and then sliced Wren, too, across the cheek, opening a long red gleaming cut, and he backpedaled, screaming, fingers on his face, but he was close enough for me to grab my .45 from his belt, though the action toppled me down on my side, onto the dance floor, chair and all, because my ankles were still tied to its legs.

I fired blindly toward Satan who became the black guy again and he had his rod halfway out of his pants when the .45 slug angled through his open yelling mouth and up through the roof of his

234

bald head, bursting it in bloody chunks like a target-range melon. Pinky Lee turned back into the stocky guy, who was pointing that sawed-off at me, his geometric shirt shifting and changing. Shirley wasn't Velda at the moment, just Shirley, standing frozen in terror, and from my fallen, chair-bound position, I managed to spin on the slick dance floor in such a way that my legs came around and caught her and she fell into the shotgun blast, which took her head off her shoulders and some of her shoulders, too. What was left of her flopped onto the floor and twitched like a dancer who'd slipped but just kept frugging, even as the soul singer's voice shouted, *"Shot-guuun!"* from high speakers.

Blood-spattered, still tied to the damn chair, I got onto my back and spread my feet apart as far as the ropes would allow, making them taut, and shot the ropes apart with the .45. Uncle Miltie, Pinky Lee, and Jesus had gone scrambling back toward the tables under a balcony overhang, and Wren had disappeared, I didn't know to where, but I somehow got the ropes and the now-broken chair off me without anybody killing me, and I stayed low as I hustled for the tiki bar. With no shoes on, I sort of skated over the dance floor, but picked up speed on the carpet under the tables with the stacked chairs, whose legs weren't dancing right now, then I dove over the counter and landed on the floor back there, breathing hard.

You're doing fine, I told myself. *You're doing fine. But who are you? What was my name? What was my fucking* name?

But then the floor began to move—it was rippling, it was breathing, and I looked up and saw a thatched roof *and I was in that island village again, hiding in that hut with the steaming jungle and Christ knew how many Japs out there, and I could hear the mocking cries of the birds up in those trees with their bladelike leaves and the rough bark and Christ it was hot, steaming hot, and when the Jap leaned through the window, I screamed at him, a scream as shrill as any jungle bird, but he was a cartoon Jap, you're a sap Mr. Jap in the*

235

Popeye cartoons, and I stopped screaming and started laughing as I put a .45 slug in his eye, and when he flopped over the counter, he was the Oriental guy with the Fu Manchu mustache, but he still had his goddamn eye shot out.

Mike Hammer. I'm Mike Hammer.

I got to my feet but stayed in a crouch, and went out through the bartender access and moved under the balcony, opposite where I'd sat for that friendly cup of coffee with the Snowbird. Music was blaring, the Rolling Stones, "Satisfaction," even an old Stan Kenton man like me knew *that* song, and I was going to get me some satisfaction, all right. I was going to hold on to my marbles and stay focused, even as the Day-Glo colors on the wall pulsed, even as my own movement made rainbow trails, like I was writing my own name in the air with my every motion.

I knew where I was headed. Unless there had been reinforcements, there were three of them left: Wren, Jesus the Marine, and Pinky Lee the stocky shit with the shotgun. I ignored the throbbing wall I moved along, and I stayed very low when I came out at the edge of the dance floor near the steps up onto the platform stage. That weird movie was still flickering and I tried to resist the images, *rotting dog, Vogue cover girl,* and stormed up those steps and hopped up into the suspended Plexiglas Go-Go Girl booth.

"There he is!" somebody shouted.

Wren was out there in the middle of the dance floor, pointing with a gun in his lacy-cuffed hand, only he was a white bird now except for that hand, a snowbird or a pigeon, but an armed one. He fired at me, but the slug whanged off the Plexiglas. Out from under the balcony at stage right came the Marine, on the run, shooting, and I reached around the side of my three-sided Plexiglas shield and fired at his head but caught him in the throat instead, but that did it, sent him down in a gurgling dance to join the sprawled headless girl who no longer heard the beat.

The guy with the shotgun had made it onto the stage, without my seeing it, and he was getting in close, because with that sawed-off he needed to get in close, and I used all my momentum to swing the cage, and it caught him in the chest and sharply swung up the shotgun, which went off, sheering off the front of his face and leaving him a ghastly wet mask and still alive enough to scream until I leaned out and shattered his skull with a .45 slug and put him out of his misery.

But I lost my balance taking that shot, and dumped myself onto the stage floor, a slug slamming into the bass drum just behind me.

Wren was still out there, in the middle of the dance floor, not a bird but a man now, having taken aim and missed. A railing across the front of the stage blocked my shot at him, and I couldn't risk standing and presenting an easy target, so I fired twice, up at where the mirrored ball was attached to the ceiling, and fired again and finally the thing came down, fast as gravity, and shatter-slammed into the dance floor, not right on top of him, but close and sending shards of glass flying.

I had only one slug left and no clip, so I was counting on that to be the distraction I needed to give me my shot. Then I was on my feet, with the .45 poised to shoot, when I saw him standing with arms outstretched, the revolver limp in his right hand. Then he let the gun slip to the floor and he staggered a step and raised his hand to his neck where the jagged shard of glass was embedded, catching the flashing lights to wink at him and me and no one else, because the rest of them were dead.

When he jerked it from his throat, the blood geysered in a perfect arc that painted a distant tabletop a colorful shimmering red that made a startling psychedelic effect when the pulsing orange and purple lights hit it.

Unless I was just seeing things.

Chapter Fourteen

FOUND MY THINGS. My hat, my coat, my wallet, my shoes, all piled in what had been Jay Wren's office. There was a couch in that office and I would have liked to stretch out and wait and ride this thing out. But at some point, employees would show up to open the Pigeon for business, and despite my unsteady grasp on reality, I somehow knew the club would open at 10:30 P.M., and realized I needed not to be there.

Apparently I remembered to go in the men's room and wash off the blood spatter, because when I got to Velda's, I didn't have any on my face and not even my clothes. She had just got home from the office and was surprised, and relieved, to see me. But she knew at once something was wrong.

"Mike—what . . . ?"

"I came in a cartoon cab."

"You what?"

"I need a bed. You need to stay with me."

She did. Sometimes sitting like a visitor at a patient's hospital bedside, sometimes curled up next to me with all her clothes on.

I would wake now and then, with a start, and see her there in the crack of light from the door she'd left ajar on the hall, and that would settle me.

I managed to sleep, and the dreams were colorful and had Woody Woodpecker and Hitler in them, but otherwise no more surreal than usual. I don't remember telling her I'd been slipped acid-laced sugar cubes, but I must have, because she already knew when I finally rolled myself out of the rack.

I figure it was about twelve hours since I'd been dosed, and felt pretty much my normal self, whatever the hell that was. Velda sat down with me in her breakfast nook, around eight A.M., and we had coffee and I was able to eat some scrambled eggs and toast.

After the meal, I told her what had happened.

"I'm not really sure what went down," I said. "I could have imagined most or all of it, after the LSD kicked in."

We were still at the table in the nook, on our second cups of coffee. She said, "Pretty sure Jesus and Pinky Lee weren't there."

"Don't bet on it."

She frowned. "Mike—what do we do about this? Do we bring Pat in?"

I shook my head. "I left no witnesses and if even half of what I remember really went down, I'd make a full-course meal for Assistant D.A. Traynor."

Her frown deepened. "You were using your .45, though. What about ballistics?"

I patted her hand. My kind of girl. "I changed barrels last month, doll, remember? That's not in the police files. Nothing to match. I'll toss this barrel down a sewer and let the rats ride it as a raft."

That got a laugh out of her, tiny, but a laugh. "With your way of looking at things, Mike, it's no wonder you took a bad trip."

"Not as bad a trip as the ones I left behind."

We decided to go in to the office, and make things look normal. We skipped the coffee and went right to work, and she brought me in some reports from Tiller and the other agencies who'd been covering for me of late, when I remembered to ask, "The Blue kid drop off an envelope for me?"

"Yes." She frowned. "He said you wanted it put in the safe, and I did. Is it important?"

"Yeah."

"That's all I get?"

"Yeah."

She shrugged and was going out when I said, "Bring it here, would you?"

She did, and I had the sealed thing in my hands as she stood there expectantly.

"Shoo," I said.

She smirked, shook her head, and the arcs of shining dark page-boy swung as she turned on her heels, muttering, "Come crying to somebody else, next time somebody slips you a mickey."

I opened the envelope and, when the phone rang, had been sitting there for maybe five minutes, staring at Dr. Harrin's handwritten words to me, which included today's date and the time and pier number for the big shipment's delivery in the form of apparently harmless ceramic molds.

"Michael Hammer," I said.

"The shit hit the fan, kid."

"Hello to you, too, Pat. What shit hit what fan?"

"Looks like Evello clipped the Snowbird's wings, big-time. It's the worst mob bloodbath since St. Valentine's Day."

"No kidding. Capone missed Bugs Moran, though—you saying Wren wasn't there?"

Pat chuckled harshly. "Oh, he was there, all right, Wren, four bodyguards, and that society girl who found out the hard way slumming with scum has its risks."

"When was this?"

"Yesterday afternoon, at that discotheque of Wren's, which was

241

closed at the time. We've reconstructed the action, at least in a preliminary fashion."

"Yeah?"

"Looks like Wren was having a sit-down with Evello and his boys, and Evello turned the tables. Would've taken at least three or four men to do this kind of damage, and nasty customers, at that."

"Takes all kinds to make a world."

"Yeah, but what a world. Anyway, this may make your life easier—we traced those two freaks who tried to hit you and took out Doc Harrin instead, and they were in the Snowbird's flock, all right. So you can safely say that Wren was the source of the attempts on your life, and the Snowbird won't be giving anybody a hard time anymore, except maybe the devil."

Nope, I thought. *The devil was on Wren's side—I saw him there, yesterday. . . .*

"I appreciate you sharing the lowdown, old buddy," I said. "Anything on the supposed big shipment?"

"There's thinking that the stuff is coming in this week, maybe even today. The T-men are blanketing the harbor."

"That would take a lot of T-men. That's a thousand miles of shoreline and maybe a dozen active ports."

"It's more narrowed down than that, Mike. Agents Radley and Dawson are checking every ship coming in from France—from passenger liners to container carriers. That's still a good number of vessels, but it can be done."

"Just because the Syndicate buys its product in France doesn't mean they shipped from there."

"No. But it's a start. Narrows down the needle hunt from the whole damn farm to a haystack."

I grunted. "Good luck to them."

He laughed in a world-weary way exclusive to longtime cops.

"Why do we bother, Mike? So we find and stop the super shipment, what then? There'll be another, and another. You can't stop a vicious circle."

"If a snake is eating its tail, chum, you can still cut it in half."

"Yeah. You ought to sew that on a sampler and hang it in your office."

He didn't know how close he was.

The Port of New York's piers have one thing in common: they stink. All that salt air gets swamped in grease and oil and dead fish and the heady bouquet of workingman body odor. Add to that the cacophony of man over nature, squawking of seagulls and lazy lapping tide drowned out by grinding machinery and cargo pallets slamming to the cement, while the toots of tugboats vainly fight the throaty whistles of steamships. Anybody confusing the New York waterfront for a beach has never seen sand.

The S.S. *Paloma* out of Marseilles docked at 1:04 P.M. on a chilly afternoon that made its nasty point that summer was over and fall was here, and live with it. Even with the canopy, women held down their skirts and men clamped their hats on, rattling down the gangplank, eight-hundred-some passengers disembarking into the waiting arms of U.S. Customs.

The Customs officers looked a little like porters only with badges on their caps and, in some cases, guns on their hips. This all took place dockside in a big brick open-sided shed, where the officers inspected every bag, looking for all the smuggler's tricks, and they knew a few.

After the passengers, the cargo—fairly limited, as this was a luxury liner not a container carrier—began its unloading process, stevedores swinging down nets of boxed and crated material and dropping them with impressive precision onto the dock. A number of trucks and vans were waiting, but so were the Customs officers, who did not turn anything over until crates had been opened and checked and weighed on a big ungainly scale that looked a little like a medieval torture rig.

This was standard procedure, but what *wasn't* standard procedure was the assembly off to one side within the brick shed of about a dozen officers in the same caps with badges, only otherwise in denim, the backs of their jackets emblazoned U.S. CUSTOMS SEARCHERS. The denim, I supposed, was for the rough, dirty work of actually having to search ships, including holds and engine rooms. But right now these guys, roughneck-looking for feds, were just milling in smoke-'em-if-you-got-'em mode.

I was milling myself, on the fringes, having moved in close to that shed and the offloading ship, after watching from behind the picket fence where people meeting passengers gathered. Despite all the T-men of various stripes—with something big obviously in the wind, beside the usual dock smells—security was nothing special, as far as getting onto the dock itself was concerned.

That was when I saw him—looking as innocuous as a ceramics mold, Mr. Elmain, the plump little guy whose gray hair had a monk's spot of baldness, wearing an off-white jumpsuit whose back said VILLAGE CERAMICS SHOPPE. Three other guys were with him, in similar jumpsuits, and they didn't look so innocuous—they might have been hoods. Or they might have been teamsters. A rose by any other thorn.

"Mr. Hammer?"

I turned and saw Agent Radley, slender, flint-eyed, and typically impeccable in yet another gray suit, with his dark blue tie flapping like a flag in the breeze. Dawson wasn't with him—probably covering another pier.

"Agent Radley. Kind of a chilly one."

He nodded, skipping the small talk. "What are you doing here?"

"Thought I might find you. Captain Chambers said you fellas

were checking every ship in from Marseilles this week. Kind of tedious work."

"We're used to it. How can I help you?"

From where I stood, I could see a Customs officer walking Mr. Elmain toward the open-walled brick shed, glancing at the bill of lading, and affixing it to a clipboard.

Radley was frowning at me. "Mr. *Hammer?* Why are you here?"

I cleared my throat. "I wanted you to know I got a package from Dr. Harrin."

His eyes and nostrils flared. "What *kind* of package, Mr. Hammer?"

Now the Customs officer was prying open the lid of a wooden crate while Mr. Elmain looked on with serene innocence. The officer stared in at the carefully stacked and excelsior-packed ceramic molds, each of which was two facing pieces strapped or rubber-banded together, varying in size and shape from as big as a medium pizza to as small as a transistor radio. The officer slipped the rubber band off one about the size of a football, only square, and I was pretty sure that mold was of a standing Santa with a bag of goodies over his shoulder.

Christmas underwrites the rest of our year, Shirley Vought had said.

"Mr. Hammer—what *kind* of package?"

"Oh, the doc sent me a framed saying—maybe you're aware, he had a bunch of those on his office walls, over at Dorchester Medical College?"

"Actually, no. Why? Is it significant?"

"I don't know. You tell me. It says, '*At the darkest moment comes the light.*'"

He shrugged, shook his head. "No. That has no special significance, as far as I can tell."

The Customs officer was having Elmain sign some papers on the clipboard.

Radley sighed, and he looked ten years older than when I'd met him, just days ago.

"I can't tell you how frustrating this case has been, Mr. Hammer. I really hoped that perhaps Dr. Harrin had shared something with you that could have made a difference here. This could be the biggest quantity of heroin ever to hit the streets of this city."

I was watching Elmain as he supervised his three burly assistants while they loaded eight wooden crates about the size of squat coffins, into the back of the Village Ceramics Shoppe van. I wondered if this was the vehicle my pal Russell Frazer used to make his deliveries.

Radley was saying in extreme frustration, "And if this is, as our intelligence indicates, pure, uncut stuff, in the hundreds of pounds? Well, it will hit with incredible impact, the biggest bang we've ever heard or seen. We'll have seen nothing of this magnitude before—it will fund and fuel the Syndicate's expansion into worldwide narcotics trafficking."

If the friends and families of the thousands who died are so consumed by rage for those who sold their loved ones this poisoned poison, they will rise up as one, and they will take down the Mafia.

"Mr. Hammer, do you have any conception of the death, the despair, the *destruction* that all of this venom would bring upon our streets?"

Elmain was at the wheel as the van rolled away from the pier.

"I can imagine," I said.